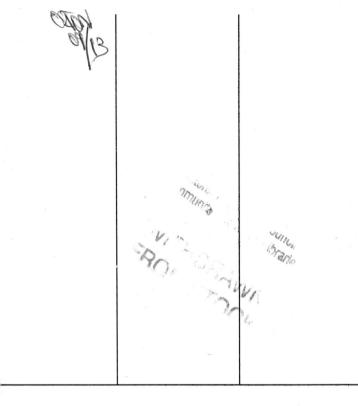

PETERBOROUGH LIBRARIES

This book is to be returned on or before the latest date shown above, but may be renewed up to three times if the book is not in demand. Ask at your local library for details

Please note that ch

D1354769

60000 0001 11236

ALSO AVAILABLE FROM CHRISTA FAUST AND TITAN BOOKS

FRINGE
THE ZODIAC PARADOX
SINS OF THE FATHER (October 2013)

CHRISTA FAUST

FRINGE

THE BURNING MAN

TITAN BOOKS

FRINGE: THE BURNING MAN
Print edition ISBN: 9781781163115
E-book edition ISBN: 9781781163122

Published by Titan Books
A division of Titan Publishing Group Ltd
144 Southwark Street, London SE1 0UP

First edition: July 2013
1 3 5 7 9 10 8 6 4 2

Did you enjoy this book?
We love to hear from our readers. Please email us at readerfeedback@
titanmail.com or write to us at Reader Feedback at the above address.

To receive advance information, news, competitions, and exclusive
offers online, please sign up for the Titan newsletter on our website
www.titanbooks.com

Olivia was playing a game with the nice doctor. This new game had rubber blocks in different shapes and colors that had to be sorted based on whether or not they were the same as the one the doctor had picked. It was kind of fun at first, but she was starting to get sick of it, and wanted to hear a story instead.

She was happy to see her mommy come through the door, but she got even more excited when she saw her daddy there, too, standing back in the doorway.

"Daddy!" Olivia cried, dropping the yellow triangle she was holding and running to hug him.

But when she reached the doorway she stopped short, because the man in the doorway wasn't her daddy at all. It was a different man, wearing her daddy's special Marine clothes.

Olivia had never seen a grown-up man cry before, but that was exactly what the strange man in her daddy's clothes did. Not real loud and snuffly like a kid would, but quietly.

"I'm sorry, Mrs. Dunham," he said softly to her mommy.

Her mommy picked her up then, and held her so that

she was sitting up high on the big bump in her mommy's tummy where her new brother or sister was sleeping. Her mommy was crying, too, as she kissed Olivia's face and squeezed her way too hard.

"Can we have a minute alone with her, Doctor Bishop?" she asked the nice doctor.

"Certainly," the doctor said. "Take your time."

The nice doctor left the room, and Olivia started to feel panicky. Whatever was going on, she didn't like it one bit.

"This is Lieutenant Kent," her mommy said. "He's your daddy's best friend, and he wants to tell you something really important, okay?"

Olivia nodded, but she wasn't really sure it was okay.

"Hi, sweetheart," the strange Marine man said. "Your daddy told me all about you."

Olivia turned her face shyly away from the stranger.

"Are you sure about this?" her mommy asked over the top of her head.

"He made me promise," the stranger said.

Her mommy nodded, rubbing Olivia's back. That felt good.

"Listen," the man said. "Your daddy gave me a message to give to you. He said he loves you more than anything, and that the world is much bigger than you think. Those were his exact words... His last words." His voice started sounding all funny, like maybe he was going to cry some more. "I don't know what he meant, but he made me promise to tell you that. So here I am."

Olivia didn't really understand anything the stranger was talking about, but what he was saying was making her mommy cry even harder, and that made her feel like crying, too.

"Where's my daddy?" Olivia asked. "I don't want

you here." She reached out and shoved at the stranger's shoulder to push him away. "I want my daddy."

"Daddy…" her mommy said. "Daddy has gone away to heaven."

Olivia looked into her mommy's face, frowning.

"He's not in heaven," she said. "He's in Beirut!"

"Not any more, honey," her mommy said. "He left Beirut and went to go live in heaven with the angels."

"No!" Olivia said, squirming and struggling against her mommy's arms. "No you're *wrong*. He's coming home soon. He promised!"

Her mommy put her down and started talking in a low voice to the man who wasn't her daddy. Then the nice doctor came back in, and her mommy talked to him, too.

That made her even angrier, so Olivia ran over to the table with the blocks on it and started picking them up and throwing them as hard as she could. Then she hid her face.

"Let me try talking to her," she heard the doctor say, but no one answered.

When Olivia looked back over at the door, her mother and the strange Marine man weren't there anymore.

Suddenly she was afraid. She ran to the door, banging on it with her fists.

"Where's my mommy?" she cried. "I want my mommy and daddy!"

"Can you tell me how you're feeling right now, Olive?" the doctor asked. "What happened to your daddy? What did your mother mean when she said he went to heaven?"

"Nothing!" Olivia said. "He's fine. He's doing a very important job in Beirut with his Marine friends but he'll be home soon. He's JUST FINE!"

The doctor went over to his machines and started

doing stuff, turning knobs and flipping switches. He did that a lot, and it made her feel like she wasn't there. Then he turned back toward her.

"Do you understand what it means when I say that someone is dead, Olive?" he asked.

"I know what *dead* means," Olivia said. "Dead means you go down the toilet like Goldie the fish."

"Will you ever see Goldie again?"

Olivia frowned. That was a stupid question.

"No," she said. "Because when you go down the toilet, you don't ever come out again."

"That's right," the doctor said, and he looked pleased at her answer. "Once someone is dead, they can't come back."

He took out a funny tiara that had lights on it, and put it on her head like she was a robot princess. It pinched, but she didn't try to take it off. One of the screens started showing a bunch of squiggly lines.

"How would you feel if I told you your father was dead, just like Goldie?" he asked.

"You're stupid," she said. "Daddy can't fit in the toilet!"

"I assure you," the doctor said, but he was looking at the machine. "It's true. Your daddy is dead, and he won't ever come back. That's what people mean when they say someone went to heaven."

"He is NOT dead," Olivia said. "You don't know *anything*."

"Why do you think your mother and Lieutenant Kent were crying?"

"Because…" Olivia clenched her fists, panic surging up the back of her throat and making it hard to breathe. "Because…"

"Tell me how you feel right now," the doctor said, looking at her, and then the machine.

"Shut up," she screeched. "*Shut up*! I hate you! I want to go home! I want my mommy!"

The pile of blocks on the floor by the table burst into sudden smoky flame.

Olivia lay in her bed, running her tongue over her split lip and listening to Rachel snore below her.

She didn't blame Doctor Walter for her busted lip. After all, he was only trying to help. He had no way of knowing that threatening to call social services would only make her stepfather angrier. Randall had started unbuckling his belt before she'd even gotten in the front door, cracking her across the face for "spreading their private family business all around town." He'd made it crystal clear that if she ever spoke to anybody again, about what went on in *their* house, she'd be sorry.

It was her own fault for asking Doctor Walter for help. She also knew, in her heart, that from now on the only person she could really count on was herself.

But as she lay there, she found herself thinking about that odd, lonely boy she'd met at the daycare center. His name had been Peter. She thought about the blimps, and white tulips, and about how strange and confusing the last few days had been.

Was it really possible to imagine herself somewhere else, or had she just made up the whole thing?

Because if it was true, if she really *could* imagine herself somewhere else, then why couldn't she do it right now? Why couldn't she take Rachel and disappear into another world, where there was no Randall?

She rolled over to look down at Rachel, sleeping on the lower trundle bed with one little hand curled against her cheek. Olivia took her sleeping sister's hand, and then squeezed her eyes closed, trying to picture the two of them lying on their backs in a never-ending field of white tulips, laughing and watching chubby white clouds and zeppelins drift across the bright blue sky.

She pictured Peter lying beside them, smiling and safe just like they were. She imagined him reaching out and taking her hand, comforting her.

Nothing happened.

"Livie?" Rachel whispered. "What are you doing?"

Olivia opened her eyes. Still in their same old bedroom. She let go of Rachel's hand.

"Nothing," she said. "Go back to sleep."

Olivia turned away from Rachel and faced the wall, feeling a dark, bitter despair wash over her. What was the point of being able to imagine yourself into another world, if you couldn't do it when you really needed to? If it had even happened at all. Maybe she had just imagined the whole thing.

She should have known it was too good to be true.

1

Jacksonville summer. Muggy and stagnant, the only breeze generated by the wings of mosquitos. Sweat pasted Randy's limp thinning hair to the back of his neck as he sat on the front porch in the late evening sun, rolling another wet beer can back and forth across his forehead.

It didn't help.

Neither did drinking the beer inside the cans, although that didn't stop Randy from trying.

"Randy…?"

That was Denise. Just hearing the sound of her whiny, nagging voice made his fingers curl into fists. The way she said his name, all stretched out and quivery, he knew what was coming. More of her bitchy little insults, disguised as questions.

Randy, don't you think you should slow down a little on them beers?

Randy, don't you think you maybe oughta try looking for a job tomorrow?

Randy, don't you think you're a worthless piece of trash who'll never amount to anything?

It didn't used to be this way with Denise. When he

first met her, she used to be fun. A good-time party girl who could drink any man under the table. Back then she'd been the quintessential blond beach babe—leggy, tan and perfect, like she just stepped out of a Coppertone ad. She'd been looking for a walk on the wild side, after her uptight military husband had kicked the bucket, and Randy was just the bad boy to take her there. She'd climbed on the back of his Harley the night they'd met and never looked back.

And the way she used to look up at him with those big blue eyes, like he was a rock star. Like he was the only man in the whole world.

Now she looked at him like he was some kind of alcoholic, just because she'd suddenly decided to stop drinking during the week. Like he was a worthless bum, even though he worked his ass off to support her and her two bratty kids. Okay, so maybe he didn't have some respectable nine-to-five type job, but he was out there hustling every day.

A little of this, a little of that. Dealing skunk weed to dumb-ass frat boys and tourists. Fencing stolen car stereos. Plus, he had a real good score lined up later that night. Something big. Something that'd change their lives and get them out of this dump. Something that would shut her whining mouth for good.

"Randy, honey," she said, pushing the creaking screen door open. "They're gonna shut the phone off tomorrow. Think you could go on down the office first thing and take care of this bill?"

"Tomorrow," Randy said, pausing to down the last of the beer. "Tomorrow I'll get you a brand-new phone in a brand-new house, how'd that be?"

"That's what you said last month," she said, and she gave him that look.

"Dammit, Denise," Randy said, crushing the beer can and tossing it out into the sandy front yard. "Why you always gotta be so negative?"

He turned to look at her, standing there in the doorway. She was dressed up all fancy in an acid-washed denim mini skirt, neon pink halter top, and high white heels. Pretty much everything hanging out like it was on sale. Hair all poofed up and bright pink lipstick like some kind of rock video tramp. He stood up, eyes narrow as he turned to face her.

"Where the *hell* you think you're going dressed like that?"

"I..." She took a tentative step back. "I told you it was Joelle's birthday tonight. Me and Lisa are throwing a little party for her down at Sandie's. You said you'd watch the girls, remember?"

He stepped into the doorway, backing her into the sweltering house. It was a good ten degrees hotter inside. Air conditioner on the fritz again.

"And I'm supposed to believe you're dressed like a slut for some chick's birthday party?" He let the screen door close, then backed her up against the living room wall. "No, no, wait a minute. Doesn't that spic ex-boyfriend of yours work at Sandie's? What was his name? José?"

"Jorge," she stuttered. "But that was way back in high school. Years ago, Randy. He's married now, with kids."

"You're married with kids," he said. "Doesn't seem to stop you from whoring around behind my back, now does it?"

"Randy, please..."

"Here's what you're gonna do," he said, keeping his voice low and even. "You're gonna go back in the bedroom and put on some decent clothes that cover up that fat ass of yours, and then you're gonna stay right here in this house and take care of your own damn kids while I go out and make us a living. How's that sound?"

She was silent for a moment, and then her eyes got wide.

"I can't take this anymore!" she screeched, her voice turning high and grating. "I've got no life because of you and your crazy jealousy. I never go anywhere. I never do *anything*. It's like I'm in goddamn prison with you."

Her shrill voice drilled into Randy's aching head, going on and on and on. Blaming him for all her problems. Swearing and squawking just like a talking parrot. A whole lot of annoying noise that didn't mean anything. He could feel sweat dripping down the center of his back, and gathering under the rim of his ball cap. His head was pounding, the nice comfortable buzz he'd been working on swiftly decimated by her bitchy little tantrum.

"Maybe I *should* use my fat ass to find a new man," she was saying. "A real man—with a *job*."

Randy punched her in the face.

There was a nice, satisfying double crunch, first his fist hitting her face and then her head snapping back and hitting the wall behind her. She slid down the wall to the spotty carpet, knees to her chest and both hands covering her bleeding nose.

He shook out his throbbing right hand, flexing the fingers.

"Talk like that to me again," he said, "Ever. I'll kill you."

He checked his watch. Nearly nine p.m. He really needed to get going if he was going to meet up with Tony for this big score.

There was a soft shuffling sound in the hallway and when he looked up he saw Denise's older daughter. She was dressed in a thin, sweat-damp nightgown, her long blond hair loose around her narrow face. The younger kid was okay, pretty quiet and easy to ignore, but this older one was a pain in Randy's ass. Just like her momma, always begging for the back of his hand. Always judging him.

She was judging him right now, staring at him like he was some kind of bad guy, when Denise was the one who started it.

"What the hell are you looking at?" he asked, glaring at her.

The girl didn't respond, but she didn't look away. She just stared at him with those spooky green eyes of hers. Like grown-up eyes in a little kid's face. He raised his hand to her, but she didn't flinch. She just narrowed her expression.

"To hell with you both," he said, almost to himself. "Somebody has to make a living around here."

He turned on his heel and left, slamming the screen door on the pathetic snuffling and boo-hooing of Denise's little pity party.

It was dark when Randy pulled his sorry-ass pickup truck into the empty parking lot of the Save Rite, and there was only one other vehicle there. Normally, he wouldn't be caught dead within a mile of a police prowler, but this was Tony's car, so Randy eased the pickup into the slot beside it and killed the engine.

Tony Orsini was the older brother of this girl Sherry he used to bang a few years back. Handsome son of a bitch with a square, comic-book hero jaw and a toothpaste commercial smile. He was five years older than Randy, but he still had a full head of thick, perfectly gelled black hair while Randy's was more like a dying lawn—thin, patchy and pale brown. Tony was the kind of guy who had a five o' clock shadow by noon. A real he-man type. Chicks couldn't get enough of him.

It took Randy a couple of months to start trusting Tony, since he was a cop and all. But it soon became clear that he was as crooked as they come. He was also a generous friend. Always picking up the tab when they went drinking, always sharing the coke he'd confiscated from some lowlife, and always offering up freebies from the working girls he kept out of jail.

Tony talked all the time about how the drug dealers he arrested had stacks of money just lying around, and how easy it would be to make that cash disappear. After all, if you rob a drug dealer, it's not like he's gonna call the cops. And even if he did, Tony *was* the cops.

All Tony needed was a good trustworthy partner. Someone he could count on to stay cool under pressure, and back him up on the score.

That's where Randy came in.

Randy got out of the pickup and slid into the passenger side of the prowler. It was nice and cool, air conditioning running at full blast. But even under the circumstances, being inside a cop car still made him sweat a little.

"You're late, Randall," Tony said, instead of a greeting.

"Sorry, man," Randy replied. "My old lady's been giving me grief all night. Practically had to chew my own leg off to get away. You'd think that bitch would be a little more appreciative, seeing as how I'm about to make her rich and all."

"Focus," Tony said. "We got a big night ahead of us." He looked over. "Let me see your gun."

Randy felt a rush of hot blood to his face.

"Goddammit," he said. "I knew I forgot something."

Tony just stared at him, flat black eyes ice-cold in his stony, expressionless face.

"Get out," Tony said.

"Now just hold on a second, Tony," Randy began.

"I said get out."

"Look, man," Randy said, palms out. "I'm sorry. I just let that whiny bitch get to me, break my concentration. Give me a second chance, willya?"

"Now you listen to me, Randall," Tony said, twisting a fistful of Randy's sweaty T-shirt and pulling him close enough to kiss. "I'm trusting you with my life here. My life will literally be in your hands, do you understand that? If you screw this up, I'm a dead man."

"I understand," Randy said, trying to keep his voice steady. "Honest. It's not a big deal. We can just swing back by my place and pick up the piece, okay? It won't take any time at all."

Tony didn't say anything for a long, drawn out moment, leaving Randy to sweat in silence. Getting in on a score like this was by far the best and most important thing that had ever happened to Randy. No more small-time action, this was his ticket to the big leagues. A score like this would change his life forever, and if he screwed it up before it even got off the ground, he didn't think he could live with himself.

"All right," Tony said finally, letting go of Randy's shirt and putting the prowler in gear. "I'm gonna let it slide, just this once. But I expect better from you from here on out."

"Absolutely," Randy said, straightening his stretched out collar. "You bet. I won't let you down. You can count on me, man."

As Tony drove back down Pearl Street toward the house, Randy had to fight to stop himself from fidgeting like an anxious kid. He'd already made such a bad impression, he needed to do everything he could to show Tony that he was cool. Trustworthy. That he really was ready for the big leagues.

When they turned the corner and the sad little white house came into view, he felt a pulse of shame. He'd been to Tony's high-rise condo, with the trendy leather furniture and the knockout view. That was the kind of place Randy wanted, not a trashy dump like this. He wanted to explain to Tony that he was better than this, that he had ambition, and that it was Denise and her nagging and lack of faith in him that kept him down. But it didn't seem like a good time. Better to just go grab the gun and get going.

When Randy walked up to the porch, the door was closed.

That's weird, he thought. The door was never closed, not in this kind of heat. But he didn't really think much about it as he pulled the screen door open and turned the knob on the wooden door behind it. He half expected it to be locked, but the handle turned easily.

When he opened the door, he saw Denise's older daughter standing there in the middle of the empty living room. Denise must have gone to lie down or something, because although she'd left behind a smeary mess of blood and snot on the wall and floor, she was nowhere to be seen.

That's when Randy noticed that the little girl had his gun.

For a fleeting second, he thought she'd realized that he forgot it, and helpfully brought it out to give to him. But he didn't remember telling the kid that he'd be needing it, and he'd never talk about that kind of stuff with a nine-year-old, anyway.

Then she raised the gun and pointed it at him, and any thoughts along those lines swiftly evaporated.

"Olivia, don't!" he said, hands held out in supplication.

The little bitch shot him.

2

Tony was starting to regret having chosen Randall as his sacrificial lamb. You'd think it would be impossible to screw up such simple instructions. Clearly he'd overestimated his victim's ability to distinguish his own sorry ass from a hole in the ground.

Tony had orchestrated this exact same bait-and-switch set up half a dozen times before, cherry-picking some loser to take the blame for the murder of one of Tony's myriad rivals and competitors. They would break into the target's house, Tony would shoot both the target and the fall guy, and from there it was a cinch to doctor up the scene to make it look like they'd killed each other during a botched robbery.

Should've been another no brainer.

But in the past few months, Tony had been suffering through a tenacious streak of bad luck. Deals going south. Sure things that didn't pan out. Worse, he'd been having these strange episodes of free-floating anxiety, combined with intense paranoia and an unshakeable conviction that very bad things were going on just outside the limits of his peripheral vision.

He figured it was probably a side effect from doing too much blow, but it was starting to mess with his composure. Making him doubt himself. And given the kinds of animals he dealt with on a daily basis, you could never show a hint of weakness, or else they'd eat you alive.

He lit a cigarette to calm himself as he watched Randall fumble around with the doorknob. This guy was really starting to get on Tony's nerves. It was going to be a pleasure to kill him.

Again, there was that icy twinge of paranoia as Tony glanced back down the street. He spotted a man standing beside the mailbox of a Pepto Bismol-colored house, on the other side of the street. He really didn't want anyone to notice him, or wonder why a petty criminal like Randall was getting into a cop car on the day that would become known as his last.

But that wasn't the only reason the guy was making Tony nervous.

By the glow of a nearby streetlight, he saw that the man was wearing a dark suit and tie, despite the sweltering heat. Also, his face—what could be seen of it—was icy pale under the rim of a black fedora. No tan—not even a hint. Clearly not a local. Some stiff from Internal Affairs?

A Fed, maybe?

Tony was starting to think that the best option was to cut his losses and drive away. He could always come back and silently execute Randall some other time. He was about to turn the ignition key when he heard the shot.

Instinct had him out of the car with his gun drawn before he had a chance to think about what a bad idea it was to get involved in Randall's domestic mess. There was a second shot and Randall fell backward through the door and onto the porch, clutching his right thigh and making a noise like an angry donkey. Tony figured the guy's bitch of a wife must have plugged him, and couldn't blame her, to be honest.

Stepping into the house, he was astounded to discover that the shooter was a little girl.

Tony had always been uncomfortable around kids. It was like they could see right through his flash and charm, and knew that there was something off about him. Something rotten. So he avoided them whenever possible.

He'd dealt with armed attackers more times than he could count, and was known in the department as a guy who always stayed cool under pressure. But he'd never faced off against a child with a gun.

"Okay, kid," he said, keeping his voice calm and even. "Why don't you just put the gun down."

The girl was breathing fast and shallow, her pale blond hair crackling with static. Her eyes were wide, with too much white around the thin green irises and dilated pupils.

"Come on, sweetheart," he said, holstering his gun and taking a cautious step closer. "Now, why don't you be a good girl and…"

He reached out and grabbed the girl's fragile little wrist, tilting the gun in her hand so it pointed up toward the ceiling.

Suddenly it felt like he had grabbed a live wire, or stuck his hand into a microwave oven. Some kind of strange blistering heat seared through Tony's fingers and up into his arm, causing the skin to bubble and blacken. He wanted to let go but it was as if his fingers had been fused to her wrist.

And in a sudden awful flash, the house was gone. The whole neighborhood was gone and he and the little girl were standing in the middle of what appeared to be a massive junkyard, with wrecked cars and washing machines and twisted metal scrap. Only all of the cars looked foreign and strangely designed, and the brand names on the various broken-down appliances were unfamiliar.

For a moment he forgot the pain. Then, before Tony could get a handle on this bizarre turn of events, he felt the intrusion of an unwanted presence inside his brain. The girl was in his *thoughts*. He could feel a weird resonant echo humming through his neurons, as if she was using them to play cat's cradle. Like the two of them were twisting together, and synching up on a molecular level.

Then, just like that, the connection was severed, and the two of them were back inside Randall's house again.

A fountain of sparks rained down from the light fixture above their heads. Light bulbs popped like corn and the dirty carpet burst into flame, releasing choking, toxic smoke.

Tony's right sleeve was on fire, too, and whatever plans he may have had for dealing with the little girl were forgotten in that instant as he spun away from her in a blind panic, shielding his face from the flames with his left hand.

As he twisted his burning right arm, Tony's uniform sleeve disintegrated into glowing ash and the fingers he'd clenched around the little girl's wrist snapped and shattered like burnt breadsticks. The heavy gun in her hand thumped to the carpet and she just stood there, wide green eyes staring.

Tony tore out into the front yard and dove to the sandy ground, rolling to smother the flames. But the feeling of burning deep inside his flesh could not be quenched. He felt as if his arm had been filled with napalm maggots that were steadily chewing their way up into his torso and head.

He grayed out for an unknown length of time, woozy

and dull with shock, but still able to hear shouting and sirens around him. Then there were hands on his body, lifting him. He tried to fight them, but there were too many. That's when he realized he was on a stretcher, about to be put into an ambulance.

"Officer Orsini?" a voice was saying. "Stay with us, okay? We're gonna get you to the hospital."

A paramedic, a woman. Broad, bland face with no makeup, hair hidden under a cap. Cold, clinical blue eyes behind pale lashes.

He turned away from her ministrations, back toward the smoky, burning house. Randall was already gone, carted away to the hospital—or the morgue, if Tony was lucky. But there was a woman and another blond girl, younger, standing together on the sidewalk. The woman looked like she had a broken nose, but seemed otherwise unharmed.

The girl was physically fine, but clearly hysterical.

Meanwhile, on his left side, another paramedic was coddling the little monster who had burned him, checking her vitals and asking if she was alright. Her eyes were still glazed over and far away.

Tony lunged toward her, ripping the IV out of his good arm and screaming.

"She did this!" he howled. "She's a monster! A demon! Get her! *She did this to me!*"

The woman paramedic tried to restrain him, but he let her have it, punching her in the gut with his good hand and then shoving her back as he climbed to his unsteady feet.

Couldn't they see that this little girl wasn't a child at all? She was the goddamn *antichrist*. He had to find a way to stop her, before the unholy power she possessed was unleashed on the unsuspecting world.

He staggered, dizzy and nauseous, sky and ground

whirling, untrustworthy as he reached instinctively for his gun. The movement sent a bolt of blinding pain through the ruined stump that remained of his right hand. He nearly blacked out again, but forced himself to hold it together, fumbling to undo the grip of the pistol with his left hand, until he was able to pull it out of its holster.

He managed to get his awkward left forefinger through the trigger and pointed the gun at that little blond monster, but then the ground seemed to spin beneath him, and his shot went laughably wide.

Behind the girl a black firefighter staggered and dropped to his knees, his heavy yellow turnout coat going crimson down one side.

Then Tony was being tackled by several enraged firefighters and restrained, howling and flailing as the red-faced woman paramedic filled a syringe. Next there was a sharp sting in the meat of his twisting arm.

Then nothing.

Olivia had no idea how she wound up out on the front lawn. The last thing she remembered was Randall.

Randall coming through the door all casual and preoccupied like nothing had happened. Like breaking her mother's nose for the third time that year and threatening to kill her was no big deal. Olivia knew her mother would never have the courage to stand up for herself, so it was up to Olivia to stand up for her. Because she believed in her heart that if she didn't, Randall really *would* kill her mother. Maybe her and Rachel, too.

So what had happened? She remembered pulling the trigger—once, then again—and Randall falling back on the porch with blood soaking through the leg of his oily jeans. Then, as a rush of intense, conflicting emotions overwhelmed her, she felt as if her consciousness was eclipsed by a roiling, electrified thundercloud.

There was a terrible smell of burning that filled her head, choking her, suffocating her. Then she was here, on the front lawn, the house behind her engulfed in smoke and flames.

Rachel!

What had happened to her little sister? What about her mother? Were they trapped inside the house?

She scrambled to her feet, only to be held back by a burly Hispanic paramedic with glasses.

"Hey, now," he said. "Take it easy."

"My sister," Olivia said, her voice rough and scratchy from the smoke.

"She's fine, honey," he said. "She's over there with your mom. Your dad has been taken to the hospital in an ambulance. He's going to be fine, too, so don't worry."

"He's…" Her voice seemed to dry up in her throat. "He's alive? But I…"

She suddenly lost all the strength in her legs, and was forced to sit straight down on the scratchy grass. She felt as if she was going to throw up.

She could see an ambulance in the driveway, and thought for a fleeting moment that she saw Randall strapped to a stretcher, but it wasn't him. It was a cop in a singed uniform. Something about him seemed eerily familiar, like déjà vu or something from a half-remembered dream. He didn't seem to be conscious, and one arm was all wrapped up and packed with ice.

"What happened?" she asked.

Before the paramedic could answer, Rachel came running out of the smoke and chaos, flinging herself so hard at Olivia that she nearly knocked her over backward.

"Hey," Olivia said. "It's okay, kiddo. We're okay."

She looked up at her mother, standing just behind Rachel. Her eyes were both swollen down to pink, puffy slits, and her nose looked like a rotten tomato. She seemed to be crying, but her face was so messed up that it was hard to tell.

Olivia stood, keeping her arms around Rachel, and pulled her mother gently into the embrace.

"We're okay," she said again.

She really hoped that it was true.

3

SEPTEMBER 1995

Olivia stood on the beach with her arm around her little sister. It was a Tuesday afternoon, at the tail end of the summer high season, and Neptune Beach was still humming with tourist activity. Mostly chubby, sunburned families with kids and leathery seniors in sun hats. A man played Frisbee with his dog while two girls Rachel's age shook sand out of their towels.

No one seemed to care what Olivia and Rachel were doing there.

The salty wind whipped Olivia's hair around her face and the warm, gentle surf bubbled around her bare feet. The sun was high and bright in a clear blue sky. Another beautiful, perfect postcard kind of day. Another day her mother would never see.

Rachel pressed her face into Olivia's shoulder, sobbing as their mother's best friend Joelle carefully unscrewed the lid on the cheap aluminum container that held all that was left of Denise Dunham.

"Should I say something?" Joelle asked, looking back at Olivia like she was the adult and Joelle was the fifteen-year-old.

Joelle was a good person, with a huge heart, but she was flighty and clueless most of the time, flapping around like a frightened chicken. Her being seven months pregnant and awash in baby hormones didn't help matters at all. Unfortunately, she was the only adult that was willing or able to help scatter Denise's ashes on the beach. Olivia and Rachel had no living family.

"Go ahead," Olivia said, her voice tight but steady.

"Denise," Joelle said, tears ruining her thick mascara. "You were my best friend since sixth grade and… um… you loved the beach. We had such fun times here, you, me, and the girls." She choked up for a minute, lips stretched thin and tight. "And now we're here, to scatter your ashes in the ocean like you wanted, so your beautiful spirit will live forever in the beautiful waves."

Olivia found her mind drifting during Joelle's awkward and corny but heartfelt speech. Drifting back to other, more vivid memories of her mother. Not tan and happy on the beach, but pale and skeletal, wrapped in an oversized hospital gown, her eyes already dead and waiting for her body to catch up.

It had all happened so fast.

Her mother always had headaches, for as long as Olivia could remember, but they got worse when Randall left.

After the "accidental" shooting that left Randall with a limp and a monster pain pill addiction, he'd come back from the hospital all smug and more insufferable than ever. Olivia just went along with his story that she had been playing with the gun, and it went off by accident, but a day didn't go by that she didn't wish her aim had been better.

Olivia ran away several times, but always ended up

coming back for Rachel's sake. She just couldn't leave her little sister alone with that abusive scumbag, because if he was going to hurt someone, Olivia preferred that it be her. She could deal with it.

Then, one day, Randall was just gone. No explanation, no goodbye, nothing. Olivia was ecstatic, convinced that her mother would finally start to live again.

But that's not what happened.

Denise withdrew even further, refusing to leave her room for days on end. She slept most of the time and when she was awake, she was like a hollow-eyed shadow of herself. Her headaches got so bad that she was unable to work, and they had to go on welfare. There was a time when Olivia came to wonder if her mother's headaches were just an excuse for her to lock herself in her room with her pills and the TV, leaving her daughters to fend for themselves.

Cleaning the house, packing lunches for Rachel, handling all the bills and groceries and everything, Olivia had been filled with deep, simmering resentment. So much so that she wanted to grab her mother by the fragile, pipe-cleaner arms and shout.

He left you, but we're still here!

The strange thing about it was that Olivia's terrible resentment somehow made her guilt-twisted love for her mother even stronger. So if her mother needed to be taken care of, then that's just what Olivia would do.

They were in the middle of another pointless, depressing argument about the overdue power bill when her mother had her first seizure.

"I told you not to open bills and leave them lying around your room, where they'll get buried and forgotten," Olivia was saying. "Just give them to me right away, okay?

"Okay?"

But her mother didn't seem to be listening. She was staring at the floor, mouth slack and eyes blinking slowly.

"Mom?" She put a hand on her mother's skinny shoulder, exasperation evaporating. "Mom? Are you okay?"

And *bang*, her mother went down, twitching, eyes rolling up in her head and urine puddling beneath her on the carpet.

The doctors wouldn't tell Olivia anything for weeks.

Inconclusive results.

More tests.

Specialists.

But Olivia knew the truth. She saw it in their faces and the way they refused to meet her gaze for more than a second at a time. And then, finally, there came a day when they couldn't hide the truth from her anymore.

It was an inoperable tumor. Cancer. Six months was a generous estimate.

They still wouldn't meet her gaze.

Standing there in the hushed hospital hallway with her inconsolable sister, Olivia had wanted desperately to scream. To punch walls and kick out windows. To shake her fist at the sky and rail against the unfairness of it all.

But she didn't. She just nodded and signed forms and accepted leaflets and the phone numbers of various child welfare agencies and grief counselors. Taking care of things, the way she always did.

Joelle shook the jar over the incoming waves and the pale, powdery ash fell like impossible snow across the water. The three of them were silent for a long minute, each one lost in their own thoughts. Joelle and Rachel cried. Olivia didn't.

On the drive back to their apartment, Joelle explained to them again how she really wanted to take them in, honest she did, but she just couldn't. She had four daughters of her own, plus her current husband Brett's two kids from a previous marriage and now this new baby on the way. There was no room at the inn.

Olivia understood, both what Joelle said and left unsaid. Like the fact that Brett was a little too fond of Olivia and had recently started complimenting her on her "development" whenever she came over to babysit. She also understood why Joelle felt the need to explain her situation over and over again. Because Joelle wasn't really explaining it to Olivia and Rachel, she was explaining it to herself.

"Okay, well…" Joelle said, pulling up in front of their familiar apartment complex. "Stay in touch. You have my number."

"Of course," Olivia replied, climbing out of Joelle's battered green minivan for what she knew would be the last time. "Thanks."

Joelle couldn't drive away fast enough.

Rachel threw herself onto the sofa in a sobbing heap while Olivia packed up the rest of her sister's things. Olivia's own meager possessions were already neatly organized and stowed inside a single rolling suitcase, but Rachel had been unable to handle packing. As if leaving her shoes and CDs strewn around the room would prevent them from having to leave their familiar home.

No such luck.

A Child Welfare agent named Leona Byers had

just arrived and was standing in the doorway, waiting impatiently for Olivia to finish. She was in her late forties, short and round with razor-thin eyebrows and a fussy little mouth. Her bushy black hair was cut into a weirdly mannish style that clashed with her tight floral dress, chandelier earrings, and garish make up.

"Look," Olivia said, "I don't understand why we can't just stay here. I can quit school and get a job. I've been taking care of all the bills and things since mom got sick, so I know what to do. We don't need foster care."

"I'm sorry, honey," Leona said, her smarmy, insincere tone making it clear that she was anything but sorry. "That's just not how it works."

"But we'll get to stay together though, right?" Rachel asked, suddenly panicky. "They're not gonna separate us are they?"

Leona smiled, flashing her disturbingly perfect little doll teeth.

"You'd better hurry up and finish packing," she said.

"They can't separate us!" Rachel cried, clutching Olivia's arm. "You won't let them, will you?"

"Here," Olivia said, handing Rachel their mother's favorite teddy bear, a panda holding a heart that read GET WELL SOON! A gift from Olivia and Rachel during the first few days of her first hospital stay, back when getting well soon still seemed like a possibility. Rachel clung to the panda like a life preserver while Olivia put her arm around her little sister and spoke close to her ear.

"If they try to separate us," she whispered, "I'll run away and come find you. I swear. Okay?"

Rachel hugged the panda even tighter and nodded.

Outside the open door, the mailman was whistling an upbeat salsa tune as he shoved letters and magazines through the mail slot of each apartment. When he reached the Dunham apartment, he raised a hand and called inside.

"Here you go," he said, holding a single envelope out to Olivia.

She turned it over in her hands. The paper was a creamy off-white, thick and expensive. In the place where a return address would be, there was just a corporate logo, a graphic three-dimensional letter M.

She opened the envelope and pulled out a single sheet of equally expensive letterhead with the same M logo.

Dear Olivia and Rachel Dunham,

We are pleased to offer you both full academic scholarships at The Deerborn Academy in Westley, Massachusetts. Room and board are included, plus a monthly stipend to cover your basic living expenses until graduation. Enclosed are two airline tickets from Jacksonville to Boston, where you will be met by a school official who will transport you to the campus.

Please note that although the date on the tickets is open ended, it would be in your best interest to leave immediately, so you may start the semester at the same time as all the other students in your respective grades.

The letter wasn't signed. As indicated, the envelope did contain a pair of airline tickets, as well as a glossy brochure extolling the virtues of the school. It looked perfect—a dream come true. Only Olivia didn't remember applying for a scholarship to any Deerborn Academy.

On the other hand, she had applied for dozens of grants and scholarships in the last desperate months of her mother's life, including several national programs that offered to find placement on behalf of gifted students experiencing personal hardships. She didn't specifically remember any of those programs having a three-dimensional M logo, but she was under such immense pressure and stress that it wasn't out of the question that she may have simply forgotten.

She looked up at Leona, who tapped the spot on her thick wrist where a watch would be, as a signal for her to hurry up.

Olivia hated being rushed into anything, but there was no time to weigh the pros and cons and come to a carefully considered conclusion. There was clearly no room for debate. Rachel needed her, and being separated wasn't an option.

She knew what she had to do.

"How about a ride to the airport?" she asked.

4

When Rachel and Olivia arrived at Logan International Airport, they had no idea what to expect.

Neither of them had ever been on a plane before, or been outside the state of Florida. Rachel seemed to think the whole thing was a grand adventure. She had been thrilled by the little packet of peanuts, and the view out the oval window, and the fact that her seat tilted backward.

Olivia, on the other hand, was wary and anxious, full of questions.

The first thing they had to do was figure out where to get their luggage. Luckily one of the flight attendants, a friendly older camp guy, helped them out, pointing them toward the baggage claim area. But right when they passed through the doors that led to baggage claim, Olivia saw a tall woman in her late fifties with obnoxiously bright, clearly dyed red hair, holding a paper sign that said DUNHAM. She had a thick, sturdy, tank-like build and was wearing a maroon, varsity style jacket that had the Deerborn Academy logo on the left breast.

As soon as she spotted them, the woman started waving frantically.

"Um... hi," Olivia said, walking up to her. "I'm Olivia Dunham."

"Of course you are," the woman replied, revealing a hard accent that Olivia guessed was Bostonian. "And this must be Rachel. So good to meet you both."

To Olivia's surprise—and slight discomfort—the woman swept the two of them up into a big three-way bear hug.

"I'm Mrs. Gilbert," she said, squeezing Olivia's shoulder with one hand and Rachel's with the other. "I'll be Olivia's dorm mother at Deerborn."

"What about me?" Rachel asked, looking up at her sister with an anxious, thundery frown forming between her pale eyebrows. "Are we going to stay together?"

"You'll be staying in the junior girls' dorm with the other seventh and eighth graders," Mrs. Gilbert said. "But don't worry, you and Olivia will still be neighbors. You can visit each other any time."

"It's okay, Rach," Olivia said. "It'll be fun. Think of all the new friends you'll make."

Rachel nodded, but still seemed a little unsure.

"Come on, girls," Mrs. Gilbert said. "Let's go get your luggage."

After retrieving their meager belongings from the revolving baggage carousel, Mrs. Gilbert stopped them right before the exit.

"You girls got coats, right?"

Olivia nodded and unzipped their suitcases to retrieve her beloved battered denim jacket and Rachel's pink Nike windbreaker.

"Those are your winter coats?" Mrs. Gilbert said, her eyebrow arched. "I guess it never gets cold in Florida, huh?"

"It does too!" Rachel said, pulling on her jacket. "It's like forty degrees in January."

"Forty, huh?" Mrs. Gilbert smiled. "It's forty out there right now. By January it'll be more like four degrees."

"Four?" Rachel said, exchanging a horrified look with Olivia.

Mrs. Gilbert smiled.

"Tell you what," she said. "I was supposed to take you shopping for winter clothes this weekend, after you got settled in, but I don't want you two freezing your little kiesters off in bikinis and flip-flops all week, so how about we stop off on the way to the school? Pick you up some real clothes."

"That would be wonderful," Olivia said. "But... well... We don't really have any money."

"Don't worry," Mrs. Gilbert said, stepping through the automatic doors and gesturing for the girls to follow. "An allowance for school clothing is included in your scholarship." Then she was off.

Frowning, Olivia took Rachel's hand and hustled to catch up with Mrs. Gilbert's brisk pace.

"Listen," she said. "About that scholarship. How did we end up qualifying for it anyway? I don't remember applying to Deerborn, so I was kind of surprised when I received the tickets in the mail." She didn't mention Leona Byers.

"Right," Mrs. Gilbert said, leading them across the street to the parking garage. "Well, the Deerborn family has always been charitably inclined, and each year they reach out to a select few gifted but financially challenged students who are experiencing personal hardships, and may not otherwise have access to the kind of high-quality education provided by the Academy." The way she said it sounded like a commercial. "Here, the van is down this way."

Olivia frowned again slightly as she followed Mrs. Gilbert to a dark green minivan with white lettering on the side that read: DEERBORN ACADEMY. Something about the explanation didn't sit right with her. It sounded *too* rehearsed, like a speech written by someone else.

"But why us?" Olivia asked, as Mrs. Gilbert took her suitcase and put it into the back of the van. "I mean, how did you know we were experiencing 'personal hardships'?"

"Beats me," Mrs. Gilbert said with a smile and a shrug. "I just work here." She closed the hatch in the back of the van and opened the sliding side door. "Come on, hop in."

Olivia and Rachel got in and she slammed the door, then went around and got in behind the wheel. Suddenly finding herself confined with a stranger, Olivia felt nervous. But for Rachel's sake she didn't say a word.

"So why don't you tell me your story," the woman said as she keyed the ignition and pulled out of the parking spot. "What sort of personal hardship brought you to us?"

"Our mom died," Rachel said. "She had cancer."

Olivia kicked Rachel's foot and shot her a warning look. She got a hurt expression in return. Her sister was like a happy puppy that would eat out of anyone's hand, but Olivia wasn't sure if they should trust this woman yet.

"Gee, that's awful," Mrs. Gilbert said. She leaned out the window to pay the parking fee to someone in a booth, and then headed out of the airport toward the highway. "I lost my mom at a young age, too. Lymphoma. I was eight."

"Wow," Rachel said. It was obvious from her face that she wanted to say more, but didn't, because of her sister's silent warning.

Olivia couldn't help thinking that maybe she was being unnecessarily paranoid. That maybe she ought to lighten up. After all, this scholarship could be the best thing that had ever happened to them. It certainly seemed like a dream come true.

Problem was, she wasn't sure she believed in dreams come true.

They stopped at a mall on the way to the school. Rachel went a little berserk and wound up with both arms full of shopping bags, while Olivia was more practical in her choices. Her only indulgence was a pair of black eight-hole Doc Martens boots, which she'd always wanted but had never been able to dream of affording.

Once they'd crammed all their purchases into the van, they headed away from the city and into the picturesque New England countryside. Rachel and Mrs. Gilbert were chatting away like they were best girlfriends, but Olivia didn't really feel like talking. She was too busy taking in the scenery.

It seemed like another world. Autumn wasn't really a thing in Florida, and was often just as hot and humid as the summer. Here, autumn was a Technicolor, multisensory experience. The air was cold and crisp and smelled like burning leaves and apples and wet stones, tempting Olivia to hang her head out the window. The leaves on the trees were just starting to turn color, a phenomenon she'd read about in science class, but had never seen in real life.

A stand of normal, green trees would be whizzing by outside the van and then suddenly a single tree would appear, ablaze with crimson and orange foliage that seemed too gaudy to be natural.

"This is Westley," Mrs. Gilbert said as they got off the highway and drove though a quaint storybook village. "The town closest to the school. There's a shuttle to take you into town on weekends, but you have to bring a chaperone. One adult for every five students. At least, until you're a senior. Then you can have a car and go wherever you like, as long as you have a driver's license, and as long as you're back by curfew."

"Does a car come with my scholarship, too?" Olivia asked, deadpan, but smiling inside. "A Corvette, maybe?"

Mrs. Gilbert laughed, hearty and genuine.

"You wish!" she said.

The Deerborn Academy had its own private driveway that seemed a hundred miles long. Then, finally, the trees parted and the school was revealed.

It looked the way Olivia pictured an Ivy League college might look. Venerable brick and stone buildings from the turn of the century. Well-kept lawns and winding, leaf-strewn walkways. There was a rippling, steel-blue lake visible between two buildings on the right, and down a hill to the left was a cluster of more modern structures along with an athletic field. It seemed like the kind of place where privileged, old-money kids played polo and dabbled in art for a few years before heading off to cushy jobs at daddy's brokerage firm or mother's fashion magazine.

In other words, it wasn't the kind of place a girl from the wrong side of Jacksonville ever imagined she would end up. Never in a million years.

Yet, there she was.

The van pulled up to a building and stopped. She got out and went to help Rachel with her bags.

5

Tony sat for the last time in Doctor Chalmers' office. Director Bloom was there too, along with a stern, shapeless woman in her sixties who Tony didn't recognize. She had a steely bob and a mouth shaped like a staple.

The room was stuffy and cramped and felt overcrowded with the four of them sitting way too close together. Tony was wracked with anxiety, but couldn't let it show. He was nearly free.

"Tell me, Tony," Doctor Chalmers said. "How do you feel about transitioning back into a more independent life?"

Doctor Chalmers really wasn't a bad guy—he was just trying to do his job. He was blond and earnest and looked way younger than the fifty years he said he was. He was a vegetarian and into fitness in that annoying, almost religious kind of way that made Tony feel like a fat slob, even though he was in pretty good shape for a guy with one arm. It was just that his psych meds made him retain water and kept him from getting real lean.

He couldn't wait to get off them.

Wouldn't be much longer now.

"Well," he said. He had a whole speech prepared in

advance, and had been practicing it in his head for weeks. "I'm excited and a little bit nervous, too, naturally. It's a big change, but I feel as though I've gained the cognitive tools I need to manage my symptoms and start really living life again."

"And what about Olivia Dunham?" Doctor Chalmers asked. "Are you finally willing to let go of your obsession with her, and accept that the loss of your arm was nothing but an unfortunate accident?"

This was it. His big Oscar-winning moment. He couldn't afford to screw it up.

"It's been a challenge," he said, allowing a little emotional quiver into his voice. It wasn't hard to fake. He always got emotional when he thought of the girl. "It seemed so real to me at the time. But I know now that I was suffering from delusions caused by my substance abuse and the underlying chemical imbalance in my brain. I realize that those obsessive thoughts may never go away completely, but I no longer feel any compulsion to act on those thoughts. I feel like I'm well on my way to becoming a whole person again."

There. That should do it.

Doctor Chalmers didn't reply, he just scribbled some notes on his little pad. The director was frowning, unmoving as a stone idol. The woman was checking over several papers in an extremely thick file. Tony could feel his heart trying to climb up his throat and make a run for it. This had to work. If his release was denied again, he really *would* go crazy.

"You've taught me so much, Doctor Chalmers," Tony added, breaking the silence. It wasn't a lie, either. The doc *had* taught him a lot, specifically what to say to make his doctors happy. "I can't tell you how grateful I am for all your help."

Doctor Chalmers looked up at him and then back down at his pad, and Tony wondered if he'd pushed it too hard with that last bit. The doc wasn't some crackhead hooker who'd never made it through the ninth grade. He was a smart, educated guy. Bullshitting a man like that took real finesse.

"I'd like to go on record," the woman said, "and state that I personally don't feel this patient should be released. His overall demeanor while in a lucid, non-agitated state remains shallow, manipulative and insincere, consistent with his diagnosis of antisocial personality disorder. While the active delusions, psychosis, and paranoia which inspired the initial offense may be effectively controlled with medication at this time, his underlying pathology does not bode well for successful integration into the community.

"There is a very high probability that this patient will reoffend within three to six months of release," she concluded.

It took every ounce of effort Tony could muster not to let the sour-faced bitch have it. He hated being talked about like he wasn't even in the room.

"Duly noted," Director Bloom said, with a tone that made it clear that he couldn't have cared less.

"In Tony's defense," Doctor Chalmers said. "He's been doing extremely well since we last tweaked his meds, and I feel that he has a genuine desire to make positive changes in his life."

"Give it a rest, David," Bloom said. "You can't save every mutt in the pound."

"My own personal reservations notwithstanding," the woman continued while Tony fumed silently, smile plastered across his frozen face. "According to our records, this patient maxed out his court-mandated sentence as of last Tuesday. Unfortunately, he doesn't have the financial resources or insurance to cover extended in-patient treatment."

The smile on Tony's face thawed and spread. He won. He'd outlasted the bastards, and there was nothing they could do to keep him. He was free. He could have kissed the staple-mouthed woman, but didn't want to push his luck.

"So what," Doctor Chalmers said. "We just dump him out on the street with no assistance or aftercare of any kind?"

"All we can do at this point," the staple-mouthed woman said, still shuffling her papers, "is provide two weeks worth of medication and a list of agencies where the patient can apply for follow-up services and other public assistance."

"Well, that's that then," Doctor Chalmers said, a deep flush creeping up from under his starched collar. "I'm sorry, Tony, but it looks like there's nothing more I can do."

He stood and extended his hand.

Tony looked down at the split-hook device at the end of his cheap prosthetic right arm, swiftly stuffing down the wave of toxic rage that welled up inside him. The urge to smash in all of their smug, judgmental faces was back with a vengeance, but he was so close to getting out of there. Nearly free.

No, this was all part of the test. He had to stay calm. Act like it didn't matter.

He forced a smile and took Doctor Chalmers' offered right hand with his left. Acknowledging his disability, but not making a big deal about it. Just a regular guy offering a normal, friendly goodbye.

"Take my number," Doctor Chalmers said, offering a

business card. "You can still call me if you need someone to talk to, okay?"

"Thanks, Doc," he replied. "I will."

"Good luck out there, Tony."

Tony smiled. He didn't need luck. He just needed will.

6

Tony checked the address of Saint Fillan House, the transitional residence in Gainesville to which he'd been assigned.

He'd almost tossed the address in the bus station trash barrel, along with the two weeks worth of meds he didn't need. But he figured he could use a place to flop for a few days while he reconnoitered and organized and fomented a plan to enact the sacred duty that had been postponed by his unfortunate incarceration.

The halfway house was in a rundown, primarily industrial neighborhood east of Main Street. It was one of the few actual houses left on a block populated mostly by cheap aluminum Quonset huts and weedy parking lots, cowering between the waste water reclamation station and a massive, thrumming power plant.

The house's exterior had been freshly painted a sad, drab grayish blue with thick white trim. There was a plastic Christmas wreath on the door and a chipped plaster nativity scene on the patchy lawn. A scrawny black man was sitting on a folding chair on the sagging porch, seeming lost inside an oversized Joe Camel T-shirt that fit him like a dress. He couldn't have been older than thirty, but had no front teeth.

"Hello!" he called out to Tony, rocking gently back and forth. "Hello, mmmm-hmm. Hello!"

Tony cranked up his smile and nodded, telling himself this was only going to be for a night or two. Just until he was able to find Olivia Dunham.

The door opened before he could knock and a heavyset strawberry blonde in her late forties greeted him. She looked like an aging biker mama with faded tattoos on her meaty arms and mannish hands. She had some of the biggest natural breasts Tony had ever seen, so big that they made her look like she was about to topple forward from the weight of them, but her hard gray eyes and no-nonsense Saint Fillan polo shirt let you know up front not to even bother looking.

"Don't need no doorbell with Shawn on duty," she said. Her voice was deep, full of nails and gravel. "Ain't that right, Shawn?"

"That's right, mmmm-hmm," the scrawny guy said, still rocking. "That's right."

"You must be Tony Orsini," she said to Tony. "I'm Maggie."

She was about to extend a welcoming hand, but noticed his prosthetic at the last second and clenched her fist, keeping it at her side.

"Pleased to meet you," Tony made himself say, keeping his expression pleasant.

"Around here," she said. "You'll answer to God first and me second. Got a problem with that?"

"No, ma'am," Tony said.

"Then come on in."

She stepped aside and motioned for him to enter.

The interior of the house was overly lit with buzzing

fluorescent lights, and smelled like moldy carpet and roach spray. The front door opened into a large common room with several mismatched couches and a small, snowy television.

There were several men there. A motley mix of ethnicities and ages with varying degrees of hygiene and social skills. They included a very young looking blond kid with thick ladders of scar up both freckled arms. An obese, light-skinned black guy with a shaved head and a lazy eye. A gray-bearded little gnome of a man who might have been Hispanic, or maybe not.

"Gentlemen," Maggie said. "Say hi to our new resident, Tony."

Some of the men waved or greeted him verbally, but more than half did not. Tony didn't care. He wasn't planning to be there long enough to bother with making friends, but he knew it was in his best interest to *appear* friendly. And it was much easier to act friendly if he pictured shooting them one by one, execution style.

"Hello, everyone," he said instead of shooting them.

"You're in bunk number four," Maggie told him. "Through here."

Tony followed her down a narrow, claustrophobic hallway and into one of two back bedrooms.

"That's you on the bottom," she said, pointing to a cheap bunk bed on the right side of the cramped room. "There's fresh sheets, a blanket, and a towel. Bathroom's at the other end of the hall, across from the chapel."

"Thanks," Tony said.

"Just so you know," she said. "We have a zero-tolerance policy for drug and alcohol use in this house. Fail your piss test, and you're out, no ifs, ands, or buts."

"Yes, ma'am," he said, smiling hard enough to crack his teeth while picturing driving a fork into her eye.

"Dinner's at six," she said. "Get settled in and cleaned up, and we'll see you then."

7

Tony lay in the narrow, lumpy bunk, going over his plans for the day, when he felt a sudden spike of resonant energy inside his brain. The neurons that Olivia had transformed with her unholy demon power were humming, singing to their mistress.

He knew that, wherever she was, she must be experiencing a rush of intense emotion, and he could feel his own rage welling up in psychic harmony. He felt her ebb and flow inside him all the time, even though her dark energy had been blunted by the thick cotton candy spun inside his skull by all his medications.

Despite this chemical interference, he had still been able to feel her emotions growing stronger and more complex than ever over the past three years. His precious little monster was a big girl now, and the flush of teenage hormones was clearly intensifying her power.

Now that the mind-numbing cocktail was starting to cycle out of Tony's system, Olivia's emotional waves hit him even harder, like a narcotic rush. It was both euphoric and terrifying. She was becoming more and more dangerous with every passing day. Tony had to stop her before she blossomed into her full adult potential.

Because once that happened, there would be no limits to her evil power.

He got himself showered and dressed, humming to himself like a man in love. He showed up in the dining room for a lousy breakfast of instant coffee, burnt eggs, and cheap white bread, chewing with his mouth closed and being personable and polite toward Maggie and the other residents. It was essential for Tony to appear easygoing and low-maintenance. There were plenty of problem children at St Fillan's to hog all the attention. Which was the way Tony liked it.

He had more important things to do.

Tony's first stop was the library at the University of Florida. He'd been able to talk Maggie into giving him a lift over to the nearby campus under the pretense of looking into some adult education programs. The library was a massive glass-fronted, red brick building that seemed like an uneasy marriage between the old and the new.

The students who filled the building reflected that conflict. Many were still sporting the familiar bright colors and big hair that Tony remembered from before his incarceration, but then he'd spot someone with a ring in their nose like an Indian broad, or someone dressed like a homeless lumberjack. He'd see girls with big clunky Frankenstein boots and boys sporting what looked like ice-skates with wheels.

He was still the same, but the outside world had gone on without him. It was time for him to play catch up.

He went straight to the periodicals room, fully intending to concentrate on his search for Olivia, but he found himself distracted by all the intriguing new current events and pop culture. War in the Balkans. The Human Genome Project. The Spice Girls.

No. He had to be disciplined and stay focused.

Sifting methodically through a variety of public records, Tony soon found the address of an apartment where Olivia and her family had lived from the time of the fire up until September of 1995. He was surprised to find an obituary for Denise Dunham, but was unable to find any information at all about what had happened to the daughters after their mother's death.

He found the name of a case worker from the Department of Children and Families, who had initially been assigned to Olivia and Rachel Dunham, but no follow-up information whatsoever. No foster home, no orphanage, nothing. If worse came to worst, he could head down to Jacksonville and pay a personal visit to Mrs. Leona Byers, but he wasn't willing to give up searching just yet.

A tall, slender girl with a long blond ponytail walked into the room pushing a cart full of magazines, and his heart clenched like a fist in his chest. It wasn't Olivia—it couldn't be her—but just for a moment, he'd felt irrationally sure it would be. Then when the girl turned toward him, she revealed a plain forgettable face with a large, narrow nose and thin lips that didn't quite cover her long, horsey teeth. She left the cart beside the librarian's desk and sat down, tapping away at a keyboard.

She looked up and caught Tony staring at her. Instead of being angry, she got up and came over to the table where he had been poring over old records.

"Can I help you find something?" she asked.

"An old dear friend of mine passed away from cancer back in September," he said. "I was serving in the military, in Bosnia at the time, and lost my arm in combat." He raised his prosthetic. She stared for a moment, then turned back to his face. He put the hook down and continued. "I only just found out about Denise's death when I got released from the veterans hospital, two days ago."

"I'm so sorry," the young librarian said, purposefully not looking at his arm.

"She didn't have any family," he said, allowing himself to tear up a little. "Other than her two beautiful little daughters. I can't find any information about what happened to those girls, and it just breaks my heart to think of them in some crummy orphanage somewhere. I was hoping, well, maybe I could find them and see about adopting them myself. I know that's what Denise would have wanted."

"That's so good of you," the librarian said, all dewy-eyed. "Especially after everything you've been through. Let me see if I can help you."

Tony had to force himself not to smile.

"Here," the librarian said. "Come with me."

She led him down the hall and into a large, brightly lit room with no windows. Inside were several modern steel desks, each one with its own large, beige plastic computer. They were all taken by students, except for the one farthest from the door.

"Here," she said, pulling an extra chair up beside the desk. "Let's try a search on the World Wide Web."

"The world wide what?" Tony took a seat in the extra chair and frowned at the monitor screen.

The librarian smiled. Way too much of her pale pink gums was visible between her upper lip and her teeth.

"Since you've been overseas," she said, all breathless and excited to be talking about what was clearly one of her favorite subjects, "you've missed out on a ton of awesome tech development back home."

Really, this was almost too easy.

"What are the names of the two girls?" she asked.

"Start with the older one," he said. "Olivia Dunham."

He spelled out the last name on a piece of yellow scrap paper.

"Got it," she said, long thin fingers flying on the keyboard. "See this is called AltaVista. You can use this cool new program to execute a search for a person or a topic or anything. But you need to narrow the results by using Boolean operators like 'AND' or 'NOT.' See, like this."

"Wow, that's amazing," Tony said, ignoring the screen completely and looking at the librarian. "Say, you're really smart. I bet a lot of guys see a pretty blonde like you and think you must be dumb. Boy, are they in for a surprise. You're the total package. Beauty and brains."

The librarian blushed and tucked her head down, a shy smile on her homely face. She didn't say anything, just kept on typing.

"Okay," she said after a few moments. "Check this out. I got a hit on the website for this prep school in Westley, Massachusetts called the Deerborn Academy. There are two Dunhams, Olivia and Rachel registered this semester. Looks like a pretty fancy place, so they must have somebody looking after them financially. Hey, check this out, here's a picture of the older one, see if that's her."

Tony's breath caught and he leaned into the monitor, desperate for a glimpse of Olivia. But the screen was mostly blank. Nothing but a little stripe of darkness at the top of the frame that was getting gradually wider one line at a time.

"I don't see any picture," Tony said.

"Give it a minute," the librarian said. "It takes time to load."

This excruciating striptease went on and on for what

felt like ages, revealing first the top of a group of heads wearing matching caps, then, line by line, their faces. The kids in the photo were holding rifles and wearing yellow-tinted eye protectors.

The photo was eventually revealed to be a group shot of the Deerborn Academy Rifle Team. There was only one female, on the far left of the top row. It had to be Olivia. She wore the same eye protectors and team cap as the rest, and the photo was pretty small, so it wasn't that easy to distinguish her features. But he could see that she was tall now, as tall as—taller even—than most of the boys on the team.

The front of her blue team uniform shirt had filled out quite nicely since their last encounter. He could make out part of a blond ponytail half hidden behind her right shoulder, so she hadn't changed her hair color, although it did seem just a little bit darker than he remembered. More of a warm golden blond than the pale tresses he remembered twisting like electrified snakes around her flushed face in the seconds before she'd burned his arm off.

"Amazing," he said softly, feeling genuinely choked up and not bothering to hide it. "That's absolutely amazing. Thank you so much for your help. I can't tell you how much this means to me."

"My pleasure," the librarian said, flashing that big gummy smile. "I need to get back to my desk now, but you're welcome to stay logged on and search around a little more on your own."

"Thanks," he said. "I think I will."

It took him some time to get the hang of the program, but he was a quick learner and soon he had called up photos of various Florida Police Academy graduates from a five-year period around the time of his own graduation. It didn't take him long to find the right man.

8

Tony's first order of business was to get his hand on some kind of firearm. He'd sketched out a workable schematic for a custom-made, bolt-on blade attachment that he could use in place of the hook on his prosthetic arm, but that wasn't what he needed for this next phase of his plan. For the more immediate caper, only a gun would do.

It didn't have to be fancy, it just had to shoot bullets.

He wasn't exactly in a position—legally or financially—to purchase a gun, so he was going to have to obtain one through more creative methods. Unfortunately, people who owned guns were generally more difficult to rob than people without them.

He'd test-driven and rejected several plans before settling on one he thought would work. He figured that a beginner's gun safety class was a great place to meet people who owned them, but had no idea how to use them.

Unfortunately, even after all these years, any savvy gun instructor would smell cop all over him, and wouldn't buy him as a novice. But if all went according to plan, Tony wouldn't need to actually *attend* the class in order to get what he needed.

The Thunder Creek Shooting Range was about fifteen miles outside of Gainesville, and the distance required Tony to steal a car in order to get there. That was just as well, since he'd need wheels to tail his chosen target, anyway. He picked a forgettable mid-range Honda sedan with an infant car seat and a yellow diamond sign in the rear window that read BABY ON BOARD. He boosted it and made it out to the range with ten minutes to spare.

Tony sauntered into the range and pretended to browse the glass cases full of ballistic candy, while the attendees at a gun safety class gathered around the instructor—a friendly, smiling older guy with a white mustache whose ample beer belly was barely contained by a tight green polo shirt. But Tony wasn't interested in the instructor, he was interested in the students.

He made small talk with the plump, older woman behind the counter, pretending to be interested in buying a membership.

"Lost my arm in Bosnia," he told her, holding up the hook. "So, now I need to start over. Teach myself to shoot with my left hand."

"God bless you, baby," she said, giving his good hand a little pat. "Let me give you a brochure."

He took the pamphlet and pretended to be interested in a story about her son who'd died for his country, God bless him, and how noble it was to make such sacrifices to protect our freedom. He smiled and nodded, all the while watching the class out of the corner of his eye, and singling out the easiest mark.

A woman, maybe early-to-mid thirties. Hispanic and pretty, a hundred pounds, tops. Little gold cross around her fragile neck. No wedding ring. She was wearing a conservative floral print dress and low heels, like she'd just gotten off her job as a receptionist—probably in a dentist's office or something.

What really drew Tony to her was that she gave off that distinct "victim" vibe. Shy, skittish, unsure of herself. The kind of woman who bought a gun because she'd been hurt before, and didn't want it to happen again.

Too bad it would.

He told the old lady that he wanted to think about it, before committing to a membership program, then went out to the Honda to wait for the class to end.

About two hours later, the woman he'd tagged came out of the range, chatting with two of the other students—a chubby redheaded man and another Hispanic female about ten years younger than his target. They stood around a battered yellow Pinto with a bumper sticker that read *JESUS ES EL SEÑOR*. After a few minutes the other two students broke off and headed toward the back of the lot, while the target got into the car. She backed out of the parking space, then drove in the direction of the exit.

Tony cranked the ignition and followed her.

He tailed her back to a pretty decent little house in a so-so neighborhood. It had a two-car driveway, but no garage. There were frilly lace curtains in the front window, and when she unlocked the door and went inside, Tony saw her walk over and greet a tiny old lady who looked related. Probably her mother or grandmother. Certainly nobody who would give him any trouble.

As he sat there, watching the two women go about their day, he felt a distracting twinge of heat resonating through his arm, singing Olivia's name. It was as if she was as impatient as he was.

Like she couldn't wait for them to be together.

Inside the little house, the target went into a back room and came out wearing a different outfit. Tight jeans and a silky blouse that actually showed a little skin at the neck. There was a short exchange between the two women, and it seemed to be about the number of buttons that should or shouldn't be open on the blouse.

Without warning, an SUV pulled into the driveway. A big, blond guy with a goatee got out and went to knock on the door.

The target answered, greeting the guy with an anxious smile, waved over her shoulder at the older lady, and then walked with the blond guy over to the passenger side of the SUV.

He opened the door for her like a gentleman, but there seemed to be some sort of hushed argument going on between them. The blond guy closed her door, and then walked around the back of the vehicle to the driver's side, shaking his head and looking aggravated.

Tony let them pull a discreet distance away, then followed the SUV to a mid-range seafood restaurant and watched them go in. By this time there was a stiff silence between them.

Finding a spot in the parking lot, he waited.

They came out sooner than he'd expected. Clearly they hadn't lingered over a romantic dinner. And from the look on her face, things had not gone well. Once again they didn't speak as they got back into the SUV.

Driving back to the house, they pulled into the driveway again. They stayed inside the parked vehicle for nearly an hour, but they weren't necking. They were fighting, arms waving and angry voices audible despite the distance and the SUV's closed doors.

Eventually, she got out and ran, crying, up to the door. The older woman was waiting and let her in, putting a comforting arm around her. The blond guy gunned the engine, backed out of the driveway, and accelerated away, burning angry rubber on the tarmac.

Tony was debating whether he should move in now, kill both of the women and get the gun, or whether he should wait and take a little more time to get to know his target and her habits. He knew he should err on the side of caution, but Olivia's hot harmonic presence inside his brain made him impatient.

He was about to get out of the car when the target came out of the house.

Behind her, the older woman was clinging to her arm, begging her not to go, but she pulled away and ran to her Pinto. As she started it up and peeled out, the older woman in the doorway crossed herself.

Curious, Tony followed the target.

She drove out of town to a large, rustic-looking house in a wooded area and parked crookedly in front, blocking the driveway. The blond guy's vehicle was in the driveway, as was a low-end silver sedan. She walked to the front door, opened it with a key, and went inside.

Tony waited with his window rolled down, idly swatting at bugs and fiddling with a fast-food napkin. He'd folded it up as small as it would get, and had just tossed it into the cup holder when a gunshot tore through the muggy silence.

He looked up at the house and saw several bright muzzle flashes through the picture window, each one accompanied by a sharp *crack*.

Seconds later, the target came running out of the front door, tossed something into the bushes on her left, and then got into her car and drove away.

Tony got out of his car and ran to the front door, squatting down and feeling through the thick, glossy bushes until his fingers found what he was looking for.

The gun.

It was a compact semi-automatic pistol, a tiny little thing that fit into the palm of his hand.

That would do nicely.

He couldn't resist peeking in through the open front door to see what had gone down. The blond guy with the goatee was on the couch with his pants down and a face full of lead. Facedown on the floor about ten feet away was a dead brunette in heels... and nothing else.

Atta girl, Tony thought, smiling to himself.

Guess she wasn't such a helpless victim after all.

9

The Deerborn Academy was like a ghost town during the winter holiday. The familiar quad was blanketed in nearly virgin snow, marred only by a single lonely trail left by a custodian's waffle-tread boots. The gargoyles lurking above the entrance to the James T. Fenwick Library wore white caps and icicle beards. The venerable old science building and the more modern, glass-fronted arts center were both dark and silent.

The four dorms were nearly empty. Most of the students and teachers were home with their families, leaving behind a skeleton crew of bachelor staff and a handful of kids with nowhere else to go. Everyone else would start tricking back in the next day, January 6th, for the start of the new semester. But that night, Olivia and Rachel pretty much had the whole campus to themselves.

Which was the way Olivia liked it.

Rachel had been camping out in Olivia's room while their respective roommates were home for the holidays. They'd celebrated a quiet Christmas together, and now it was time for another family celebration.

"Happy birthday to you!" Rachel sang, holding out

a homemade chocolate cupcake with a single pink candle stuck in the center. "Happy birthday, dear Olivia, happy birthday to *youuuuuu!*"

"Thanks, sis," Olivia said, squeezing Rachel into a sideways hug.

"Mrs. Lehman let me use the oven in the cafeteria," Rachel told her. "Make a wish!"

Olivia didn't really have a wish, other than a generalized desire to make sure that Rachel would always be taken care of, no matter what. But she blew the candle out anyway.

"Do you feel sixteen?" Rachel asked, setting the cupcake on Olivia's desk.

Olivia shook her head, and smiled.

"Feels the same, I guess," she said.

She didn't tell Rachel that she had felt thirty since she was thirteen. That she didn't even know what being a teenager was supposed to be like. She also didn't tell Rachel that she hated her birthday. That she dreaded it every year. While everyone else was celebrating New Year's Eve, making resolutions and toasting to the future, Olivia was haunted by the past.

Randall.

She hadn't opened his annual birthday card yet, because she didn't have the stomach. How had that bastard managed to find her at Deerborn? Would she never be rid of him? She kept telling herself that she should just throw the envelope away unopened, but somehow she never did. Every year she opened that card, and just the sight of his childish, semi-literate handwriting made her physically sick.

He never wrote anything negative or overtly hostile inside those sappy, generic cards, just the phrase "Thinking of you." But the unwritten message was loud and clear.

I'm still here.

Just a few inches to the left, and that second bullet would have hit his femoral artery, causing him to bleed out before the ambulance arrived. In the years since that terrible night, Olivia had become a champion skeet and trap shooter, and was the current co-captain of the Deerborn Academy Rifle Team. She was driven to excel at the sport—so much so that Coach Lowenbruck had recently started pushing her to try out for the Olympics.

But for Olivia it was too little, too late. Because she'd been so scared that night, so overwhelmed with emotion—and when it really mattered, she'd failed.

It was a failure Randall would never let her forget.

His yearly reminder sat on Olivia's desk beside Rachel's charmingly lopsided cupcake. She reached for the pastry and casually slid the envelope under her history textbook, so her little sister wouldn't see it and get upset. Rachel was sensitive and deeply superstitious. A girl who loved birthdays and cupcakes and presents. Olivia didn't want to ruin that for her, so she never told Rachel about the cards.

Olivia made herself smile and took a bite of the cupcake, leaving chocolate and sprinkles smeared across her lips.

"Delicious," she said. "Thanks, Rach."

There was a tentative knock on the half-open door, and she jumped involuntarily. Then Kieran McKie stuck his shaggy head into the room.

Kieran was a tall, lanky senior who looked kind of like what you'd get if a teenage mad scientist had joined a grunge band. His unruly brown hair was at that awkward, still-growing-out shoulder length, and his bony wrists always stuck way out of his too-short sleeves. He wore heavy, vintage horn-rimmed glasses and the eyes behind them were the exact same shade of green as Olivia's.

He wasn't an orphan, but he may as well have been. His single mother was Kristie McKie, the celebrity fitness trainer. She was always busy jet-setting all over the world, shooting her bestselling workout videos and whipping her famous clients into shape. Holidays were her busiest time, since everyone was being tempted by all that wicked holiday food, and needed to work it off.

As a result Kieran was stuck there at Deerborn with the rest of the holiday orphans. Olivia met him during the Thanksgiving break, and he had quickly become her one and only real friend. She was actually kind of glad to have him around, although she would rather die than admit it.

"Hey," he said, holding up a festively wrapped package. "Happy birthday!"

Olivia set the half-eaten cupcake down and accepted the present. She could tell from the feel and weight that it was books. She smiled.

"If my powers of deduction serve me well…" She carefully removed the wrapping paper and grinned at the cloth cover revealed beneath. "Oooh, nice."

"They're from the 1920s, I think," he said. "Not fancy first editions or anything like that, but they're in great condition. That's *A Study in Scarlet*, *The White Company*, and *The Sign of Four*, plus a few extra short stories, too."

Kieran always joked that she was Sherlock Holmes, and he was her loyal Watson. He wanted to be a writer and she wanted to be an FBI agent. She would solve crimes, he said, and he would write about them.

"Wow, that's awesome," Rachel said. "But you know what, I'd better…"

She made a wordless gesture toward the dorm room door, then swiftly made herself scarce, flashing a conspiratorial wink on the way out.

Olivia rolled her eyes. Ever since Thanksgiving, Rachel was endlessly scheming to get Olivia and Kieran together—even though Olivia had told her sister a hundred times that they were just friends. Then, when Kieran's girlfriend had dumped him right before winter break, Rachel had redoubled her efforts.

True, Olivia really liked Kieran. Trusted him and enjoyed hanging out with him, but she just didn't have time for a boyfriend. Rachel had a new crush every other week and seemed to think life wasn't worth living if you weren't in love. But Olivia had her studies to worry about—maintaining her grade point average, organizing meets for her shooting team and, of course, keeping an eye on her little sister.

There just wasn't room in her head for romance.

But she was starting to get the feeling that Kieran had other ideas. She saw it in his eyes when he thought she wasn't looking. She was pretty sure that was part of the reason his previous girlfriend had dumped him. Because she didn't want to share him with another girl.

She set the books on her desk. She could still see the corner of Randall's card sticking out from under the history book. Without thinking, she scowled.

"What's wrong?" Kieran asked, a concerned frown creasing his pale forehead.

Damn him for being able to read her so easily. She steeled herself, deliberately smoothing her face to a calm, blank mask.

"Nothing," she replied, picking up the cupcake. "Want some of this? It's delicious."

"Okay," he said with a funny little half-smile, obviously not buying her dodge, but graciously allowing her to change the subject.

She broke off a piece of the cupcake and held it out to

him. To her surprise, he bent down and ate the cake out of her hand, his lips brushing against her fingers.

"It's good," he said, knuckling some stray crumbs from the corner of his mouth.

For a long, awkward moment, neither of them said anything. Olivia was still holding the last sticky chunk of cake in her other hand. She didn't really want to eat it, but didn't know what else to do with it. All she could think about was how close Kieran was standing to her, and how there was hardly anyone else in the entire deserted dorm.

"Do you want more?" she asked, because she couldn't come up with anything else to say. She must have been blushing, because her face felt like a frying pan. "Cake, I mean."

This was getting way out of control, way too fast.

He took a clumsy half step closer to her, big feet shuffling in his battered Chuck Taylors. He was blushing, too, green eyes like hers overflowing with something raw, intense, and unnamable. She looked away, heart racing.

"Listen, I..." he began.

There was a sudden sharp *pop*, like a small caliber gunshot, and the light on Olivia's desk blew out in a shower of sparks, throwing the room into darkness. Without even realizing she'd done it, she dropped the rest of the cupcake and shoved Kieran protectively behind her, even though he was four inches taller than her, and thirty pounds heavier.

"Jeez, Liv," he said. "It's just a lamp." He laid a gentle hand on her shoulder. "Stand down, soldier."

She turned to face him in the dark. They were even closer now, almost touching, and she could feel the heat of his body burning through that scant inch of space between them. His hand was still on her shoulder, but it had started sliding tentatively up under her hair to cup the back of her neck.

Oh my god, she thought. *He's gonna kiss me.*

I want him to kiss me.

"Olivia? Is everything all right?"

Light from the hallway spilled into the room as Mrs. Gilbert picked that moment to push the door open. From the moment Olivia had arrived, Mrs. Gilbert had taken her under her wing, and while Olivia had been suspicious of the older woman at first, she had quickly warmed up to her.

Now she was the closest thing Olivia had to a mother—even more so than her own fragile and helpless mother had been when she was still alive.

Mrs. Gilbert reached in and switched on the overhead light, then frowned dramatically.

"You," she said to Kieran. "*Out!* Olivia, you know male visitors are *not* allowed in dorm rooms."

"Sorry, Mrs. G," Kieran said, backing away from Olivia and showing his palms. "I just came by to give Olivia her birthday present."

"Well," Mrs. Gilbert said, blue eyes sparkling with barely suppressed mirth. "It's a good thing I arrived before you had a chance to deliver. Now get the hell out of here, before I kick your scrawny ass into next week."

Kieran nodded quickly and moved to obey.

"See you later, Liv," he said, lingering for a minute in the doorway before turning to go.

Once he had gone, Mrs. Gilbert turned to look at her, a concerned expression on her face.

"What happened, honey?" she asked.

"Nothing," Olivia said, crouching down to clean the dropped cupcake off the floor beside her desk. "We're just friends."

"I wasn't born yesterday, you know," the older

woman said. "I've got three grown kids and a pretty good idea where they came from—but that's not what I'm talking about. I'm talking about that firecracker sound—like a little explosion in here." She waved a ring-laden hand in front of her face. "Do you smell that weird metallic odor? Sort of like... ozone."

"My desk light blew out," Olivia told her. "Must have been a short or something."

Mrs. Gilbert frowned, looking from the burnt-out lamp to Olivia and back again.

"Tell me exactly what happened," she said, sounding very serious.

"I don't know," Olivia said, feeling inexplicably defensive all of a sudden. "It just... blew up."

"What happened right before that?" Mrs. Gilbert pressed.

"Nothing," Olivia said warily. "I opened my birthday present, and we had some cake, and then..." She shrugged. "How should I know what caused the light to blow up? I'm not an electrician."

"Okay, okay," Mrs. Gilbert said, unplugging the lamp and winding the cord around the base. "I'll get you a new one. And I don't want to see that boy in your room again, or you'll get Saturday detention."

"Don't worry," Olivia said. "It won't happen again."

Lorna Gilbert sat in her office with the phone receiver stuck between her shoulder and cheek. She had wrapped the broken lamp in newspaper and was carefully placing it in a box filled with packing peanuts.

"Yes," she said. "I'm sending the lamp over to the lab right now. She's unwilling to admit it, but I suspect sexual activity of some kind was occurring in the minutes leading up to the event." She paused, sealing the box and applying a pre-paid sticker addressed to the New York offices of Massive Dynamic. "I understand. Of course. Will do."

She hung up the phone.

Rachel didn't know what her sister's problem was. She loved Olivia more than anyone else in the world, but sometimes she wished that she would just lighten up.

Olivia had always seemed different than other girls, but Rachel could never put her finger on the difference. When she was young, she used to pretend that she and Olivia were actually magical elves who had been left with human parents by accident. But as boring and ordinary as Rachel really was, there had always been something a little otherworldly about her sister. Something in her eyes, in the way strange, inexplicable things sometimes happened when she was around.

Rachel always thought that their stepfather had been able to sense that otherness in Olivia, too. He sensed it, and he hated her for it. He'd been mean and violent toward Rachel, of course, but Olivia had been like a magnet for his wrath, and always got punished twice as hard.

They'd been through so much together, Rachel and Olivia, but that was over now. Things were better—perfect, really. Rachel had never really liked school before, but she actually looked forward to going to classes now. Especially art class, which was her favorite. Her art teacher, Ms. Dandine, was really cool. She had a tattoo and swore a lot and drove a vintage purple Karmann Ghia. She let the kids draw comic books and taught them how to make monster masks. Plus there was a really cute boy in her art class named Nathaniel who was from England and had this fantastic accent. Which she probably shouldn't be noticing, since she'd been casually, sort-of-but-not-really seeing Brandon Ardmore since last Tuesday.

But whatever, he knew it wasn't serious.

Rachel walked down the path to the junior girls' dorm with her chilly hands stuck deep in her pockets, wondering what was going on back in Olivia's room. She didn't like being in her own building when it was nearly deserted, which was why she spent so much time in Olivia's room. But Mrs. Lamquist was there, and she was okay, although she was kind of fussy and got really wigged out if anything got moved around or left in a mess.

She figured maybe she'd get Mrs. L. to let her watch a movie or something while she gave her sister time alone with Kieran.

Rachel just didn't understand why Olivia was so reluctant to admit that she was into Kieran. He was so obviously into her, and she could deny it all she wanted, but Rachel knew that Olivia liked him back.

It seemed like a no brainer.

But Olivia had never had a boyfriend. Never had any friends at all really, except for this one kid named Nick who went to the daycare center with her when she was younger. But that was like a million years ago. Which was why Rachel was so bound and determined to get Kieran and Olivia together. It didn't seem healthy or normal to be sixteen and not have a boyfriend. What was she so afraid of anyway?

Afraid she might like it?

10

It was 5:30 a.m., still dark and quiet. Tony watched his target from across the street as the man loaded a pair of suitcases into the trunk of an old white Datsun.

The man was a cop, a detective. His name was Jimmy Obejas, age thirty-six, Cuban-American, divorced father of three, and reformed alcoholic. He had dark hair and eyes, like Tony. He had the same complexion, same height, and same build—give or take an arm. A little younger than Tony might have wanted, but everything else about him was ideal. Especially the reformed alcoholic part.

Jimmy was on his way to pick up his son and daughter for a visit to Disney World. He didn't know it, but he was about to fall off the wagon again. His ex-wife and kids wouldn't be at all surprised when he failed to show up for the promised trip. He'd taken a week off work for this family vacation, so no one in the department would wonder where he was, until long after Tony had gotten what he needed.

But the guy kept screwing around, forgetting things and double-checking things and making Tony crazy. The longer he waited, the lighter the sky would get. There was already a delicate flush of pink along the violet bellies of the clouds crowding the eastern sky. But finally, after the third trip back into his first-floor apartment, Jimmy came back out again with a bag from the toy store and an insulated thermos cup, and locked his front door. He put the toy bag on the passenger seat, took a swig from the cup, checked his watch, and then got in behind the wheel.

Tony let him get a block-and-a-half head start before keying the big sedan he'd stolen and following the smaller white Datsun. He'd been tailing his target for weeks, learning his routine and watching his every move, so he already knew what route Jimmy usually took to pick up his kids at his ex's house just outside of Haines City. There was a perfect spot along Old Polk City Road where he and his target would meet for the first and last time. It was a ballsy move, taking the target out in the morning, early though it may be. But the circumstances were just too ideal.

He'd known from the beginning that he had divine forces on his side, and finally getting a lucky break like this just proved him right.

He hummed softly to himself along the way, feeling the subdued heat of Olivia's power throbbing gently in the remaining bones of his right arm. It was almost a weird kind of comfort, that heat. A reminder of his destiny. Ahead of him, the white car turned onto Old Polk, and he was close behind.

He was ready.

Pulling a rumpled map out of the glove box, he held it against the wheel and pretended to be trying to read it while driving. A lost, absent-minded tourist, trying to find his way to the ocean. When they reached the long, empty stretch of road that Tony had selected, he sped up until he was beside his quarry. He pushed the button to roll down the passenger window and gripped the wheel with his hook, using his good hand to make a window rolling motion at Jimmy and flashing his most disarming smile.

He could feel Olivia inside him, flowing sinuously like smoke through the convolutions of his brain.

Jimmy rolled his own window down and returned the smile.

"You lost?" he called out across the purr of the wind.

"Nope," Tony said, raising his gun and pulling the trigger.

Olivia pulled the car over to the side of a deserted stretch of road and got out. She could taste the swampy humid air of her home state, and hear the familiar soporific buzz of cicadas in the low, scrubby trees. It was dawn, and still cool, the lazy red sun just raising its head to peer through the eastern clouds.

She walked purposefully back along the empty road, toward a crumpled break in the tree line about a hundred yards away. When she got closer, she noticed the tail end of a white automobile sticking out of the brush. The smell of crushed leaves, sweet bay, and strangler fig mingling uneasily with the harsh odor of burnt brakes and leaking gasoline.

She pushed her way through the broken branches to reach the driver's side door. The window was open and the man behind the wheel was almost unrecognizable behind a mask of blood.

But he wasn't dead.

He was slumped against his seatbelt and barely breathing, but when he saw Olivia, his eyes went wide. He held out a shaking hand in desperate, wordless supplication.

She felt nothing for the dying man. No pity. No

remorse. He was merely an obstacle to be overcome in the pursuit of a sacred mission.

There was a gun in Olivia's hand. Her left hand.

She raised the gun and pressed it to the man's forehead, right between his pleading eyes.

She pulled the trigger.

Blood and brains showered the car's neat, well-maintained interior, pooling in the concave top of a thermos sitting in the cup holder. The man's head rocked back on his neck and bounced off the headrest, and then he slid down sideways and over the gear shift until his leaking forehead came to rest against a colorful bag in the passenger seat.

Olivia watched him die like she was waiting for a bus. It took a little longer than she was expecting, but soon enough he stopped breathing. Still she felt nothing.

She woke with a swallowed gasp, sitting up in her bed with the vivid horror of that dream clinging to her mind like an oil slick suffocating a sea bird. It was the most awful, most inexplicable dream she'd ever had.

She'd often talked with Kieran about how important it was in law enforcement to be able to see into minds of killers. She had read dozens of books on the subject of psychopathology and psychological profiling, but she'd never imagined anything even remotely like the kind of casual, careless boredom she'd felt in that dream.

What did it say about her own mind, that she was able to dredge something like that up from the depths of her subconscious? Or had she just been reading too much Thomas Harris?

Olivia pulled her blanket around her shoulders, shivering. Already, the details of the dream were unraveling, slipping away. She looked at her clock radio. It would be going off in two minutes, to wake her for her first period German class. There was a test that day, a minor quiz, but Olivia took every test very seriously and had stayed up late the night before studying.

She concentrated, and before long thoughts of German conjugation filled her head, washing away the last clinging fragments of her terrible, murderous dream.

The seductive whisper of Olivia's presence inside Tony's brain dissipated like fog as he pulled Jimmy's body upright in the driver's seat. He shook his head to clear it, and then went through the target's pockets, removing his wallet and badge. He also removed the keys from the ignition and used them to open the trunk. He took the larger of the two suitcases and set it to one side, then closed the trunk and set about meticulously covering the back end of the car with branches, making it virtually invisible from the road.

He had a bad moment when he heard a car coming down the road, but if the driver noticed anything odd, they didn't bother to stop and check it out. Tony held his breath as they passed, heart thumping, and tried to blend into the greenery as the sound of the car's engine faded into the distance.

He was in the clear, for now, but he'd ditch his own car at the earliest opportunity, just to be on the safe side.

That opportunity came at a rest stop east of Tampa, where he was able to score a green minivan. He ditched the gun in an overflowing dumpster, took only a brief detour to a neighborhood liquor store, and then drove the new vehicle back to Jimmy's apartment. He parked across the street and headed up the walkway, all ready to be confronted by nosy neighbors. He'd prepared an explanation about how he'd promised to water Jimmy's plants while he was at Disney World.

Turned out that nobody really cared about anyone else in the crummy little complex. Which was just the way Tony liked it.

Carrying a clinking bag from the liquor store, he let himself into the stuffy apartment and quickly discovered that his excuse wouldn't have worked, anyhow. There were no plants. In fact, there were hardly any decorations of any kind. The fire-sale sofa, a dull, unappealing plaid, was shoved up against the far wall like the homely girl no one wants to dance with. A second-hand recliner that looked like it got way more mileage than the sofa. Generic table, cluttered with mail and magazines and unwashed coffee mugs. Clearly the house of a recently divorced male who had been used to letting his wife handle things around the house.

Tony didn't linger. He was on a mission.

He found Jimmy's gun and shoulder holster hanging inside the closet door. It was a nice rig, comfortable, well-worn leather that fit him perfectly. He was disappointed to find that Jimmy didn't have any other firearms conveniently stashed around the house, but he did have plenty of ammo for the .38, and a nice buck knife that might come in handy.

He also took 500 dollars that he found hidden in a sock drawer, a tan, summer-weight blazer, and a brand-new pair of those Air Jordan sneakers that the kids were crazy for all of a sudden.

Tony walked through an open archway and into the kitchen, carrying the liquor store bag. He emptied two bottles of vodka down the sink and left them, empty, on the counter. Then he took the third bottle, dumped out a little more than half and used it to prop the apartment door open on his way out.

If anyone came looking, they'd notice the bottle, assume Jimmy had gone off on another bender, and wouldn't give it a second thought.

In the meanwhile, Jimmy would be in Massachusetts, hunting down a juvenile arson suspect from Jacksonville.

1 1

It had taken Tony three days to drive a series of stolen cars from Florida to snowy Westley, Massachusetts.

Having grown up in north Florida, snow was something he'd rarely seen outside of illustrated Christmas cards, and driving through it was a real challenge. But thoughts of Olivia kept him warm.

They also distracted him from the road. The snow turned to rain, and by the time he realized that his tires were sliding uselessly sideways on the icy tarmac, he was unable to avoid plowing into a sign that advertised the local Butchie Burger. When he hit the front leg of the billboard, the large anthropomorphic Boston terrier came crashing down on his hood, shattering the windshield and peppering Tony with cubes of glass.

He struggled to unfasten his seatbelt, but every bone in his body felt like it had been replaced with razor wire. He could taste blood, and feel it burning in his eyes.

Freezing wind clawed at him through the broken windshield, spitting icy rain in his face. He tried the door and found that it had been crushed closed.

Rage welled up in the back of his throat. He was

furious at himself for letting something like this happen.

Then the passenger side door was wrenched open and a guy bundled up like a flannel Michelin Man stuck his pink face into the car.

"Had yourself a hell of a crash," he said loudly. "You all right, mister?"

Tony reached out with his prosthetic arm, catching and twisting the man's scarf with the hook on the end. The guy's astonished look would have been funny if Tony wasn't in such a bad mood. He pulled the knife out of his pocket, thumbed it open, and jammed it into the Good Samaritan's thick, wattled neck.

At least his blood was warm.

Tony stabbed the guy way more times than he needed to, but it felt good. Like each stab was draining away not only the man's pointless life, but also Tony's rage. By the time the guy was dead, Tony felt calm and centered again. He kicked the body out of the car and climbed over it.

It was still horribly cold, but now the wind felt almost bracing, even invigorating. There was no sign of civilization that he could see. No houses or buildings. No people anywhere. There was the Samaritan's empty car up on the side of the road. The door was hanging open, and the interior of the man's car seemed warm and inviting in the frozen night, lit by the friendly yellow glow of the automatic overhead light.

Tony grabbed his duffle bag and his map, and got into the man's car. It was a brand-new Mystique, green with a tan interior. Still had that new-car smell. The guy must've just been down to the Butchie Burger and there was a warm sack of chow on the passenger seat. The radio was on, playing "golden oldies."

Like any time was really golden. Like the world wasn't always like this.

He twisted the knob until he found a generic rock station. He'd never really cared one way or the other about music, but it made the long drive seem less lonely. He helped himself to a Butchie Burger and drove away.

1 2

"Hey, Han," Chelsea said as she whirled with a dramatic flourish into the dorm room she shared with Olivia, swinging her leopard print roller suitcase up onto her bed. "Did you hear about the peeper? Disgusting!"

Chelsea Speigelman wasn't bad, as far as roommates go, but she could be exhausting. She drank too much espresso and talked a mile a minute, always delighting in the latest hot gossip. She was a proud New Yorker, raised on Manhattan's Upper West Side, although she'd actually been born in Russia and adopted as an infant. A tall, leggy, blue-eyed blonde who looked like she could have been related to Olivia and Rachel—far more so than the short, chubby, dark-haired parents she towered over in all of the snapshots.

"What peeper?" Olivia asked, looking up from *The Sign of Four*.

"God," Chelsea said. "I just got back and I already know more than you. And you've been here the whole time!" She unzipped the suitcase and started pulling out sheer frilly articles of clothing. "Lisa M. saw him outside her window. He had a hook for a hand!"

"Oh, come on," Olivia said, rolling her eyes. "You've got to be kidding. A hook? Was he wearing a hockey mask, too?"

"Not a hook like a pirate hook," Chelsea said. "Like one of those prosthetic metal pincher things." She made her first two fingers into hooks and pinched the air in front of Olivia's face, then used them to mimic masturbation while peeping through an imaginary window.

"Ew, gross," Olivia said.

"Yeah, right?" Chelsea said, and she laughed. "Think he ever pinched himself by mistake, in a moment of passion?"

Olivia made a face.

"Would you knock it off?" she said. "That's an image I don't need in my head."

"They're going to issue a warning to all of the female students," Chelsea continued. "We're all supposed to keep our curtains closed until hook-man gets caught." She cupped her hands over her nearly flat chest. "Not like I have anything to peep at, anyway. At least not until I turn eighteen, and don't need my stupid parents' permission to get a boob job."

"Don't you think this sounds a little made up?" Olivia asked. "Honestly—a man with a hook? It's too corny to be real. You'd think a girl like Lisa would have a better imagination. Like the story she told about losing her virginity on Concorde, with her forty-year-old French boyfriend. That, at least, was semi-believable."

"It sure was—I met Philippe," Chelsea said. "He was pretty hot. You know, for an old guy. Can't swear by the Concorde thing, though."

"You're missing the point," Olivia said. "I'm just saying that I don't buy the whole hook-man thing. It seems... I don't know... too over the top. Like the urban legend."

"Speaking of wild stories—" Chelsea plopped herself down on the bed and folded her long legs up into a lotus pose. "—What's this I hear about you and Kieran getting caught in the dorm after hours? Don't tell me you finally agreed to throw the poor boy a bone."

"No!" Olivia snapped her book shut and got up. "Of course not. Who told you that?"

"So…" She smirked, picking at the glitter polish on her big toe. "Are you planning to die a virgin, or what?"

"That's none of your business," Olivia said. She could tell that she was blushing, and knowing it just made it worse. "Anyway, nothing happened."

"He's totally in love with you, you know."

"He is not." Olivia turned away, wrapping her arms around her body. "We're just friends."

"You could do worse," Chelsea said. "He's cute, in a geeky sort of way. Smart, funny, and sincere, and you can tell he worships the ground you walk on. You don't have to marry him or anything, just have a little fun.

"You could use a little fun," she added.

"Fun?" Olivia smiled and shook her head. "What's this strange concept you call fun? I must have missed that class, while I was cramming for midterms."

"Seriously, Olivia," Chelsea said, refusing to be put off. "You're, like, the most uptight person I've ever met. Like if you let your guard down for *one* second, the whole world will come to an end."

"I'm not uptight," Olivia said. "I'm just careful."

"Want to be careful?" Chelsea asked, rummaging in her suitcase. "Use this."

She tossed Olivia a condom wrapped in a pink and black wrapper.

Olivia caught it out of the air, stifling a giggle.

"Pervert," she said, pocketing the little packet and

grabbing her neatly folded towel. "I'm gonna go take a shower. I need to wash your filthy thoughts off my pure virgin soul."

"Yeah, right," Chelsea said. "Scrub real hard. Especially down there."

Olivia was starting to turn into a prune, standing there in the streaming hot water, but it was so hard to motivate herself to get out of the shower. It was so peaceful and private. All her worries and day-to-day drama seemed so far away, forgotten and lost in the fragrant steam.

Except for Kieran.

The more she tried not to think about him, the more he snuck into her head. She kept thinking about the night of her birthday, and what had almost happened before Mrs. G. showed up to check on her. Thinking about what might have happened if Mrs. G. *hadn't* showed up. About what Olivia wanted to happen.

She'd been avoiding him for days, and in turn avoiding her own feelings about him, but she couldn't hide forever.

Funny how she'd been insisting to everyone that she and Kieran were "just friends," but seeing as she didn't have any other friends besides him, she didn't really have any standard of comparison. Sure, Chelsea was her roommate, and she was okay. And there was Rachel, but that was different—she was her sister.

In fact, the last person who'd really felt like a friend was that little boy named Peter, in the strange year before she'd shot Randall. In a way, Kieran reminded her of that boy. His charming awkwardness, the way he never seemed totally at home in the world around him. Like an exchange student from an unknown country with a population of one.

That odd, existential loneliness made her want to reach out to him. To connect, physically. To ground him—and herself, in the process. But she was afraid, too. Afraid to be vulnerable, to trust. To open herself up to almost certain disappointment.

Then she frowned. As usual, she was probably overthinking this. Rachel would tell her to go for it. To open herself to the possibility of love, and follow her heart. But girls like Rachel were able to follow their hearts because they had girls like Olivia to watch out for them, and catch them when they stumbled.

Who was going to watch out for Olivia?

13

Kieran sat on his bed with his notebook open, but he wasn't writing. He'd only written a single word on the fresh new page.

Enigma.

Enigma was one of the characters in his sprawling, endlessly revised novel, a beautiful blond vigilante with mysterious green eyes and a dark secret. A thinly veiled fictional version of Olivia.

Olivia the enigma, the lonely badass. Fiercely intelligent and driven by unknowable private demons. Heroic, but always at arms length.

Until that moment when her desk lamp blew out. He'd been so close. Close enough to smell her clean hair and feel her warm breath on his skin. He'd almost kissed her, and he was almost sure that she wanted to kiss him back. Almost.

Still an enigma.

Nicole, his ex, had been bitterly jealous of Olivia and her fictional counterpart. She'd demanded to know why there wasn't a character based on her in his novel. Truth was, she had a good heart, but she just wasn't hero material.

Nicole was smart and ambitious and wanted to be a pediatrician, but struggled with self-esteem issues and anorexia. She'd decided to date Kieran with the same Mother Teresa instinct she might have shown by picking out a sad, special-needs mutt at the shelter, instead of a cute puppy. It was easier to go along with her than to go against her, and Kieran didn't want to be a virgin forever.

But he quickly tired of being her charity lay. He was almost relieved when she found a graphic love scene between Enigma and his first-person protagonist, and dumped him for a kid with a T8 spinal injury. That way, he could go back to pining over Olivia, full-time.

He'd always had trouble with women. Starting with the most important one. His mother.

Kristie McKie had grown up dirt-poor in Glasgow, Scotland, with eleven brothers and sisters. Even though she'd made her first million as a model before she was twenty-one, and ran her own wildly successful fitness business, she was still terrified of being thought of as inferior to all of her rich celebrity friends. She was convinced that a fitness trainer, no matter how famous, was nothing more than a glorified servant, and that everyone else would see it that way.

As a result, she was always trying desperately to fit in, wearing the right designer clothes and donating money to the right charities, and taking vocal coaching to Americanize her Glaswegian accent. She even went so far as to get knocked up through artifical insemination because she wanted to have a cute trophy baby, like all her trendy clients, but couldn't be bothered with the headache of a relationship.

But somehow, she could never make Kieran fit in, no matter how hard she tried. It was as if all the pampered rich kids could smell his trashy, lower-class DNA, no matter how many expensive outfits his mother bought him. He desperately wanted to make her happy, but always failed to measure up to her expectations.

Starting with the day he was born.

He'd been born with aortic stenosis—essentially a fancy name for a bum ticker. Nothing life-threatening, just enough to keep him out of gym class. As a result he was uncoordinated, underweight, and embarrassingly unfit in his mother's eyes. To make matters worse, he was also shy and myopic, and always managed to button his shirt wrong, or knock his glass over, or say the wrong thing. By the time he was old enough to go to boarding school, his mother had pretty much given up and started systematically distancing herself from him. It was as if she finally realized that her brainy, awkward boy was never going to be the cute little matching accessory she had wanted.

So she bought a Pomeranian instead, and warehoused Kieran in cold storage here at Deerborn.

He couldn't help but wonder if he had gotten so hung up on Olivia because he was used to pining for the love of distant blondes who never seemed to have enough time for him.

But really, Olivia was so different—unlike anyone else he'd ever met. She possessed a quiet confidence that his endlessly dieting, pumping, and sculpting mother could never achieve. She had a sharp eye and clear deductive mind, and was nearly impossible to deceive. Yet, unlike her coldly logical detective idol, she was deeply empathetic, and even weirdly maternal. He saw it in the way she protected her sister, Rachel. Not so much maternal like a mother hen. More like a mother bear.

Mess with her cubs, and she'd tear your throat out.

He shut the notebook and put it on the bedside table.

There was no way he was going to be able to concentrate on his novel that night.

His mind kept on returning to the moment just before the light blew out, replaying it over and over again, analyzing it and picking it apart. Did he really see something in her guarded eyes, or was it just wishful thinking? She didn't push his hand away when he touched her neck, and he was almost positive that she had even leaned in a little, but he couldn't be sure.

A muffled series of thumps in the hallway outside his door made him jump. The rest of the dorm was almost completely uninhabited at the moment. His roommate Justin wasn't due back at school until tomorrow, and there were plenty of other kids who wouldn't arrive until Sunday night. The only other living soul in the narrow, L-shaped building was Mr. Hohulsten, the residence supervisor, and his apartment was on the opposite end of the L.

Kieran got up and stood with his hand on the doorknob, waiting for another sound. For a moment, there was nothing, then some stifled laughter and shushing.

He opened the door and peered down the hallway.

It was Brent Pell and Tyler Mattox, his neighbors across the hall and personal tormentors.

Tyler was a junior, tall and handsome in a forgettable, made-for-TV-movie kind of way. Thick blond hair like an animal's pelt and big, perfect white teeth in a soft, feminine mouth. He was almost tolerable if you could get him alone, but you usually couldn't. He was the type of guy who was born to be someone's sidekick. Although unmotivated and gutless on his own, he was an attack dog when the right hand was on his leash.

And that hand was Brent Pell's.

Pell was the great-great-grandson of Harrison

Deerborn, the founder of The Deerborn Academy, which was the one and only reason he was currently enrolled at the school. He was barely literate and academically lackadaisical at best, belligerently taking up classroom space that should have gone to another hungry scholarship student like Olivia, who actually wanted to learn. He even sucked at football, although that fact didn't keep him off the team any more than his lack of stature and piss-poor grade point average did.

Not only was he a Deerborn, but his father was Massachusetts state Senator Michael Pell, who'd recently been under investigation for misappropriating public funds and alleged sexual harassment of several barely legal female interns. Clearly Brent got his sense of entitlement and flexible morals from his father's side of the family.

He was 5'6" and stocky with mean, close-set blue eyes under heavy eyebrows that were always bunched together from trying to figure out if whatever you'd just said was an insult. He had a preppy, Young Republican haircut and a weak chin, plus an affinity for polo shirts and sucker punches. And he had a special hatred for Kieran, fueled inexplicably by what Brent referred to as his "gay name."

Kieran had been an abuse magnet his whole life, so Brent's attentions were nothing new. The world was depressingly full of Brents, and although Kieran often entertained fantasies of learning martial arts or buying a samurai sword or something like that, in real life he just did his best to avoid bullies whenever possible.

Unfortunately, now wasn't one of those times.

When he opened his dorm room door and looked out into the hallway, Brent and Tyler spotted him immediately, heads snapping toward him like predators spotting a kill.

They were both bundled up in colorful down parkas and jaunty wool scarves, as if they'd just stepped out of the L.L. Bean winter catalog. Their boots were dripping with slush, leaving long wet trails down the polished wood floor.

There was someone with them.

It was a girl, a skinny little thing with puke in her curly blond hair and a short, floral print slip dress. She didn't have a coat or shoes. Her pale skin was blotched pink from the cold and her bare feet were dusky blue and caked with snow. She lolled in Tyler's arms like a broken doll, wet hair swinging in her face.

Rule number one: Never, ever initiate conversation with bullies. This rule was so deeply ingrained in Kieran that when he heard the sound of his own voice echoing down the hallway, he was almost startled, as if it belonged to someone else.

"Is she okay?" he asked.

"Get lost, retard," Tyler said, shifting his grip on the slouching, seemingly boneless girl.

"She's fine," Brent said, opening the door to their room and motioning for Tyler to bring her in. "Which is more than I can say for you if you don't get your ass back in your room and keep your goddamn mouth shut."

Partying. That's what they were calling it. Kieran wondered if the girl had any idea that she had been invited to the party.

Brent and Tyler had a revolving entourage of females in and out of their room all semester, most of whom were clearly under the influence. Which made a certain degree of sense, since Kieran couldn't imagine a sober girl actually wanting to sleep with Brent. But this girl seemed really sick, maybe even suffering from hypothermia. Her poor little feet were so blue.

Torn, Kieran hesitated in the doorway. Brent lunged

toward him and he instinctively ducked back, slamming and locking the door. His heart was hammering in his chest, and he hated himself for being such a coward. He thought immediately of Olivia. Olivia would have stood up for that girl. He wished desperately that she were there with him.

She wouldn't hesitate to do the right thing.

He paused for a long moment with the palm of his hand pressed against the door, as if he could feel vibrations through the wood and use them to judge what lay on the other side. Was Brent right outside, waiting to punch him in the stomach as soon as he showed himself? Or had he gone into his own room?

Kieran waited for a few more seconds, then slowly, carefully eased the door open.

The hallway was deserted.

He could hear some sort of music playing inside Brent and Tyler's room, everything but the chunky, throbbing bassline muffled by the thick walls. If the girl was making any sounds, of either pleasure or distress, Kieran couldn't hear them.

This is none of your business.

Maybe she's okay.

Just walk away.

That was fear talking. Making excuses not to stand up and do the right thing. But there was another voice in his head. Olivia's voice, calm and steady.

You know what you have to do.

The walk down the hall felt like the longest trek of Kieran's life.

Mr. Hohulsten's apartment door at the far end of the building looked exactly the same as everyone else's. Same glossy dark wood, same eye-level metal frame for the name tag of whoever was living there that semester.

Inside, however, he had two big rooms, a kitchenette, and a private bathroom. He lived there in the fall and winter, then turned the apartment over to Mr. Reese for the spring and summer.

Kieran paused in front of the door, hand closed into a fist and ready to knock. He felt sick with adrenalin, unsure and second-guessing himself. Mr. Hohulsten was the kind of guy who took this job because he never wanted to leave high school. He was thirty-six but still considered himself one of the guys, and was notoriously lenient about curfew and visitors. He'd never struck Kieran as a bad person, just kind of immature and clueless with his ponytail and grunge rock T-shirts.

Mr. Reese, on the other hand, was a real hardass with an unbending dedication to his job and enforcing the rules with relish. As much as Kieran disliked him as a human being, he really wished that Mr. Reese were there now. He could be counted on to kick ass and take names when it came to rule breakers, where as Kieran had absolutely no idea how Mr. Hohulsten would react to a situation like this.

Only one way to find out.

He knocked.

It took Mr. Hohulsten a moment to come to the door. When he did, he was wearing sweats and a baggy T-shirt, his hair all coming out of his ponytail in frizzy wisps around his face. He looked tired, squinting and holding his glasses in one hand.

"What's up, buddy?" he asked, putting them on and smoothing his hair back. "Everything okay?"

It wasn't too late to back down. To keep his mouth shut like Brent had told him to.

"Um," Kieran said. "Well…"

Mr. Hohulsten frowned.

"Something wrong?" he said.

"There's a girl in the dorm," Kieran replied, all in a rush as if ripping off a bandage. "I think she's sick."

"A girl?" Mr. Hohulsten slipped his sock feet into a pair of boots by the door and came out into the hallway. "What, you mean a student?"

"I don't recognize her," Kieran said. "But she seemed really out of it. Throwing up. I think she might need a doctor."

"Where is she now?" Mr. Hohulsten asked, closing his door. "In the bathroom?"

This was the moment where it would go bad. This was where Kieran crossed the line from loser to a snitch.

Kieran looked down at his feet.

"Brent and Tyler brought her in," he said. "She's in their room right now."

Mr. Hohulsten shook his head and smiled, stroking his goatee.

"Those guys," he said, as if they were discussing a pair of loveable puppies that had chewed up a shoe. "They aren't even supposed to be back yet. I swear, they could find a way to smuggle girls into Alcatraz."

"It's not just that," Kieran said. "I think this girl needs help. She's really sick. She didn't even have shoes!"

"Well," Mr. Hohulsten said, "in that case, she's better off in a warm dorm than out in the cold night, right? Just let her sleep it off and I'll kick her out in the morning."

"Do you not get it?" Kieran asked, frustration making his voice crack. "They're doing things to her while she's like that!"

"You don't know that," Mr. Hohulsten said, face suddenly serious.

"Will you please just check?" Kieran pleaded.

For an endless moment, Mr. Hohulsten didn't say

anything. Kieran couldn't read his expression and the waiting felt like a death sentence.

"Fine," he finally said. "I'll check. Go back to your room."

In the safety of his tiny room, Kieran didn't feel all that safe. He felt like he was waiting for the end of the world. Like he'd just lit the fuse and was waiting for the dynamite to explode.

He stood by the door, listening with every fiber of his being, but their dorm was one of the oldest buildings on campus and had strong, thick walls and heavy doors. Deerborn had been an all-boys school until 1969, when the more modern girls' dorms had been built, but this was the building where the class of 1911 had slept. It was built to last, all venerable stone and secrets.

Kieran could hear voices in the hallway, but couldn't make out exactly what they were saying.

Then nothing.

Kieran looked over at his clock radio, watching the numerals flip with a clunking sound from 10:59 to 11:00. Nothing, nothing and more nothing. No sirens. No paramedics coming to pump the girl's stomach. No cops coming to investigate. Nothing. Just the low, rhythmic thumping of the old steam heater in the corner and the counterpoint of Kieran's anxious heartbeat.

Then a small, folded sheet of paper slid under his door, bumping up against his foot. He let it sit there for a good long minute, waiting to see if anything else would happen.

Nothing.

He bent and picked up the note, dread sitting like bile in the back of his throat.

YOUR DEAD.

He wanted to laugh at the bad grammar, but couldn't

summon the breath. He just crumpled the piece of paper in his fist and flung it toward the waste paper basket beside his desk. It bounced off the rim and rolled under his bed. But its message remained, branded into Kieran's head.

He was dead.

14

Kieran really had to piss.

He'd had to piss since 6:30 a.m., and it was now almost 8:00. He was already late to his creative writing workshop, but he couldn't leave his room.

When he'd cracked the door open at around 6:45, sure enough there were Brent and Tyler, standing outside their door. Waiting for him.

Kieran had actually considered pissing out the window, but his room faced the busy quad, with various newly arrived students and teachers heading off on their various morning rounds. He really didn't feel like flashing the whole school, especially not in this freezing cold weather.

He'd also scoured his room for any kind of container he might be able to use, but his messy roommate wasn't back from winter break yet, so the usual clutter of soda bottles and coffee cups was unfortunately absent. Their wire mesh wastepaper basket had been emptied the night before. Kieran cursed his own compulsive neatness, but the only empty container he could find was an aspirin bottle.

That just wasn't going to cut it.

He was going to have to leave the room sooner or later or he was going to burst.

Listening by the door, he decided that the next time he heard a group of voices in the hallway, he was going to run for it in the hope that his archenemies would be reluctant to really whale on him in front of an audience. Maybe he could get away with just a quick shove, or being tripped. Though if Brent punched him in the stomach right now, his jeans would be soaked instantly.

He waited as long as he could, and ten minutes more. Then, when he heard a rowdy crowd of boys clatter down the hallway toward the exit, he made a desperate break for it, shoving his door open and running for the bathroom.

Brent and Tyler were gone.

He only had a split second to register this fact as he ran past their door, but his sense of relief was overwhelming.

That was nothing, however, compared to the relief he felt when he ducked into the bathroom and hit the urinal. For a long drawn out moment, nothing else mattered.

He had just zipped up and was about to go wash his hands when he heard that loathsome voice behind him.

Brent.

"We were starting to think you were avoiding us."

Before he could turn to face his tormentors, Brent grabbed Kieran's hair and smashed his face into the top of the urinal, splitting his lip and sending fiery pinwheels across his vision.

"What part of 'keep your retard mouth' shut did you not understand?" Brent hissed into his ear. He kept his grip on Kieran's hair and used his other hand to grab the back of the waistband of Kieran's jeans. He used this two-handed grip to give Kieran a bum's rush, dragging him the length of the narrow bathroom and throwing him into the shower stalls.

Kieran banged his head against the tap and everything went red and woozy for a moment. He crumpled in a heap on the cold tile, and when his vision cleared, he saw something that filled him with icy terror.

Tyler was dragging the heavy steel garbage can over to the door and wedging it under the knob. Which meant this wasn't going to be a quick drive-by beating with a wedgie thrown in for good measure. They were settling in for a long, leisurely torture session.

Kieran was trapped. No chance of Mr. H. or other students interrupting the bullies before they had their fill.

He really was dead.

He got his wobbly legs under him and ran to the single, small frosted window, knowing that it wouldn't open, that it had been stuck since he was a freshman and wasn't going to magically cooperate now. But he had to try something.

Brent and Tyler exchanged amused glances while he scrabbled around the window frame and pushed as hard as he could. Of course it didn't budge.

He considered making a run for one of the toilet stalls and trying to lock himself inside, but Brent anticipated that move and stepped to the left so that he was squarely in the way. Backing away, Kieran's eyes darted around, as he desperately searched every inch of the bathroom for anything that could be used as a weapon.

A forgotten, nearly empty bottle of dandruff shampoo.

An extra roll of toilet paper.

That was it.

At that point, Kieran knew that he would just have to resign himself to the abuse. It wasn't the first time, and it wouldn't be the last. All he could do was try to go away in his head, make himself as small as possible, and try to survive until it was over.

Still, that first punch to the face was always the worst. No matter how ready for it he thought he was, it was always way worse than he remembered. First there was the bright shock of it, water filling his eyes and blood welling up inside his nose. The roaring red pain kicked in, eclipsing any kind of rational thought.

Then the raging emotion, the fear and the fury. The hate, the anger and the shame at his own weakness.

He staggered back and to the left, as Brent followed up with a punch to the gut, and then a swift uppercut that nearly knocked Kieran's lower jaw loose from its hinges. He fell to his knees and Tyler kicked him in the center of the chest, knocking him over on his back. Kieran turned to his side, turtling up with his arms over his head as the two bullies kicked him again and again.

"Why you gotta be such a little snitch-bitch?" Brent asked, punctuating the question with another kick.

"What do you care anyway?" Tyler said, kicking Kieran again. "You don't know her."

"Yeah," Brent said, with another kick. "What do you care about a skank like that?" Another kick. "She's, like, not even a person."

Kieran knew better than to try to respond. Questions like that weren't requests for actual information. They were just aggressive sounds, like dogs barking or chimpanzees grunting. Instead, he kept his head covered and stared at the tiny octagonal black and white floor tiles visible between his forearms.

He tried to list the next ten movies he wanted to order from his Hong Kong tape trader. Or decide what to do about that eleventh chapter in his novel that had been giving him so much trouble—the one where Enigma goes back to her old home town and has to confront demons from her childhood. Or anything other than the relentless blows filling his mouth with blood and his battered body with searing agony.

Just when Kieran thought he couldn't stand another second, the barrage of abuse ceased. He heard one of his tormentors hock up a thick, juicy loogie, and he felt it splat against his temple, dripping down his cheek. Then he heard receding footsteps and the sound of the trash can being dragged away from the door.

Then, nothing.

He waited for a second, then another. Waiting to see what would happen next.

Still nothing.

He risked a glance through his protectively held arms. He was alone in the bathroom.

He got slowly, painfully to his feet. His body felt like a bag of rocks and broken glass. His poor heart was thumping desperately like a trapped rabbit. His flannel shirt was stained and smeared with blood, so he took it off and threw it into the trash. He didn't want to look in the mirror, but he couldn't help himself.

His lower lip was twice the normal size, with a raw, bleeding split. He had a fat mouse under one eye that was going to blacken fast, and his chest and sides were blotchy with red, shoe-shaped marks where he had been stomped and kicked. This was going to go down in his personal history as the worst beating of his life so far.

He ran water in the sink and splashed it on his stinging face, washing away the spit clinging to his cheek and the blood crusted under his nose. But he couldn't wash away the anger. The hot, impotent fury that made him want to put his fist through a wall and smash everything in sight.

Particularly Brent and Tyler's faces.

He ran back to his room, grabbed a clean shirt and his coat and got the hell out of the dorm. No way of knowing when the bullies might decide to come back for more.

He had a wool cap in his pocket and pulled it down low over his eyes so the other students wouldn't see his bruised face, and headed over to the math and computer science building.

It was one of the newer buildings, built in the late seventies. Kieran thought it looked like it had been borrowed from the set of a British science fiction series about a future utopia where people of all colors and creeds wear togas and enjoy peaceful intellectual discourse. It looked kind of like a pair of concrete igloos connected by a glassed-in walkway. Students called it "the Tits."

It was one of Kieran's favorite places on campus, because guys like Brent and Tyler wouldn't be caught dead there. They contented themselves to snigger at the building's silhouette from the football field.

Once inside, Kieran ducked into the empty solid geometry lab and sat down at one of the metal worktables to pull himself together. There was a large spindly model of an isotropic vector matrix sitting in the middle of the table, and Kieran picked it up, turning it over in his hands.

All he could think about was Olivia.

He didn't want to go to class or to lunch or really anywhere on campus, because he didn't want Olivia to see his bruises and know how weak he was. He'd really tried to help that girl, tried to do the right thing like he knew Olivia would have wanted. But in the end it was all for nothing.

He was a failure.

A weak, useless loser who can't even protect himself.

"Oh, hey." A male voice came from the doorway. "I didn't realize anyone was in here."

Kieran looked up and saw Mr. Bennett, the geometry teacher. He was short and chunky with thinning, light-brown hair and glasses. He didn't have a pocket protector in the breast pocket of his white button-down shirt, but he may as well have.

"Man," he said when he saw Kieran's face. "You okay?"

"Fine," Kieran said, setting the geometry model down on the table. "Same old same old, you know."

"I do," Mr. Bennett said, coming forward and sitting down beside him. "Believe me I do. You know, this may come as a shock, but I wasn't always the studly chick magnet you see before you today. In fact, I used to get my butt kicked all the time, back in high school."

Kieran laughed and shook his head.

"Hey, look," Mr. Bennett said. "You can report this if you want to. I'll back you up on it."

Kieran frowned and was surprised by how much that expression hurt.

"I can't," Kieran said, raising his hand to touch his burning eyebrow. "That will only make it worse. You oughta know that. Guys like them, they can do whatever they want and never have to pick up the check."

"Okay," Mr. Bennett said. "But trust me, it does get better. Maybe not perfect, but better."

"Thanks," Kieran said. "I'm just gonna stay here by myself for a while, if you don't mind."

"Sure," Mr. Bennett said. "Take as much time as you need."

15

Olivia sat in the library with a neatly organized stack of books on the long wooden table in front of her. It was a warm, cozy sanctuary from the bitter New England winter, all rich, polished wood and worn leather and the musty perfume of foxed paper.

She was restless, and eagerly looking forward to the spring and summer, when her favorite outdoor activities—like mountain biking, track, and skeet shooting—would start up again. But for a displaced Florida girl still unused to the cold, spending the evening in the warm library suited her just fine.

The books were all about Allan Pinkerton and the Pinkerton National Detective Agency. She was supposed to be doing research for a social studies paper, but her mind kept wandering back to Kieran.

She hadn't seen him at lunch or dinner, which seemed odd since they always sat together. And if you missed meals at Deerborn, you were stuck eating out of the rec hall snack machine. It wasn't like you just popped out for a burger. It was a twenty-minute drive into town, and even though Kieran had a car, one his mother had bought him, seniors were normally only allowed off-campus on the weekends.

They usually saw each other briefly between sixth and seventh periods, too, as she was leaving her chemistry class and he was heading up to the biology lab for his senior science project. He hadn't been there, and Olivia had to leave to make seventh period english lit.

She was starting to worry about him. She'd even stopped by the school nurse to see if he might have been sick, or having problems with his heart.

No one had seen him.

Then, as if summoned by her thoughts, Kieran appeared from behind a tall bookcase. He wore a black knit cap and was slouching in his oversized black parka, looking like a turtle trying to pull its head into its shell. He wasn't wearing his glasses, and the narrow strip of face that was showing between the coat's turned-up collar and the rim of the cap was a lurid rainbow in every shade of bruise.

One eye was swollen completely shut. The eyebrow above it was crusted with a scab, and so was the bridge of his nose.

Olivia got to her feet in an instant, thorny, complicated emotions surging through her body.

"Kieran," she said. "What the hell happened?"

"You smoking in the library, Liv?" he asked, with a shaky and unconvincing laugh.

"What are you talking about?" she asked, frowning.

He gestured to the narrow burn scarring the maple syrup finish of the antique table where her hand had been seconds before. Funny, she hadn't noticed a cigarette burn when she sat down, and from the smell, it had to be recent.

But she shook her head, and turned back. She was way more worried about Kieran.

"Don't change the subject," she said, reaching out to touch his cheek. "Who did this to you?"

He pulled away from her, his one good eye shiny with stifled tears.

"I didn't even save her," he said, tears spilling over. "I wanted to, but…"

He turned and slammed a fist into the impassive wooden flank of the nearest bookshelf. A book on the classification and evolution of the phylum *Cnidaria* tumbled to the floor and landed open to a weirdly beautiful illustration—jellyfish reproductive organs.

"Whoa, hey," Olivia said. "Take it easy." She grabbed his hand to stop it from hitting the shelf again, and led him over to one of the chairs. He sank into it, and she took a seat beside him. "There's no point in putting any more stress on your heart."

With that she put her hand in the center of his chest. She could feel his heart thumping like a wounded bird trying to get off the ground. She wanted to pull him close and promise him she would never let anyone hurt him again, but she hesitated, unnerved by the sudden strength of that desire.

"Why don't you just tell me what happened," she said instead.

As the distraught Kieran told his story about the drugged girl who had been with his dorm-mates, Olivia could feel a terrible cold fury brewing inside her. That girl could have been Rachel. Or anyone. Privileged scumbags like those two needed to be made to answer for their actions, and face the consequences.

"According to Mr. H," Kieran said. "They told him that she was a friend from town who had too much to drink, and they were letting her sleep it off in their room so she wouldn't have to drive. But I know them. There's no way those guys just let her sleep." He pushed shaking fingers through his hair. "The worst part about it is that I have no idea who she was or if she's okay. When I woke up the next morning, she was just gone. Like she'd never existed, and I got the crap kicked out of me for nothing." He looked away. "I couldn't save her."

"You tried," Olivia said, gripping his chin and turning his face back to her. "It took a lot of courage to stand up to those guys. You did the right thing."

"But they got away with it!" Kieran shook his head, frowning. "What's the point of doing the right thing if the bad guys win anyway?"

"Look," Olivia said. "This isn't the first I've heard of something like this going on with those two. Chelsea is always telling me these awful stories, but none of the girls are ever willing to press charges, because they don't want their parents to find out they were drinking." Olivia stood and turned away, the bare bones of a plan forming inside her head. "Maybe we couldn't do anything to help that one girl, but I have an idea for how to put those losers out of business, and for good."

She reached into her backpack, took out the tiny tape recorder she used to record lectures and make notes to herself. She set it on the table in front of Kieran.

"There's a welcome-back party tonight in the recreation hall tonight. Chelsea and Stacia are organizing it, so you know there'll be drinking going on. I'm sure Brent and Tyler will be there sniffing out drunk chicks for their own private parties.

"I'll make sure they pick me," she added.

"What?" Kieran asked. "Are you crazy?"

"I'm not really going to get obliterated," Olivia said. "I'll fake it. I'll hide this tape recorder in my boot and while I'm with them, I'll try to get them to say something

I can take to the police. And even if I can't, if they try anything with me, I'll be happy to report them. I don't have parents to disappoint, so I've got nothing to lose."

"If they try to do anything to you," Kieran said. "You'll be visiting me in jail, because I'll kill them."

"That's very chivalrous of you," Olivia said with a grim smile, "but I can handle myself. Besides, you can't just go around killing people, no matter how badly they deserve it. You have to go through proper channels."

"Okay," Kieran said. "Maybe that came out wrong. I just meant… well…"

He looked up at her, tears gone now and replaced by something hot and painfully earnest.

"Be my girlfriend," he said.

"Wait… what?" Olivia frowned, uncertain she had heard him right.

"I mean…" He shrugged with a little self-deprecating smile. "This probably isn't the best time to ask, but I'm already beat up, so I figure I have nothing to lose. Still, don't punch me or anything, okay?"

"I'm not going to punch you," she said. "I just…"

She looked away, a deep flush creeping up from under the neck of her sweater.

"You don't have to… do anything," he said. "You know, if you don't want to."

"It's not that," she said, reaching up to touch the side of his jaw that was the least bruised. "I do want to." She couldn't believe she was actually saying those words out loud. "It's just… complicated."

"I really want to kiss you," he said. "But my lip's all busted open and gross."

She burst out laughing, the relief of it like a weight lifted.

"You're so romantic," she said.

He slid his arms around her waist.

"That's nothing," he said. "Wait till you hear my a capella rendition of 'Mandy' outside your window at midnight."

"If I do," she said, leaning into him. "I really will punch you."

"Fair enough," he said, brushing her hair back from her face. "I should have known you're more of a Neil Diamond fan."

She laughed softly, rolling her eyes and shaking her head. For a long minute neither of them said anything, and the reality started to sink in. Kieran's embrace felt warm and safe in this cold, wintery world where so few things did. But it also felt like a gateway to a strange new world with its own mysterious language and unfamiliar customs.

"I tell you what," she said, breaking the silence. "We can talk about this whole 'girlfriend' thing later, okay? Right now we need to concentrate on Brent."

"Okay," he said, although she could feel how reluctant he was to let go. "Just be careful, Olivia."

"I was born careful," she replied. "Trust me."

16

Chelsea was totally behind Olivia's idea to set up Brent and Tyler, but it had nothing to do with morality or a sense of justice. It was all about the fact that—for the first time—Olivia had finally agreed to allow her roommate to dress her up.

"You're letting me do your makeup, too," Chelsea said. "It's already decided, so don't argue."

Olivia, whose concept of makeup was usually limited to mascara and chapstick, had no choice but to go along with this undercover makeover.

"Your feet are bigger than mine," Chelsea said, giving Olivia a critical once-over. "So you'll have to wear your own Docs."

She rummaged through an open drawer and flung something plaid in Olivia's general direction. Olivia caught it out of the air and discovered it was a pleated skirt so short it looked more like a belt.

"You've got to be kidding," she said, holding the little red piece of tartan up to her waist.

"You have killer legs," Chelsea said. "I've seen them. Why not share your secret with the rest of the world."

She tossed Olivia a pair of black socks that were folded together. "Try it with these."

Olivia pulled down her old comfortable jeans and shimmied into the skirt. She'd worn bathing suits that were more modest. The socks turned out to be extra long, reaching well above her knees, and had little bows with silver skulls.

"What am I supposed to be?" she asked. "A goth schoolgirl stripper?"

"You said you wanted to look slutty," Chelsea said. "Your wish is my command."

Olivia laced up her Doc Martens boots over the socks, already feeling like someone else.

"I'm gonna freeze my ass off," she said.

"It's a short walk," Chelsea responded. "Here, try this sweater." She passed Olivia a handful of black fluff. "But first, get rid of that dreary, Soviet Olympian sports bra you're wearing. That thing is like a crime against humanity. You'll just have to go without for now, but we are so going lingerie shopping this weekend. It's time for you to experience the miracle of the push-up."

Olivia removed her bra, and then pulled the black sweater on over her bare chest.

"It's too small for me," she said, yanking at the hem. It stubbornly remained several inches above the waistband of the skirt.

"It's perfect," Chelsea said without even looking. "Now, let me do your makeup."

She held Olivia's chin in between her thumb and forefinger, turning her face one way and then the other, then pulled a large plastic tub of cosmetics out from under her bed and went to work.

"Look up," she said, running a black pencil along the inner rim of Olivia's lower eyelid.

Olivia did as she was told. It felt weird, and it was a struggle not to blink defensively. Chelsea dusted her lids with charcoal shadow and slicked her lips with something sticky and vanilla scented. She did Olivia's hair, too, shielding her eyes with a cupped hand while dousing her head in bubblegum-scented hairspray.

After several long minutes of fuss and fluffy brushes, Chelsea finally seemed to be satisfied with the beautiful monster she had created.

"Check you out," she said, gesturing toward the full-length mirror.

Olivia almost didn't recognize the girl she saw there. Smoky eyes, black-cherry lips, and mile-high legs. Chelsea had pinned Olivia's long blond locks into twin buns like mouse ears, each with a little fan of stiffly sprayed hair poking out of the center. The only familiar things in the mirror were Olivia's trusty Docs, so her gaze kept going back to them, like that would ground her somehow. Make her feel less like a stranger.

Tearing her gaze away, she walked over to the bed, took the little tape recorder out of her bag, and slipped it down the side of her right boot.

"What about you?" she asked Chelsea. "What are you going to wear?"

Chelsea picked up Olivia's discarded jeans and wriggled into them.

"Me?" She smiled and buttoned the jeans. "I'm dressing down. This is your show, Han."

She pulled her favorite leopard print faux-fur jacket out of the closet and handed it to Olivia. Olivia slipped her arms into the sleeves and pulled it tight at her waist. It smelled like Chelsea, like jasmine oil and cigarettes. Like a bad girl.

It made her feel like she could do this.

▲

Outside, the cold wind on Olivia's bare thighs made her gasp.

"Come on," she said to Chelsea. "Hurry." Her roommate didn't even seem to notice the chill.

Olivia held out a little flashlight to show the way as they took a shortcut. It illuminated the snow along the path. They were about halfway through a little spur of woods and over to the back of the rec hall when Chelsea stopped short.

"Dammit," she said. "I forgot the camera."

"I told you you'd forget it if you didn't put it in your purse," Olivia said. "We need that camera, so you can get some photos of me with Brent and Tyler!"

"Chill, will you?" Chelsea said. "I'll go get it."

"Well, I'm not going back," Olivia said. "It's too damn cold. I'll just see you there."

"Fine," Chelsea replied. "God!" She turned around and headed back toward the dorm, while Olivia continued on to the party.

Chelsea was such a bubblehead. Honestly, Olivia had probably made a mistake relying on her to be part of such an important mission. Knowing her roomie, she'd probably meet some cute guy on the way back to the dorm, and decide to go do tequila shots out of his navel. Then drive down to New York for bagels. She was always pulling stunts like that, and skating by without any consequences.

It'd probably be better to figure out a way to make this work without the photos.

Still, Chelsea had done such a great job on the hair and makeup, and Olivia couldn't really stay mad at her.

17

When Tony saw the girls split up, he knew this was his chance.

He should have been scared, standing there in the darkness, so close to the demoness who had destroyed his life, but he felt unnaturally calm. The night was bitter cold, but he felt warm all over. He could feel his brain humming from Olivia's closeness, with a phantom burning that was pulsing through the hand and arm he no longer possessed.

He raised what he had instead, the seven-inch hunting knife he'd carefully modified and bolted to the business end of his prosthetic. The blade was matte black and nearly invisible—a deadly shadow, like the vengeful ghost of a fist.

Olivia's trampy roommate held a tiny flashlight, and Tony watched its delicate fairy ring of illumination drift away through the naked winter trees for a few seconds. Then he was alone with Olivia.

He had to act quickly. In just a few more feet, she'd be out of the dark woods and out into the open. Reaching out to grab her felt inevitable, like falling.

He stepped onto the narrow trail behind her and clamped his good gloved hand over her mouth. She let out a surprised squeak, muffled down to nothing against his palm. He could feel her hot breath through the leather.

She was so tall now. Almost as tall as he was, he mused as he cranked her chin up and back. She felt like a woman as she struggled against him. He had clearly caught her just in time. The devil child was well on her way to becoming a full-grown monster.

He brought up the blade and drew it swiftly across her exposed throat, cutting all the way down to the bone and releasing a bubbling hiss of escaping steam.

Her last breath, he thought. *Now I'll be free.*

She sagged in his embrace, boneless and empty as her lifeblood soaked into the snow around their feet. He let her drop and took a deep shaky swallow of the icy night air.

His arm still burned.

Panic set in, driving his heart like a whipped horse. He could still feel her razor-edged glitter shimmering inside his skull. Her poisonous heat still burned through him even as her body grew cold at his feet. He clutched at the place where his flesh met the dull rubber of the prosthetic, overwhelmed with a sudden conviction that he really *was* crazy.

Could Doctor Chalmers have been right? Was his psychic connection with the devil child really all in his head?

It couldn't be. It felt so real. So true.

But if it was real, how could he still feel her, even after she was dead?

He fell to his knees beside her and turned her body face up. Her features were caked with bloody pink snow. Her familiar coat had fallen open and the shirt beneath was crimson with sticky gore.

But something wasn't right.

It just wasn't right.

Her bloody, steaming shirt clung to her body, revealing a flat, almost boyish chest beneath. Olivia was no Dolly Parton, but she had more than this.

Tony combed his fingers through the snow, fumbling for her fallen purse. When he finally found it, he unzipped the main compartment and pulled out a fluffy fake fur wallet and a disposable lighter.

He couldn't hold the lighter and go through the wallet at the same time, so he had to take each plastic card out in the dark, set it on the snowy ground between his knees, and then spark the lighter to read it.

The first one was a video rental ID. The next was a credit card. Then a Deerborn student ID. They all had the same name.

Chelsea Speigelman.

He'd screwed up. Big time.

18

Olivia was walking around the back of the rec hall toward the entrance, when a sudden spike of a headache pulsed behind her right eye. She'd always been a little scared of headaches, after what her mother had been through. She often wondered if her mother's condition might be dormant inside her own head, like a hungry seed, just waiting to blossom.

But this felt different from anything else she'd experienced. More like the way your ears hurt if a noise was too loud. It was like her brain was trying to squint against some painfully intense stimulation. She staggered a bit. The snow all around her boots suddenly melted in a warm rush, revealing the frozen yellow grass beneath.

But as quickly as the strange headache appeared, it was gone. And she was so keyed up, going over and over her plan, that she quickly put it out of her mind and started walking again.

She took a surreptitious swig from the flat pint bottle of cheap gin Kieran had given her, swished the nasty, medicinal-tasting liquid around in her mouth, then spat it into the snowy bushes. She cupped her bare hand in front of her lips and sniffed at her steaming breath. She could detect a hint of the junipery floor-cleaner scent of gin, but wasn't sure it was strong enough, or how long it would last.

So she dabbed some behind her ears and into her exposed cleavage like perfume, and was instantly sorry. The alcohol evaporated rapidly in the cold night air, chilling her skin. She shivered, and figured she would have to rely on her backup plan. She had five white Good-n-Plenty candies she'd put into an old bottle of Vicodin Chelsea had nicked from her mother. She'd need to make sure she was seen swallowing those.

There was music playing, 'Good' by Better Than Ezra, and she could hear a group of girls laughing. Someone else was throwing up. Olivia had never been all that much into parties, and always felt slightly uncomfortable in large groups, hence Chelsea's nickname for her—"Han Solo." But the thick make up and borrowed clothes made her feel like an undercover agent on a secret mission.

Which, essentially, she was.

She'd known ever since the day she shot Randall that she wanted to be an FBI agent. The very next day she'd gone to the library and found a book with a list of the qualifications required to become a special agent. She'd photocopied it and had kept it in her pocket or purse ever since, meticulously updating it by hand as the qualifications were modified or enhanced over the years. That soft, ragged, and endlessly refolded piece of paper became a kind of talisman that she went back to whenever she felt unsure of herself.

She was constantly pushing herself to drop a few seconds off her 300-meter sprint, or add one or two more sit ups to her one-minute limit, not because she wanted to look good or be healthy, but because she wanted to make sure she aced the physical fitness test. She planned to join the Marines as soon as she graduated from high school, not just to get money for college or because her late father had been a Marine, but because military service would give her a leg up in the FBI application process.

It was as if her whole life was geared toward achieving that goal. And even though she couldn't exactly put this kind of thing on her application, her little sting operation felt like the perfect way to hone the skills she would need later in life.

Not *if* she was accepted into the FBI, but *when*.

Tony hooked his arms under the imposter's armpits, and dragged her corpse down to the edge of the lake.

He'd underestimated his quarry's fiendish intelligence. She had sent this decoy to trick him, to mislead him and allow her to slip—unscathed as quicksilver—between his fingers. And now he had this mess to deal with. If this girl's body was found, it would create a media frenzy, followed by a security crackdown that would make it difficult—if not impossible—to get to Olivia.

He didn't need months, or even weeks. He felt confident that he'd find a way to be alone with her within the next forty-eight hours, maybe less.

This girl would need to be missing for that long before the local police would initiate any kind of search. By then, Tony would have done his sacred duty.

After that, nothing else mattered. He'd go to the gas chamber with a smile on his face, knowing that the demoness had been vanquished, and the world was safe.

There was a fat, impassive moon hanging in the cold sky, veiled by an icy scrim of cloud, and its light made the dead girl's skin seem to glow with a gentle, translucent beauty she'd never possessed while she was alive. Tony laid her out across a long, flat rock on the wooded shore and used one of its fellows to smash a hole in the thick ice. The water beneath was as black as the sky, and probably no deeper than waist high where he was standing. But it didn't need to be deeper. It just had to be deep enough for him to slip the inconvenient body under the cloudy ice, where it would remain undiscovered until the spring thaw.

He used the rock to chip away the edges of the hole, in order to accommodate the width of her shoulders. A series of resonant cracks echoed across the frozen surface, and he had a bad moment where he thought the ice might give out beneath his feet. So he made himself stand completely still with his arms spread wide. After a few anxious seconds, the sounds subsided and the snowy hush returned.

Tony looked out over the surface of the frozen lake. There were a few scattered lights on the far shore, too far away to be a concern. The rowing team's dock was visible to his left, but it was dark and deserted this time of year. The only real illumination came from the indifferent moon and the faint glow of the old-fashioned gas lamps that lit the winding paths of Deerborn.

Even though he was alone, Tony didn't feel that way. He could still feel Olivia close by, her heart beating in tandem with his own. He carefully skirted the edges of the hole and went back up to the shore, where he'd left the impostor's body.

There was a thin dusting of snow on the surface of her open eyes, making them seem to sparkle in the dim moonlight. He didn't bother to carry her, just dragged her by her ankles over to the hole, and shoved her head first into the dark water.

Sure enough, her shoulders were a tight fit, but once

they were through, the rest of her slipped beneath the ice with no trouble at all. Her body lingered in the water just beneath the hole, Olivia's puffy coat bright and visible like a warning flag, so he got a sturdy branch from the shore and used it to push the body out of sight. That hole would be gone by morning, and the imposter would be perfectly entombed.

That was all Tony needed to buy him a few precious hours.

19

Inside the main hall, pretty much the entire Junior and Senior classes were crammed cheek and jowl, with a generous handful of underclassmen sniffing around the perimeter. There was a billiards table in the middle of the room that was currently being used as a throne from which a languid Stacia was holding court.

Stacia Mason wasn't exactly the most beautiful girl at Deerborn, but she was by far the most desirable. Looking at her objectively, Olivia couldn't figure out what all the boys saw in her. Chelsea was much prettier, yet when Stacia was in the room, guys acted like Chelsea didn't exist. Her dimensions were average in every direction, neither fat, nor thin. Five feet five inches, with a longer torso and short, sturdy legs. B-cup chest. Even her face was plain, eyes just a little too small and nose just a little too long. Her brown hair was shoulder length and forgettably styled. If you saw her in a still photograph, you'd forget what she looked like the minute the photo was taken away.

But in person, Stacia smoldered. She gave off a trail of steamy pheromones as if it was incense, and moved with a come-hither bump and grind that turned any male within a mile radius into a leering cartoon wolf. Stacia knew it, too, and used it ruthlessly to her advantage.

Luckily for Olivia, Brent and Taylor would have no interest in an alpha she-wolf like Stacia—she was way too intimidating to victimize. Like all predators, they singled out the weaker members of the herd.

Although Olivia was viewed as a white-trash outsider at Deerborn, and didn't have a lot of friends, she was far from an easy mark in the eyes of a guy like Brent. He tended to prefer girls who had a reputation for being "sluts" so that if it came down to her word against his, no one would believe a girl like that.

It would be up to Olivia to make him believe that she would get in some kind of trouble if she were caught drinking. Then to convincingly pretend to be passed out drunk.

When she spotted her targets standing over by the snack machine, she felt a thrilling pulse of adrenalin that sharpened her senses and made her heart hammer in her chest. Here she was, hunting a hunter, just like she'd always dreamed she would do. It felt so right. Like her destiny.

They hadn't spotted her yet, so she took a few moments to plan her approach. She looked around for Chelsea, but didn't see her. She thought that she might wait a few minutes for her roommate to arrive with the camera, but then again, she might be waiting all night.

Then Brent was pointing to the door, seeming to be indicating a desire to leave.

Olivia couldn't wait any longer. She had to act quickly.

She turned and backed toward the two of them, her bottle of fake pills open and ready. Then she made herself stumble, bumping into Brent and spilling the candy out onto the floor.

"Oopsie," she said. "Let me just…"

She got down on her hands and knees and started crawling around Brent's legs collecting the fallen candy. Brent and Tyler snickered, elbowing each other and nodding at her raised ass and short skirt.

"Hold this," she said, thrusting the empty bottle into Brent's hand and hoping he'd read the label.

"No problem, Han," he said. "Take your time down there."

Bristling inwardly at his use of her nickname, she kept her feelings hidden and gathered up most of the candies. At the same time she slipped one hand into her boot, quickly enough that they didn't notice.

Then she turned her face upward so Brent and Tyler could see her, and then popped them all into her mouth at once, cringing a little at the thought of eating anything off the floor, but grimly determined to do whatever it took to pull off this charade.

"Atta girl!" Tyler said.

"You missed one," Brent said, toeing the last candy with his boot.

Olivia picked up the muddy candy and held it out to Brent.

"You want it?" she asked. Before he could answer, she giggled and shook her head. "Too bad."

She swallowed the last candy and pretended to wash it down with a swig from the nearly empty gin bottle.

"Need a hand?" Brent asked, reaching down to help her up with one hand while sliding the other up under her sweater, brushing against a breast.

She shuddered with revulsion at his touch, but made herself act like she didn't notice. She had to think of it like eating the dirty candy. A necessary evil for the greater good.

"Don't tell Coach Lowenbruck that I've been partying," she said, leaning heavily against Brent. "If he finds out, he'll totally kick me off the team."

She put her finger to her lips and made a loud, wet, shushing sound, and then pretended to fade out for a moment, letting her eyelids flutter closed, but still watching his face through her eyelashes.

He looked over at Tyler and smirked.

Olivia knew the hook was in, but he wasn't in the boat. Not yet anyway.

She jerked her eyes open and looked up.

"I'd better…" She waved her fingers in the direction of the door. "I should go home now. I think I feel sick."

"Here, baby," Brent said, wrapping a python-like arm around her waist. "Let us help you." Tyler stepped up to the other side and did the same.

"You're so sweet," she said, stumbling against him. "I feel kinda queasy. I think I need some bacon. Can we get some bacon sandwiches?"

"Don't worry," Brent told her. "We're here for you."

Tyler covered his mouth with the back of his hand and snickered. Olivia had to stifle an urge to punch his leering face. Instead she pulled away from him and spun around, hands in the air.

"Oh my god I LOVE this song! WHOO-HOOO!"

She didn't even recognize the song that was playing— something with a girl singer—but it didn't matter.

"Yeah," Brent said, pressing up against her under the pretense of dancing. "Shake it baby!"

Tyler pushed up against her from behind, crushing her between them, and she felt a flush of claustrophobic panic, but she pushed it down inside, steeling herself for what had to be done. She let out a slushy giggle and sagged against Brent as if she'd nodded out.

"Is she out?" Tyler said, his hands up under her little skirt. "I don't want her to wake up in the middle, like that last one. What's her name again?"

It took every ounce of determination and will to stay completely still and not to flinch away from his touch. The urge to elbow him in the nuts was almost overwhelming.

"Her name is Han Solo," Brent said. "But after tonight, I think her name will be Han Trio."

"How about if we just call her Whore?"

"Good idea. It's so much easier when they all have the same name. That way you don't accidentally say the wrong one when you're nailing them!"

Olivia let her body go heavy and limp, and when Brent failed to hold her up, she let herself slide to the floor.

"Oh my god!" an unfamiliar female voice said. "She's totally wrecked."

"No worries," Brent was saying, lifting her with his hands in her armpits. "We'll take her back to the dorm."

Olivia kept her eyes closed, but felt the icy shock of the night air as she was dragged out of the rec hall. They propped her up against the outside wall of the building for a moment, while they made some sort of adjustments.

"This one is definitely ready for her ride on the stud train," Brent said, lifting one of her limp hands and then dropping it. "Stick a fork in her, because she is *done!*"

Tyler snickered, lifting her other arm and slinging it over his shoulder.

"I'll stick my fork in her as soon as we get her back to our room!"

Olivia cheered silently. Not only did she have them talking about previous assaults, but she also had them outlining their plans for her, right there on tape. She just needed a little bit more and she'd be ready to "wake up."

"Evening, gentlemen," a deep voice said from behind

them. "What's wrong with your ladyfriend?"

Brent spun to face the voice, dragging Olivia around with him. The voice belonged to an older guy with thick black hair that was just starting to gray at the temples, and cold dark eyes. He was dressed in a cheap down jacket, the little T-shaped plastic tab that used to hold a price tag sticking out of one sleeve. Bulky leather gloves, but no hat or scarf.

Instead of boots, he wore an incongruous pair of fancy, expensive sneakers, currently caked with snow. He might as well have been wearing a sign that read NOT FROM AROUND HERE.

Looking at him through slitted eyes, Olivia felt the swift return of the strange, spiky headache she'd felt earlier, followed by a flash image of blood on snow. It was like a double exposure, gone before she could get a handle on it.

"Who the hell are you?" Brent asked, the tight panicky tone of his voice undermining the intended toughness.

"I'm the guy who's taking that girl off your horny little hands, tiger." The man held out a slim leather wallet in his left hand and flipped it open, flashing a badge too quickly for them to read it. "You got a problem with that?"

"Whoa," Tyler said, backing away from Olivia like she was on fire.

"Hey," Brent said. "We don't want any trouble, officer. We were just helping her get home safe."

"And she lives in the boys' dorm, huh?" He smiled. "Right."

"Listen," Olivia said, standing up straight and pulling away from Brent, keeping her voice clear, calm, and normal. "I'm fine. We were just goofing around, really."

Brent looked at her like she'd suddenly grown an eye in the middle of her forehead, but she ignored him.

Her gaze was drawn to the man's right hand, to the little price tag hanger. There was something strange about the glove. It looked hollow, like he only had one long finger in the middle and the rest were empty.

Brent and Tyler were idiots who wouldn't notice an oncoming train until it hit them, but Olivia could tell that this man was bad news. The man seemed to sense her suspicion and smiled even wider.

The smile never reached his eyes.

"Yeah, well," Brent said. "We're gonna get going, then. Right, Ty?"

"No wait," Olivia said, reaching out to take Tyler's arm. She never thought that she'd be desperate to stay with Brent and Tyler. "Don't go. Let's go back to the party."

"No way, man," Tyler said, pulling away from her and walking away as fast as he could without running.

"It's okay, Olivia," the black-haired man said. "I'll walk you home."

20

Tony was finally alone with Olivia.

He hated the way that she was dressed, with all that makeup and everything, and decided that he would take time to wash her face. He'd do it after he knocked her out, but before he killed her. Just so that he could see that pretty young girl's face the way he remembered it.

It seemed so crazy that his whole life had been leading up to this moment and now he was here, living it. It was real.

She was real.

"Olivia?" A woman's voice. "You okay, honey?"

Tony felt that hot, corrosive rage boiling up inside him. It was that nosy old biddy from the dorm. She was wearing an ugly, ankle-length, purple down coat and a matching angora hat that made her look like that fat purple creature that used to sell hamburgers to kids.

"Mrs. G," Olivia said. "I'm fine. I was just heading back to the dorm."

The older woman stepped up to Tony like a suspicious bulldog trying to decide whether to bark or bite. She had her right hand in her pocket, arm stiff and held at a sharp right angle. She didn't pull her gun, but she didn't have to. Tony knew it was there. He could smell it.

"Who are you?" she asked.

"Detective Jimmy Obejas," Tony said, flashing the badge again. "I'm investigating a cold case, ma'am."

"Cold case?" She squinted at him, clearly not buying his story. "Let me see that badge again."

He looked over at Olivia, but she had her face turned away, locking him out. He could still feel the burning of her closeness.

He took the badge from his pocket and opened it again. The old bulldog frowned at it, studying it as if there was going to be a test.

He'd dismissed the woman when he first saw her around the dorm, but now he was realizing that he had seriously underestimated her as a potential threat. She wasn't regular police, more like some kind of private security. But on whose payroll?

"Tampa," she said with a scowl. "What's a Florida dick doing all the way up here? And what does it have to do with Olivia?"

"I'm not at liberty to discuss the details of the case," he said.

The woman arched a red painted eyebrow.

"If you want to interview any one of my students," she said, her flat Southie accent swiftly replaced by the smooth, generic tones of a radio newscaster, "you are welcome to do so during specific hours, in the presence of one or more school officials. If that is not acceptable, you may obtain an arrest warrant and conduct the interview at the local police station, in the presence of her lawyer. What you may *not* do is accost my students alone in the woods in the middle of the night.

"Do I make myself clear?"

"Clear as crystal, ma'am," Tony said, pocketing the badge and backing away. "Just make sure she gets home safe."

"Oh, I will," the woman replied. "You can believe that."

She put a puffy purple arm around Olivia and led her away.

"What was that about?" Mrs. Gilbert asked.

"I have no idea," Olivia replied. "I've never seen that guy before in my life."

It wasn't exactly a lie. She just couldn't put her finger on where she might have seen him before. But there was something disturbingly familiar about him. Something that made her feel anxious, and a little nauseous.

Mostly, she just wanted to get back to her room and listen to the tape.

"Okay, listen," Mrs. Gilbert said. "I'm gonna look into this, and see what I can find out about this so-called detective. Meanwhile, I want you to be extremely careful. Don't go anywhere alone. Got it?"

"Got it," Olivia replied.

When they got back to the dorm, Olivia was not surprised to find the camera on Chelsea's desk, and Chelsea herself absent. That girl was the queen of distraction. Especially male distraction.

"Have you seen Chelsea?" she asked Mrs. Gilbert.

Mrs. Gilbert shook her head.

"If she doesn't show up by midnight, you let me know," she said. "That will be her third time breaking curfew, just this month."

"I will," Olivia lied. She didn't bother to contradict Mrs. Gilbert, but Chelsea had, in fact, stayed out all night twice that many times, and hadn't been caught.

"Olivia," Mrs. Gilbert said, pausing with her hand on

the door to the room. "Is there something going on with you that I ought to know about?"

Olivia shook her head.

"I'm fine," she said.

She hoped it was true. But as soon as Mrs. Gilbert had closed the door, she pulled the little tape recorder from her boot, and forgot all about the mysterious detective.

21

Kieran had been determined to go with Olivia to the police station, but she argued that she'd be much better off on her own. Eventually, she'd won the argument by agreeing to let him drive her into town, and wait for her in the car.

When she arrived, she had a hard time suppressing her excitement. This was her calling—what she was meant to do with her life. Any opportunity to work with law enforcement in the administration of justice made her feel like she was in her element.

The station was a small, unassuming, white-brick building that looked more like the office of an upscale pediatrician than a place that dealt with crime and death. There was a parking lot in the back for the two clean, well-maintained patrol cars, as well as a hidden rear entrance. Probably so the occasional ne'er-do-well who got arrested for public intoxication could be ushered into the building without besmirching the Norman Rockwell set-dressing.

Olivia walked around to the front.

There she found a neat, old-fashioned and almost apologetic sign that read TOWN OF WESTLEY POLICE

DEPARTMENT. If it had been summer, the pretty leaded-glass front door would have been wreathed in flowering vines. Now, in the harsh grip of winter, the twisted vines were bare and thorned with ice.

Inside there was a small waiting area and an antique desk with a rosy-cheeked young man wearing a pristine navy-blue uniform that looked like he'd just bought it that morning.

She strode purposefully up to the desk, head held high.

"I'd like to report a series of assaults at the Deerborn Academy," she said.

The young officer's pretty blue eyes went huge, his pink cheeks turning pinker.

"Oh," he said. "Well, um, okay, miss." He picked up the phone and fumbled with the buttons like he'd forgotten what they were for. "Please have a seat, and someone will be with you shortly."

Olivia did what he asked, choosing the sleek leather chair closest to the door and setting her messenger bag on the glossy floor at her feet. The young man muttered something into the phone, and then went to work meticulously rearranging the three items on his desk. He scrupulously avoided looking at Olivia.

After about five minutes, a woman appeared in the doorway behind the desk. She wore a dowdy tan suit instead of a uniform, and had her thin, shoulder-length blond hair tucked behind her large ears. Her face was birdy and sharp, with very pale blue eyes behind nearly invisible blond lashes. No makeup. Her gaze was direct, no nonsense.

"Detective Elyse Sherman," she said, putting out a ringless hand for Olivia to shake.

Olivia stood and took the offered hand. It was cool, her grip just a little too firm.

"Olivia Dunham," she said.

"Follow me, please."

She led Olivia past the desk and down a narrow hallway to an unmarked door. Inside was a nearly bare room with a bolted down metal table and two chairs. On the right side of the room was a large mirror. Obviously two-way glass, Olivia mused.

An interrogation room.

"Sorry to have to bring you in here," Detective Sherman said. "But our facilities are very limited, and I figured you'd feel more comfortable talking here in private, instead of in the office I share with my male colleagues."

"Thank you," Olivia said, taking a seat in one of the two chairs. "It's okay."

"Good," Detective Sherman said. "Why don't you go ahead and tell me why you're here."

"Well," Olivia said, putting her bag on the table and removing a large red file folder. "I've prepared a detailed written statement, including information about both my own experience with the perpetrators, just last night, and a previous assault against an unknown female which occurred on the evening of January 7th, for which I have eyewitness testimony.

"I've also provided a copy of the audio cassette I recorded of the perpetrators discussing their intentions, and joking about past incidents. Here, you can see that I transcribed the tape for you, as well. The sound quality isn't all that great because I had to hide the recorder in my boot."

"Slow down a second, kid," Detective Sherman said, a small thin smile appearing in one corner of her narrow lips. "You after my job here, or what?"

"Well," Olivia said with a sheepish shrug. "I guess I kind of am. When I get older anyway."

"We could use more women on the job," the detective said, the smile widening and pale eyes crinkling at their corners. "But that's not what matters right now. Right now, I just need you to tell me—in your own words— exactly what happened to you."

There was a knock on the door, and a balding guy with glasses stuck his head into the room.

"Elyse?" he said. "Can I please have a word with you?"

"Now?" Detective Sherman frowned.

"*Now*," the bald guy said.

"Sorry, kid," she said to Olivia. "Just give me a minute, okay?"

"Sure," Olivia said, straightening her papers.

Detective Sherman slipped out of the room, leaving her alone.

She sat there for several minutes, going over her statement and thinking about the look on Brent's face when the cops showed up at school to arrest him.

Then the door to the interrogation room opened, but it wasn't Detective Sherman, or even the bald guy.

It was the man who'd scared off Brent and Tyler the night before. The dark-haired cop from Tampa, who'd said his name was Jimmy Obejas.

He smiled at her.

"Hello, Olivia," he said.

22

Olivia just sat there, stunned for a moment. Then she stood up slowly, backing away from him.

"What are you doing here?" she asked.

"My job," he replied. He was holding a pair of handcuffs in his left hand.

Detective Sherman appeared in the doorway behind him. Her eyes were narrowed, and she was wearing a slight frown.

"I'm taking this juvenile into custody," Obejas said over his shoulder. Before the words could sink in, he stepped over to Olivia and slapped the handcuffs on her wrists. "She's wanted on an outstanding arson warrant from Jacksonville, Florida."

"Arson?" Olivia frowned. "Are you crazy? *What* arson?" She turned toward the detective. "Can't you see this isn't right? This guy was hanging around my school in the middle of the night. Following me."

"Nothing personal," he said with a big, smarmy smile. "I told you, it's just my job." Then he manhandled her out into the hallway, were the bald guy was waiting, and looking nervous.

"You can't just let him take me!" Olivia protested, struggling and shifting her gaze back and forth between Detective Sherman and the bald guy. "Where are the interstate extradition documents? Doesn't the indictment need to be certified by the governor, before he's allowed to take me? I want to talk to a lawyer!"

"You're still a juvenile," Obejas said. "So official certification isn't required. And don't worry, you'll be allowed to speak with an attorney as soon as we get back to Jacksonville."

"This isn't right!" Olivia said again, planting her feet and turning toward Detective Sherman. "It's not right, is it? Please don't let him do this! Just take a little time to look into this. Make some calls. I can wait in the fish tank and you can put an armed guard on me so I don't try to escape. You can even handcuff me to the table."

The lights flickered for a moment, and a hint of fear seemed to flit across Obejas's face. Olivia paused and took a deep breath to calm herself.

"If it's all on the level, and you find out that I'm really a fugitive, then I'll go quietly, I swear. What does it matter if he takes me back to Jacksonville now, or in an hour?"

"She's right, Jim," the detective said. "Maybe we should…"

"Listen, honey," the bald guy replied, cutting her off. "Obejas warned me she'd try something. She's pulled scams like this down in Florida—he gave me the full details.

"This is a quiet little town," he continued, "and it's my job to make sure it stays that way. The sooner this mess is out of my jurisdiction, the happier I'll be. And the happier I am, the happier you'll be." He turned back to Olivia and gave her a sneering once-over, then nodded to the dark-haired man.

"Detective Obejas, I hereby remand this juvenile into your custody. You're free to go."

"Good call," Obejas said. "It's nice to deal with a professional." He shot Detective Sherman a condescending look, and the bald guy just smiled.

"No!" Olivia cried. "No, wait, please."

Obejas gave a jerk that pulled her off-balance, dragging her away. She fought, grim and silent, against the cold steel cuffs and his implacable gloved grip on her upper arm.

"Wait," the bald guy said.

Olivia froze, her heart leaping.

"Take her out through the back door," he said, pointing down the hall in the opposite direction. "Please. Let's not have an ugly public scene."

As Obejas dragged her toward the exit, she twisted back to look for Detective Sherman. The woman was looking down, cheeks flushed an angry crimson.

She wouldn't look at Olivia.

The creepy cop held Olivia's arm with his left hand and led her out the back door, into the parking lot. As soon as they were out of sight, he used his teeth and pulled the glove off his right hand, revealing a prosthetic hook. She stared in shock.

"Do you remember me now, Olivia?" he asked.

This was Chelsea's one-armed peeper. The urban legend bogeyman with a hook for a hand.

But why was he asking her if she remembered him? She'd never seen him before last night. Or had she? She felt a sudden sharp pulse in her skull—that same strange headache she'd experienced the night before, but it was gone as quickly as it came.

She barely had a second to process this jumble of

thoughts when he used the hook to grab her ponytail, wrenching her chin up high and steering her by the hair while his good hand gripped her upper right arm. He was very careful to stay far to the side and slightly behind her. She thought she might be able to land a heel to the shin, or maybe stomp on his foot, but was afraid it would just piss him off.

The building was blocking Kieran from seeing her and her predicament. Her mind raced, trying to come up with some method to signal him, but couldn't think of anything.

The one-armed cop propelled her toward a dark blue sedan, and she was sure that once he got her in that car, he could do anything he wanted with her.

Obejas opened the passenger side door and shoved her inside, using her ponytail as a handle to push her head down.

Sitting on the passenger seat with her cuffed hands squashed against the small of her back, heart pounding and sick from adrenalin, she realized that she only had one chance for escape. She felt like a trapped animal, so she did the only thing she could think of.

She gave up—stopped resisting, and made it clear that she was beaten.

When he started to close the door, he bent down to look in through the window at her, a smug smile on his face. Then she bent her legs, pivoted swiftly on her hips and planted both feet against the door, shoving as hard as she could.

Because he had been bending down slightly, the corner of the door nailed him in the temple instead of the chest. He went down, splayed out on the concrete like he'd been shot.

Olivia lunged out of the car, rolled to her feet, and ran.

23

Kieran was reading *Watchmen*. He had the engine running to keep warm while he waited for Olivia to come out of the police station, but he was having trouble concentrating on the story. He kept on looking up to check that vine-covered doorway.

He had to admit that he was excited by the idea of being off-campus with her. It was almost like a date. Perhaps after she was done at the station, he would just casually ask if she was hungry and see if she wanted to stop at the Copper Pot for some breakfast. Not make a big deal out of it or anything, just get a bite.

Not like a *real* date or anything.

Except that he wanted it to be a date. He wanted people in the restaurant to see him with her, to watch him pull out her chair so she could sit down, and wish they were him.

These were the pleasant thoughts drifting through his head when a sudden frantic thumping on the driver's side door made him jump so abruptly that he banged his head.

It was Olivia!

She was kicking his door, hands behind her back

and her face pale and frantic. He pressed the button to roll down the window, wondering how she'd gotten out of the station without him seeing her. But any questions were obliterated by adrenalin when she unexpectedly dove through the open window, sprawling across his lap.

"*Drive!*" she hollered.

Before he could react, the rear windshield of the car shattered, safety glass flying everywhere like cubist snow. The bright yellow graphic novel flew from his hands, bounced off the dash and landed in the space where the passenger's feet go.

"*DRIVE!*"

He grabbed the wheel and threw the car into gear. He stomped on the gas, one hand on Olivia's back as her legs kicked wildly out through his still-open window.

That's when he noticed that she was handcuffed.

He hung a screaming, slippery left at the end of the block, icy wind whipping his hair around and stinging his cheeks.

"Holy crap!" he said, glancing up into the rearview mirror. "Was somebody shooting at us? Why are you in handcuffs?"

He took another sharp turn and had to concentrate to keep control as Olivia pulled her legs into the car and squirmed over into the passenger seat, sliding and slamming against the passenger door.

"We have to go get Rachel," Olivia said, ignoring his questions.

When they got back to the campus, Kieran pulled over, got out, and went around to the passenger side to open the door. He took off his coat and draped it around Olivia's shoulders to hide the cuffs, helping her to her feet. That's when he noticed that the graphic novel lying on the on the floor had a hole in it—a bullet hole through the eye of the smiley face on the cover.

He shuddered, realizing how close he'd come to dying. This wasn't some kind of cool action movie. This was real.

Too real.

Olivia stubbornly refused to explain anything, and it was really starting to bug Kieran. He felt like he deserved to know what was going on. But he gave her space— didn't press the issue. The most important thing was that she needed him.

They walked as quickly as they could without running, and hightailed it to the metal shop. It was housed inside a large, low brick building that used to be a garage for old man Deerborn's fancy automobiles. It also housed the wood shop, auto shop, and the pottery shop.

There wasn't a class on at the moment, but a girl Kieran didn't know was there working on some kind of decorative ironwork project. She was a tiny little thing, with stoplight-red hair scraped up into two stubby pigtails, and she had her back to them, headphones on and totally engrossed in her work.

She didn't even notice Kieran when he reached up to steal a small hacksaw off its peg on the wall.

"Come on," he said, pulling Olivia into the single, unisex bathroom in the building and locking the door.

He took off the jacket to expose the cuffs. She twisted her head to look over her shoulder at her hands.

"Hurry," she whispered.

He went to work sawing through the cuffs. At first he was too tentative—he was afraid the saw blade would slip and cut her pale wrists. So it took much longer than he expected just to get through one cuff.

But he kept at it, sawing furiously with sweating hands. When the second cuff finally dropped off, Olivia spun around and threw her arms around him. Holding her, he could almost forget everything crazy that was happening.

Almost.

"Thank you," she said, pressing his face between her cold hands for a brief moment. He hoped that she might kiss him, but she didn't. "Let's go!"

Kieran left the hacksaw in the bathroom, but stashed the broken cuffs in his backpack with the vague, unformed thought that maybe he shouldn't let anyone find them. By the time he was done Olivia was way ahead of him, and he practically had to sprint to keep up with her.

"Should we…" Kieran began breathlessly. "I mean… If people are going to be shooting at us… Well… Maybe you should get your rifle?"

Olivia shook her head, a terse dismissal.

"I can't check it out of the gun locker without Coach Lowenbruck's signature," she said. "I don't want him to get in any trouble over this."

Somehow that seemed like the least of their worries, but Kieran didn't say anything.

They ran across the quad and down to the junior girls' dorm.

Rachel.

She was in her room, reading a book with her headphones on. When she saw Olivia and Kieran, disheveled and breathing heavily, she pulled the headphones off. At first she looked pleased, but then a quizzical look crossed her face.

"What's going on?" she asked.

"Rach," Olivia said. "Pack a bag, right now. We're leaving."

Rachel looked up at Olivia, and then hugged her

hard. She didn't even pause to ask questions. She just did what she was told.

The trust and love that Olivia saw in her little sister's face made her feel painfully inadequate. What if she failed? What if that crazy cop found them? Was Olivia actually putting Rachel in harm's way by keeping them together? Would she—and Kieran—be better off away from Olivia?

"Come on," she said to Rachel, still terribly uncertain but unwilling to let it show. "Let's go."

24

In Kieran's car, Rachel sat in the back seat, but leaned forward so her head was between Kieran and Olivia. She'd cleared a space on the seat so she wouldn't have to sit on the broken glass—safety or not.

"Are you gonna tell me what's going on?" she asked, voiced raised to be heard over the cold wind howling through the broken window.

"Seriously, Liv," Kieran echoed. "What happened to you?"

"Okay," Olivia said. "Look, I'm sorry for freaking everyone out, but here's what's going on. There's this weird guy following me around. He claims to be a cop, but I don't believe him. He's got a missing arm. I'm pretty sure he's the guy who's been peeping around the school and…"

She stopped in mid-sentence, hand flying involuntarily to her mouth, her eyes wide.

She couldn't believe she hadn't thought of it sooner.

"Chelsea!" she said from between her fingers. "My god, he got Chelsea!"

"What are you talking about," Kieran asked. "I thought you said she was with some boyfriend?"

"I thought…" Olivia began, but she couldn't find the words to finish.

Poor silly, shallow, hypercaffeinated Chelsea.

Chelsea, who had believed the one-armed stalker story, while Olivia had dismissed it as a goofy rumor.

Chelsea, who hadn't been anywhere to be seen that morning…

"Pull up at that gas station," she said.

"Sure, but…" Kieran slowed and turned into the station. "Jesus. This is serious. What are we going to do?"

"Shouldn't we call the cops?" Rachel asked.

"Look what happened last time I tried to talk to the cops," Olivia said. She pointed through the window. "Pull up by that phone."

Kieran did as she asked and she got out, going through her pockets for change as she walked over to the pay phone.

She did the only thing that made sense. She called Mrs. Gilbert.

"Mrs. G," she said as soon as the woman answered. "It's Olivia. Listen, Chelsea never came home last night, and she wasn't in class this morning. Remember that weird guy from last night? I think he might have done something, hurt her or… worse. You need to call the police."

"Olivia, where are you calling from?" she asked. "What the hell is going on? You're not allowed to be off-campus without a chaperone."

"Never mind that," Olivia said. "Please just call the police and tell them that Chelsea is missing. I gotta go now."

She hung up, pre-empting Mrs. Gilbert's torrent of questions, feeling sick to her stomach with adrenalin and fear. She looked back over her shoulder at the car, at Kieran and Rachel, and was struck again with the idea that she should run as far as she could away from them.

That she'd already gotten her roommate hurt—or maybe even killed.

And she didn't even know why.

Mrs. Gilbert slammed the phone back into the cradle, and then immediately dialed another call.

"It's worse than we thought," she said, wedging the phone between her shoulder and ear, pulling her gun from a locked drawer in her desk and putting it into her purse. "The subject has gone AWOL, and I have reason to suspect that the man calling himself Obejas may be after her.

"Set up intercept teams at the bus and railway stations, and I'll fax you the license plate number of a car registered to a boy who may be aiding her. I'll have the cellular phone, and will check-in on the road."

She checked the charge on the brand-new cell phone, and put it in her purse with the gun.

"I understand," she said. "She won't get far."

Olivia got back into the car, feeling numb and cold.

What was she doing? Where were they going? She didn't have a plan, just this terrible urge to run fast and far.

"I think we need to ditch this car," Kieran was saying. "If this guy after you is a cop, he'll probably have other cops looking for you, too. They'll know I'm with you, and be on alert. Plus we'll freeze to death with this missing rear windshield."

"Maybe we can get bus tickets or something," Rachel suggested.

"What about the train?" Kieran said.

Olivia couldn't seem to concentrate. She kept

thinking about Chelsea. But she forced herself to focus.

"Maybe we should split up," she said. "Maybe you should take Rachel to your mom's place in the Hamptons. I'll go to New York City or something, to draw him away from you guys."

"Hell, no," Kieran said. "No way. You can't fight this guy alone."

"I'm not going with him," Rachel said. "I'm staying with you!"

"We should definitely stay together," Kieran said. "But the beach house in the Hamptons is a great idea. That whole neighborhood will be pretty much deserted this time of year. No one will think to look for us there."

Olivia wished she could think of a better plan, but couldn't.

When they arrived at the train station, Olivia eyed every single person with suspicion. Was that guy with the briefcase staring at them? Was that woman on the payphone just pretending to talk to a dead receiver, while she clocked Olivia getting out of Kieran's car?

She put her arm around Rachel's shoulders and led her across the lot to the station entrance, feeling as if she had a bullseye on her forehead. She swiveled her neck around, trying to watch the whole lot at once. They were almost to the entrance when a police car pulled in.

Olivia ducked into the doorway and pulled Rachel in with her. Kieran was right behind them.

"Cops," he said.

"I know," Olivia said. "I saw them."

Kieran peered out through the glass doors.

"Is that Mrs. G?" he asked, frowning.

Olivia risked a glance out through the doors and

saw that Kieran was right. It *was* Mrs. G. The woman was leaning over the driver's side of the cop car, talking to the two policemen inside.

A thin twist of anxiety took hold of Olivia. Why was Mrs. G talking to the cops? This was starting to feel like some sort of conspiracy. Was she in it? But how could she be? She had always been so friendly and caring toward Olivia.

Maybe too friendly.

Olivia felt like an idiot for being so trusting.

Suddenly *nothing* seemed trustworthy, as if her whole life was being revealed as an elaborate stage play. Could she even trust Kieran?

No, she was letting paranoia get the better of her. She had to keep a level head and not get carried away. She had to concentrate on keeping Rachel safe, and staying one step ahead of everyone who was after her.

She looked up at the monitor screen.

"There's a southbound train due in three minutes," Olivia said. "We should go up onto the pedestrian bridge and wait for it. When it pulls in, we run down and get on at the last possible minute. We can pay for tickets on the train."

"Okay," Kieran said, squeezing her hand. "Let's go."

When they reached the top of the stairs and entered the glassed-in pedestrian bridge that led over the train tracks, Olivia could see both platforms. It was precisely why she'd chosen it as a place to wait.

On the northbound side, standing near the stairs, she could see Mrs. Gilbert, two uniformed cops, and three neckless guys in suits who looked like private security goons. Two were older, white, and similar as brothers with matching gray politician haircuts and bland, forgettable faces. But the third was younger than his buddies, black and movie-star handsome despite a thick scar running up his left cheek and into his close-cropped hairline.

As far as she was concerned, all three looked like trouble. She watched them for a few seconds, and they didn't seem to see her. But when she turned to scan the southbound side, she spotted the one-armed cop standing at the far end of the platform.

None of their various pursuers had spotted them yet, but there was nowhere for them to go from there. It was a devil's choice.

The frying pan or the fire.

"Okay, listen," Olivia said to Kieran. "Here's what I want you to do. Take Rachel down the northbound stairs. If you're careful, you can make it to the northern side exit without being spotted by those goons. Take her back to the car and drive down to the next station. I'll meet you there."

"But that cop will see us," Kieran said, nodding toward the one-armed man.

"No he won't," Olivia said, heading toward the right hand stairway. "Because he'll be following me."

"No!" Rachel cried. She glanced around, and spoke again quietly. "That's crazy, Liv. We should stay together!"

"Hurry!" Olivia said without looking back.

She took the stairs two at a time, and when she got down to the platform, she leaned out over the edge as if looking for the train. She kept her back to the one-armed cop, but she could feel his gaze on her. It chilled her and made her nauseous with adrenalin.

She was desperate to look over and see if Kieran and Rachel had made it to the exit yet, but she didn't want to give their position away.

Fists clenched at her side and breath caught in her aching chest, she made herself wait, counting slowly to ten before turning and ducking out through the doorway that led to the ticket booth.

She shot an anxious glance back over her shoulder toward the platform doorway. The one-armed cop wasn't there. Was he not following her?

Where the hell was he?

When she got to the ticket booth, he pretended to study the timetable on the wall beside the doorway, but each passing second was excruciating. The more time that passed without him coming through the doorway, the more nervous she became. Eventually, she was compelled to check back out on the platform.

He wasn't there.

He couldn't have gone past without her seeing him. There was only one other way he could have gone. Up across the bridge, and onto the other side.

He'd gone after Kieran and Rachel.

She sprinted across the platform and jumped down onto the tracks, bypassing the other platform and running straight for the parking lot.

She had to get to them first.

25

Kieran had a protective arm around Rachel as he unlocked the passenger side of the car.

It struck him how absurd it had been to lock the door, what with the back window missing.

"She's gonna be fine," he said, wishing he believed it himself.

"What about us?" Rachel asked.

Kieran didn't have an answer for that.

"Let's go," he said instead, opening the door and gesturing for her to get in.

She did as she was told. Kieran shut the door and walked around to the driver's side. He was sick with worry about Olivia. The fact that she was much tougher than he was didn't stop him from feeling this primal caveman urge to protect her—at all cost. It didn't feel right to let her go off alone.

But at the same time, Rachel needed him, too, and he had promised to look out for her. If he couldn't protect Olivia, he could still protect her sister.

He opened the driver's side door and got in behind the wheel. He was about to shut the door when the one-armed cop stepped out of nowhere and pushed in between the door and the frame, stopping it from closing.

He jammed a gun up under Kieran's chin.

"Get out," he said.

Rachel let out a breathless shriek, pressing herself against the passenger door and balling her body up on the seat, with her knees pulled up under her chin. Her eyes were huge in her pale face.

"Run, Rachel!" Kieran cried, twisting his body to keep it between Rachel and the gunman.

"Stay right where you are, Rachel," the cop said. "Unless you want to wear your buddy's brains."

"Please," Kieran said, his heart thumping erratically inside the prison of his ribs. "Do whatever you want to me, but let her go. She's just a kid."

But the man wasn't listening.

"Are you getting out, or am I throwing you out?"

"Don't," he said. "Please…"

The cop used the metal hook then, to grab Kieran's shirt, and brought the butt of the pistol down on the bridge of his still-healing nose. Pain exploded in his head.

26

When Olivia reached the parking lot, she found the car gone, and Kieran lying on the tarmac with a pool of blood around his head.

"Oh, *god*," she said, running to his side. "Kieran, where's Rachel?"

"Olivia…?" His eyelids fluttered. "I…"

He rolled on his side and started vomiting.

"Kieran," she said, hand on his lower back and pushing his hair out his face. "You have to tell me what happened. *Where is Rachel?*"

"She…" Kieran looked up at Olivia, his eyes unfocused and bile dripping from his chin. "I don't know. I don't remember. Where's my car?"

Olivia felt like screaming. She'd read about people who experienced concussion, then lost the immediate past in traumatic amnesia. But for it to happen *now*…

She gathered him up into her arms, aching with fury and frustration. That's when she noticed the note.

There was a folded sheet of yellow paper sticking out of Kieran's left coat pocket. It hadn't been there before—when she left him and Rachel on the bridge. She was sure of it.

She pulled the note out of his pocket and unfolded it.

Dearest Demon Olivia,

Meet me at the place where we first met. The place where you shot your stepfather, and burned away my arm. Rachel and I will be waiting for you.

Do not call the police. Do not bring anyone else with you. Do not try anything stupid.

You have forty-eight hours to get there. That's forty-eight hours before I start hurting your little sister in ways that will only leave scars on the inside. Forty-eight hours to trade your life for hers.

Love always,
Tony

For a moment, all Olivia could do was stare at the note in stunned disbelief. Understanding dawned within her.

This guy was the same cop who'd had a nervous breakdown at the scene of the fire, and taken wild potshots at her, spouting some kind of nonsense about demons. He'd been institutionalized after that incident, and she'd assumed he'd never be allowed to go free.

At first she'd been hung up on failing to kill Randall, and then her mother's subsequent deterioration. So she never really gave the crazy cop a second thought.

But he'd obviously been thinking about her.

Why did he think she was responsible for what happened to his arm? She had no idea what had caused his injury.

When she looked up from the awful note, she saw Mrs. Gilbert and her goons on the far side of the lot. They were looking around, but didn't seem to have noticed her. In another second, though, she would be spotted. She didn't want to leave poor Kieran—not in the state he was in—but she couldn't let herself be caught.

Rachel needed her.

"Kieran," she said, clutching his hand. "Listen to me. Mrs. G. will find you and take care of your injuries, but I have to go. I have to save Rachel."

"I'm going with you," Kieran protested, struggling to stand but unable to do so.

"No," Olivia said, gently laying him back down on the tarmac. "I have to go alone. If you want to help me, count to ten and then call for Mrs. G, okay?"

"Wait…" he said, but she didn't wait to hear the rest.

She ducked behind a white minivan and waited to see if Kieran would do what she asked. By the time she'd counted to nine, she heard his voice.

"Mrs. Gilbert!" he called out weakly. "Help me!"

Olivia waited another few seconds for Mrs. G to respond. When she peered around the rear bumper of the van and saw the woman and her security guys running to Kieran, she headed the opposite way, up toward the street.

There was a middle-aged woman in a green square-back pulling up in front of a liquor store across the street. She had a strange, spiky, bleached hairstyle that didn't seem to go with her soccer mom duds and frumpy beige coat. She got out of the car and went in to the store, leaving the engine running.

Olivia didn't hesitate. She dashed across the street, causing an oncoming pick-up truck to stomp on the breaks, horn blaring. When she reached the square-back, she ducked down and got in behind the wheel.

She had just started driver's education classes, and didn't have her learner's permit yet. She'd never operated a motor vehicle outside of the school parking lot. The interior of the car was laid out differently than the practice vehicle they'd been using in her classes.

But there was no time for hesitation. If she started thinking about all the traffic on the street—the pedestrians and other obstacles she'd need to navigate—she'd be paralyzed with self-doubt. She needed to think of Rachel, and nothing else.

The gearshift and the gas pedal were both pretty much in the same place as usual. So she pushed down the brake, and then carefully moved the gearshift from P to D. Her heart was pounding as she cautiously pressed down on the gas pedal.

The car leapt forward, and banged into the SUV parked in front of her.

Her heart was racing, cold sweat gathering under the collar of her coat. She cast an anxious glance back at the door to the liquor store, and shoved the gearshift to R, cranking the wheel and pressing the gas.

She must have turned the wheel the wrong way, because the back end of the car swung out toward the street and dented the left corner of the bumper on the Skylark behind her.

As she lifted her foot off the accelerator, she heard a shout.

The woman with the spiky hair came running out of the store with a carton of cigarettes, shaking her fist and swearing. She came running toward the car, and Olivia slammed the gearshift back into drive. Then she punched the gas.

There was a terrible squealing sound as she scraped the whole right side of the car against the rear corner of the SUV in front of her, taking off the passenger side mirror and several coats of paint in the process.

Miraculously, there was a lull in the traffic, and Olivia was able to pull out into the street without hitting or being hit by any other cars. She knew she was going way too fast, but couldn't seem to make her foot ease off the gas. Her senses all felt cranked up to eleven, her eyes darting all over the road, hyper vigilant and terrified.

She followed the same street for several minutes, afraid to try and make any turns, but eventually she realized that she couldn't just drive in a wild panic, with no direction or plan. She needed to pull over, figure out where she was going, and how she was going to get to Jacksonville. Driving a banged-up stolen car all the way to Florida wouldn't be a great idea, even if she was an experienced driver.

Without Kieran and his credit cards, she didn't have enough money for a plane ticket. She was feeling gun-shy about taking the train, and couldn't risk trying to hitchhike, so that only left one other option.

She had to find a bus station. It was far from ideal, but it was her only hope of making it to Jacksonville in forty-eight hours or less.

27

Tony didn't know if he really needed to hog-tie the little sister or not, since she'd been pretty much paralyzed with fear since he'd pistol-whipped that geeky loser back in the train station parking lot, and taken his car. Still, he figured it was best to be on the safe side.

He pulled around behind an old warehouse and turned to the shivering and terrified girl.

"You try anything funny, and I'll cut your eyes out," he said. "Do you believe me?"

The girl nodded, keeping her face turned away toward the window, her body curled into a trembling C shape.

He got out of the car and scanned the weedy lot. There was no one around. It was bordered by two-story buildings on two sides, and a windowless, graffitied flank of an adult bookshop. No security cameras.

Perfect.

He popped the trunk and walked around to the back of the car. It was empty—nothing but a set of jumper cables, a flashlight, and a blue plastic tarp.

Walking to the passenger side, he pulled open the

door and grabbed the girl by her fuzzy pink jacket. She let out a little animal whimper and stumbled against the car as he marched her around to the open trunk.

"Get in," he said, shoving her toward the opening.

Her eyes went huge, head whipping back and forth in a wordless negative as she tried to squirm away. He cracked her in the temple with his prosthetic arm, knocking her stupid, but not completely out. She slumped against him, head lolling, and he caught her with his good arm before she could slide down to the concrete.

He shoved her upper body into the trunk, and then lifted her legs and tossed them in after it.

He'd brought along a small roll of duct tape for just such an occasion. He used it to bind her skinny little ankles and wrists. Then he bent her legs at the knees and fastened her ankles to her wrists. Lastly, he tore off a strip with his teeth and slapped it over her mouth.

She was just starting to get her wits about her again, twisting her head from side to side and moaning behind the tape gag. As he watched her become aware of her predicament, it occurred to him that he could just kill her, and not have to worry about the practical challenges posed by transporting an underage hostage across state lines.

But he was worried about what Olivia might do if she came into the old house and didn't see her sister there. Not only that, but he had this strange feeling of pride in being a man of his word. He was on the side of good, and Olivia was pure evil. It was as if they were destined to meet in this way, and any deviation from the plan would result in disaster.

He closed the trunk, ignoring the scuffle and thumps coming from the interior, and walked back around to the driver's side.

As he got in behind the wheel, he was already making plans for getting rid of this car and procuring a new one. Something nice and roomy for the long haul. Preferably with an intact rear windshield.

If he didn't sleep, they could be in Jacksonville by tomorrow morning. Then, all he would have to do is wait.

Olivia sat on a Greyhound bus, leaning against the window and watching the bare, leafless trees go whizzing by. The ride was long and dull, and she had nothing to do but think.

She felt simultaneously keyed up and utterly exhausted, and had absolutely no idea what she was going to do when she got to the old house. She wanted to try to come up with some clever plan, but couldn't seem to focus. Instead, she kept running awful scenarios in her head of what might be happening to Rachel.

If anything bad happened to her sister, she didn't think she would ever be able to forgive herself.

She was also terribly worried about Kieran. She wanted desperately to call him and make sure that he was okay, but another part of her felt that she should distance herself from him right now. That being close to her was clearly dangerous, and he was better off staying as far away from her as possible.

Again and again, she found herself wishing that she were older. She already felt like an adult, and had for some time, but while she had shouldered many adult responsibilities in her young life, she didn't have any of the privileges and freedom given to most adults.

Most significantly, the privilege to purchase a rifle without parental permission.

If only she could find a way to get her hands on one,

she had a perfect plan. She could hide across the street from the old house and wait for that one-armed bastard to show his face, so she could put a bullet between his eyes.

She had no doubt that she could hit the target. Shooting was as natural to her as breathing, and she'd made plenty of tougher shots in the past without breaking a sweat. But since she was preparing to join the Marines as soon as she graduated, she'd often wondered if she'd still be able to make a shot, knowing it would end the life of a fellow human being.

Now, knowing that her sister was in danger, Olivia had no doubt that she could pull the trigger—without hesitation or remorse.

Only she would never get the chance, because she had no way of getting access to any kind of firearm. Even if she were old enough, or able to find some unscrupulous person willing to overlook her age, she'd spent almost all her money on the bus ticket.

So she had to come up with some kind of plan that relied only on her bare hands, and her wits.

For the moment, however, the exhaustion was winning, and she found herself drifting. Not quite asleep, but not quite lucid. Drifting, eyes half shut, random, dream-like thoughts flapping like trapped bats inside her skull.

Tony cased several suburban neighborhoods around the outskirts of Boston before he found one he liked. It was generic, middle class, and mostly white. A complacent neighborhood, just nice enough to make the residents feel safe, but not nice enough that the homeowners would take paranoid measures in order to protect their possessions.

Most of the houses on the sleepy residential block

he chose had two-car garages, which was his first requirement. The second requirement was that the garage in the target house have only one car in it. Third, he wanted a dwelling with a single, preferably female occupant with no kids or dogs.

It took some doing, but by mid-afternoon he'd located the perfect target.

It was a neat little place, yellow with flowerboxes and wind chimes. There was ceramic duck by the mailbox and a wrought iron sign that read WELCOME TO GRANDMA'S HOUSE.

He parked the kid's car around the corner and walked around to the back of the house, pulling a latex glove over his good hand. The back door wasn't locked.

Perfect.

The door led him into a small, tidy kitchen that smelled like cookies. The harvest gold appliances were dated, but well maintained. Children's drawings were stuck to the refrigerator with magnets shaped like fruit. A stained-glass cross hung in the window, casting patches of colored light across the worn orange linoleum. He could hear the television nattering in another room, and silently made his way down a carpeted hallway toward the sound.

He found the occupant sitting in a blue velvet easy chair in the living room. He'd glimpsed the back of her white head through the window, and now that he could see her face, it was pretty much exactly what he expected. Big, owlish glasses balanced on a thin, aristocratic nose. Deeply wrinkled lips painted garish pink, and fake choppers that were way too white. Hair like dandelion fluff that looked like it might be blown off her head by a light breeze.

She was dressed in a bulky magenta sweater and a

pair of white velour trackpants. She had a gaudy polyester scarf loosely knotted around her wattled neck and furry pink slippers on her tiny feet.

When she saw Tony, she seemed more baffled than frightened. At first, anyway.

Olivia had a gun stuck in the waistband of her jeans, but she didn't want to use it on the old woman because of the noise. But that scarf around her neck gave Olivia an idea.

She lifted the woman up like a ragdoll and threw her to the dusty carpet, jumping on top of her so that her knees were on the old woman's shoulders. The lady was starting to make noises like a frightened turkey, so Olivia punched her in the face. That shut her up, but Olivia instantly regretted the action because the old woman's big false teeth cut into her left knuckles.

She shook out her stinging hand and then grabbed the woman's scarf and cinched it tight around her wrinkly neck.

As she choked the life out of the flailing figure, she found her attention drifting to the television screen. Some kind of talk show. Two pregnant women were shoving each other while a lascivious male host hovered over them, clutching his microphone and grinning. A frightened man with stringy hair and a scraggly beard hovered nearby.

By the time the fight between the women had been broken up by a pair of handsy security guards, the old woman was dead.

Olivia stayed on top of her for a few more minutes, though, watching the television, curious to see the paternity results for the angry pregnant women. When it was revealed that neither baby had been fathered by guy with the stringy hair, Olivia shrugged and went to find the old woman's car keys.

Olivia woke with a little aborted cry stuck in her throat. She was soaked with sweat, her heart racing, and she was suddenly afraid that she was going to throw up.

She shook her head and tried to calm her pounding heart.

She was under tremendous stress, but that didn't explain the recurrence of these terrible dreams. Was she losing her mind? Cracking under the pressure?

Maybe it was a manifestation of her murderous thoughts about the dark-haired man. That might have led to her latest nightmare, but what about the earlier ones?

There was no way of knowing, but she couldn't let herself be rattled by dreams. She had more than enough bad reality ahead of her.

Tony found the dead woman's keys in a ceramic dish full of candy and change. He took only the car keys and left the rest, including the *I Love My Grandbabies* key chain with a photo of a couple of pale, potato-faced brats.

At the far side of the kitchen he found the door leading to the garage. Turning on the light, he let himself into a blue '91 Vista he'd spotted through the dirty garage window. There was an automatic garage door opener, which he pocketed, along with the keys.

He went back through the kitchen and out the back door, and walked back to the kid's car. He didn't hear any sounds coming from the trunk, and hoped it was just because Rachel had worn herself out struggling. But he couldn't worry about that now. This next bit would be tricky, and he had to stay focused.

He got into the car and started it up, then drove around to the front of the dead woman's house. He circled the block twice, just to be sure there was no one watching, and then on the third pass he used the garage door opener to let himself in. He parked next to her sedan, and then killed the engine and popped the trunk. He got out went around the back to check on Rachel.

The girl had wet her pants—the sharp reek of it was like a slap in the face when he leaned in over her. She was shivering, cheeks pink with shame, and wouldn't meet his gaze.

"I tell you what," he said, opening the trunk of the old lady's sedan. "You be a good girl for the next thirty minutes or so, and I might let you clean up. Try anything stupid, and you can lie in your own filth until we get to Jacksonville. *Capice?*"

She nodded, but her face was still turned away.

He lifted her out of the trunk, wrinkling his nose and reluctant to touch the wet spot on her jeans even with his gloved hand. Then he transferred her over to the new trunk. She made some kind of pleading noise behind her tape gag, tangled hair falling over her desperate eyes, but he closed the lid anyway.

He went back into the house.

In the living room, he quickly wrapped the dead woman in an ugly crocheted blanket and carried her into the garage. She barely weighed a hundred pounds and felt like a bundle of sticks in his arms. When he got into the garage, he put her body in the kid's trunk and closed the lid.

Getting in and keying the engine, he knew this would be another risky moment. But he felt more exhilarated than anxious. He felt closer to Olivia than ever.

He opened the garage door and drove the kid's car several blocks to a small park he'd previously chosen. He'd originally thought it would be good to leave the car in the parking lot of a supermarket or big box store, but the two closest lots had surveillance cameras. This sad little park was perfect. It was nearly empty, thanks to the chilly weather, the rickety old swing sets and rusted jungle gym long abandoned in favor of a new, more modern playground just a few blocks to the west.

Tony parked in the last slot, farthest away from the park entrance. There was only one other car in the lot—a battered white station wagon that was filled to bursting with bundles of newspapers and magazines. The wagon's owner was nowhere in sight.

Giving one last glance around the lot, he got out of the car and swiftly walked away.

Back at the dead woman's house, Tony headed into the garage to check on Rachel. She was still curled up in the trunk like a good girl, so true to his word, he carried her into the house and threw her into the shower stall, turning the water on full blast.

She let out a muffled yelp, twisting her face away from the spray, but then started to relax as the water warmed up. Tony left her there for a minute and went to locate some clean clothes, a plastic garbage bag, and a pair of scissors.

When he returned, he was pleased to find that she hadn't moved an inch. She just lay there, right where he left her, compliant and still. He turned the water off, and then used the scissors to cut her free.

"Take off those clothes," he said, "And put them in this trash bag."

"Do you have to watch?" she asked, frowning and clutching her wet jacket up under her chin.

"Yes," he said, "I do. But don't worry. I couldn't care less about your body."

She reluctantly peeled off her sodden layers, trying to keep one arm across her chest, even though she hardly had anything to cover. The duct tape had really done a number on her wrists, leaving behind thick bracelets of irritated red skin. Once she'd shoved all her old clothes into the trash bag, he handed her a towel.

"Thanks," she said reflexively, taking the towel and using it to dry her hair.

It was kind of absurdly cute that she had such good manners, given the circumstances. Tony figured that growing up with a fearsome demoness for an older sister meant she'd learned at young age to be polite, and not sass back. Still, he didn't want her to get too comfortable with him, so he kicked her as hard as he could in the naked stomach.

She let out a breathless gasp and doubled over, clutching the towel to her belly, tears filling her eyes.

"I'm not your friend," he said. "Remember that."

He threw the clothes he'd chosen into her face, and waited silently for her to dress.

28

Olivia had to switch buses for the third time in Raleigh, North Carolina. She'd been on the road for nearly twenty-four hours now, at times stuck waiting in interchangeable bus terminals. She slept in spurts, but her gnawing anxiety kept her from getting any real rest.

She had a few extra minutes, so she ducked into a low-rent burger joint to grab a quick bite. She couldn't remember the last time she'd eaten, and was starting to feel a little woozy.

The food was unsurprisingly lousy, but she wolfed it down quickly and efficiently, washing it down with bottled water. On her way to board her new bus, she spotted a bank of pay phones, and was hit with a desperate need to call Kieran, to make sure that he was okay. She knew it wasn't a good idea, because someone might have a trace on his dorm phone, but that didn't stop her from wanting to hear his voice.

She paused for a moment beside the last phone in the row. Even allowed herself to reach out and rest her hand on the receiver. But she knew she was just being silly. Weak. She had to stay strong and not let herself get distracted.

Looking up at the digital clock above the bus schedule, she noticed that she had allowed far too much time to slip away while she was having her little moment of uncertainty. She only had a minute left to make her connection.

She sprinted toward the gate, but pulled up short right before the swinging glass door that led out to the spot where the bus was parked and waiting.

Standing by the open door and talking to the bus driver was the handsome black guy with the distinctive scar on his face. The private security guy she'd seen with Mrs. Gilbert at the train station.

Who *was* that guy? And how had he tracked her down?

What the hell was going on?

She backed slowly away from the door, brain working overtime to come up with some clever plan of action. Something better than *run like hell and hope for the best.*

Nothing came to mind, so she ran like hell.

She had a vague idea that maybe she'd try to hitch a ride outside the station or something, but when she reached the main entrance, she found it jammed with kids her age. They were pouring into the station through all four doors, herded by several hassled and distracted adults wearing T-shirts that read SAWBRIDGE HIGH SCHOOL on the front and CHAPERONE on the back.

Behind her, the handsome security guy had come back into the station and was looking around for her. He hadn't spotted her yet, but he would any second now. She was sure of it.

Olivia looked over the heads of the incoming students at the cars idling out front. Weighing her chances of scoring a lift, and not liking her odds. But the giggling, rough-housing students gave her a much better idea. She had to act fast.

She slipped into the crowd of students, slouching

down and falling in step beside a tall, fat kid in a black T-shirt decorated with the image of a masked wrestler on the front. He had thick, dark frizzy hair that stuck out every which way, close-set hazel eyes, and an aggressive outbreak of virulent acne. She could have kissed him.

"Are you excited about the trip?" she asked, trying to act nonchalant while keeping his massive body in between her and the spot where she'd last seen her pursuer.

"I guess," he said, shrugging. "I don't know. I mean, Disney World. Whatever. I've already been, like, a billion times when I was a kid."

Olivia cheered silently.

Perfect.

"Still," she said. "It beats school, right?"

"Are you in Mrs. Himmel's homeroom?" he asked.

"Um… yeah," she said. "How about you?"

"Mr. Ulster," he said. "What's your name?"

"Rachel," she said. "You?"

"Andy Metzger," he said. "Mindy is my sister."

He said that like it was supposed to mean something, like everybody knew Mindy Metzger.

"Oh, right," Olivia said, nodding. "Sure."

She risked a peek around Andy's bulky shoulder and saw that the security guy was less than ten feet away, scanning the crowd of kids.

Her heart skittered against her ribs and she ducked down like she needed to tie her shoe, waiting for his gaze to pass over them like a searchlight.

When she popped her head back up, she saw that the security guy was headed for the door. She swiftly duck-walked to catch up with her new pal Andy, keeping her head low.

"This way," a male chaperone said, gesturing toward one of two waiting buses.

Olivia impulsively turned toward the one indicated by the male chaperone, figuring he obviously wasn't Mrs. Himmel and so it would be less awkward if he didn't recognize her.

"Come on," she said to Andy, hooking her arm through his and leading him toward the bus she had chosen. "We can sit together."

He looked at her with naked incredulity.

"Hurry," she said. "We don't want to get stuck sitting next to the toilet!"

She boarded the bus, waving casually at the chaperone and the driver.

She nearly had a heart attack when the chaperone called after her.

"Hey," he said. "Who are you with?"

But to her amazement, her new pal in the wrestling T-shirt came to her rescue.

"She's with Mrs. Himmel," he said. "But she can ride with us, right?"

The chaperone eyed Olivia with suspicion for a moment, but then seemed to relent and waved her on.

"Here," she said to Andy, choosing a window seat about halfway back. "You're pretty tall, I bet you want the aisle seat."

"Thanks for saying 'tall' and not ' fat,'" he said with a self-deprecating grin. "But yeah, the aisle is better."

As the bus pulled out of the station, she saw the security guy standing on a street corner, talking into a cellular phone. She tucked her chin down and turned away from the window, covering her face with her hand.

"Paparazzi?" Andy asked with an arched eyebrow.

Olivia smiled and shrugged.

"You aren't in Mrs. Himmel's class are you?" he asked. When she didn't answer right away, he said,

"Don't worry, your secret's safe with me."

"Busted," Olivia said, hands up in surrender. "I'm just broke, and trying to score a free ride to Jacksonville. My little sister's gotten herself into some trouble, and needs my help."

"What kind of trouble?" Andy asked.

Olivia shrugged and looked away, out the window.

"I'd rather not talk about it."

He nodded, looking thoughtful.

"That's okay," he said.

They were both silent for a few minutes as the bus got onto the highway and headed out of town.

"I knew you weren't from Sawbridge," Andy said eventually, half to himself. "No girl from Sawbridge would be caught dead sitting next to me."

29

"Eat something," Tony said, nudging the bag of Butchie Burgers along the bench seat of the '65 Olds they were currently driving. It was an ugly ride, and drank up gas like it was happy hour, but the damn thing was solid as a tank and had plenty of room to stretch out. The late owner had probably bought it new the year it came out.

Tony had left the old fart to bleed out in a rest stop toilet off Interstate 95.

Rachel cringed away from the food like it was a bag of snakes, turning her face toward the dark window.

"You gotta eat, or your sister's gonna be all pissed off," he said. "She'll think I'm mistreating you."

"You are mistreating me," she said without turning to face him. Her voice was a dull monotone, emotionless and shut down.

"Honey," he said, "when I start mistreating you, you'll know it."

She didn't respond. He shrugged and turned on the radio. He twisted the dial until he found a bubbly pop song with a female singer.

"There," he said. "I bet you like this, huh?"

Still no response.

"So what kind of music do you like then?" he asked. "New wave? Heavy metal?"

"No!" she said, her teenage contempt finally overruling her sullen silence. "God, wake up and smell the '90s."

"I knew that would get you talking," he said with a grin. "Tell you what, why don't you pick a radio station for us to listen to?"

"Forget it," she said, wrapping her arms around her body.

He lashed out at her with his prosthetic arm, cracking it across her mouth and splitting her lip. She squealed and covered her face with both hands, tears welling up in her eyes as she jammed herself against the passenger door in an attempt to get as far away from him as possible.

"I said *pick a radio station*," he said.

She reached a shaking, bloody hand toward the radio dial. She turned it to the very next station, a fire and brimstone religious station, and then pressed herself back against the door.

"This is what you want to listen to?" he asked, smirking and shaking his head.

She nodded.

"'Cause I'm not gonna change it until we get to Jacksonville."

She didn't respond.

He shrugged and turned the volume up.

"Okay," he said. "Your wish is my command."

In a weird way, her choice was perfect. The preacher on the radio was female, with the warm, honeyed voice of a phone sex operator, and all this talk about hell and the devil just reinforced his commitment to destiny. He could feel Olivia's heat echoing inside him, knowing she was out there on the road somewhere, moving toward the place where they met, just like he was.

They were like two celestial bodies about to cross orbits and achieve an auspicious, once in a lifetime conjunction. If he failed, the demon Olivia would mature into an unstoppable monster and the world would be destroyed in a fiery Armageddon not unlike the one being lovingly described by the sexy preacher on the radio.

Tony felt better than he had in months, calm and centered and ready. He felt righteous.

When the bus made a stop in Jacksonville to refuel, and let the kids stretch their legs and load up on junk food, Olivia bid farewell to Andy. He looked sorry to see her go, but seemed happy to have had an unexpected adventure, however vicarious.

After a quick visit to the ladies' room, she found it easy to lose herself in the crowd of tourists and families—those chaperones weren't very good at their jobs, she noted.

She kept her eyes open for the security guy she'd seen in Raleigh while letting the tide of people carry her away from the school kids and out through the main doors.

There was a line for taxis, and she didn't want to wait so she hopped a city bus that she knew would drop her off close enough to the old house that she could walk the rest of the way.

Sitting there in the back right window seat of the grungy bus, she thought about what she was walking into, and the full weight of it started to hit her. She wished for the thousandth time that she had some ace up her sleeve, some brilliant plan that would guarantee Rachel's safety and bring her abductor to justice. All she had, however, was this mounting sense of desperation.

She scanned the faces of her fellow riders, wondering if any of them could sense her fear, but they all seemed preoccupied with their own troubles.

That's when she had a sudden strange flash, a vivid vision like a double exposure over her view of the bus. She saw a grubby, bearded man—homeless, judging by the look of his stained clothes and questionable grooming habits. His skin was a muddy, grayish brown that could have been due to genetics, exposure to the sun, layers of dirt, or all of the above.

He had a mostly bald head, with a fringe of wispy white hair around the edge and a woman's cheap clip-on earring on one ear, like a pirate. His toothless mouth was open in a silent scream as blood poured from a deep slit in his throat.

She must have let out a not-so-silent scream herself, because everyone on the bus turned back to look at her. Just as quickly, they lost interest—as if screaming nut cases were a regular occurrence on the Jacksonville public transit system.

Olivia shuddered and sank back into the seat, wondering what had gotten into her. It was bad enough that she was having murderous nightmares in her sleep. But having them while she was awake—that was a whole other thing. Something infinitely more troubling.

But she pushed the thoughts to the back of her mind. She got off the bus a stop earlier than she had intended, just to give herself time to walk off the ugly vision and clear her spinning head.

She had to keep it together. She had Rachel to think of.

Tony stood over the body of the homeless man he'd found squatting in Olivia's house. He was still reeling from the demon girl's sudden active intrusion into his brain. She'd been there in the background, of course, the way she always was, smoldering like a nest of banked coals. Then, out of nowhere, she'd flared up and eclipsed his perception with her own, making him doubt his own identity for a vertiginous moment.

If the blade hadn't been bolted to his prosthetic arm, he would have dropped it.

He pressed his good hand to his temple and took a crooked, stagger-step back from the body. When he turned back to Rachel, she was gone, and the front door was swinging shut.

He swore and took off after the little bitch. How could he have let this happen? Clearly, he'd allowed himself to become complacent with her whipped puppy routine, thinking that she was too scared to try anything.

When he got out to the street, he spotted her desperately banging her little fists on the door of the house next door. A young black woman with lots of long, thin braids twisted together into a fat one was opening the door just as Tony came barreling up the porch steps.

He grabbed Rachel by the hair and shoved her in, knocking the frightened woman backward and stepping into the house, slamming the door behind him.

The woman was crawling away from Tony, and Rachel was cowering off to the right beside a playpen that held a silent, owl-eyed toddler in a pink T-shirt and a diaper.

Tony leapt on top of the woman, covered her mouth with his good hand and stabbed her repeatedly in the chest and neck until she stopped moving.

When he was done dealing with her, he sucked

in a long, deep breath to center himself, taking in the surroundings and situation that Rachel had put him in.

The interior of the house was laid out very much like Olivia's. The front door opened into a large living room, and the kitchen was visible through an archway to the left.

The living room was cheaply but thoughtfully furnished and decorated with family photographs and a few unframed abstract oil paintings that showed some potential, but were still a little bit rough and immature. It was clean and tidy with a warm Christmassy smell of scented candles.

There was a scatter of textbooks and handwritten notes on the low coffee table, and an easel in one corner with a half-completed canvas that looked like it was shaping up to be a real quantum leap in skill, compared to the other ones. Too bad it would never be completed.

Surprisingly, the toddler wasn't crying. She just sucked her little brown fist and stared at Tony in that creepy way that he hated.

He shuddered and turned to Rachel. Time for an important life lesson.

He gripped her hair and dragged her over to the corpse, thrusting her face down until it was inches from the dead woman's agonized rictus.

"Do you see what you did?" Tony asked.

Rachel tried to twist her face away, but he pressed the knife against her neck and made her turn back.

"Take a real good look at what you did," he said.

She was shaking and sobbing, almost silently.

"You killed this nice lady," he said. "It's your fault that she's dead now. Your selfishness means that she'll never get her degree or finish that painting, and that little girl gets to grow up without a mommy.

"I hope you're happy."

Tony threw Rachel toward the playpen. The girl fell awkwardly on her side and just lay there shivering.

"Pick up your baby," he said.

She looked up at him with a baffled expression, and so he kicked her in the stomach.

"I said. Pick. Up. Your. *Baby*."

Rachel hunched her back, a small dribble of bile leaking from her mouth as she clutched her stomach, but she struggled to her feet and picked up the eerily silent toddler. She wrapped her arms around the little girl, turning to place her own body between Tony and the child.

"You killed her mommy," Tony said. "So she's your baby now. If you try anything stupid, like that little stunt you just pulled, I can't be responsible for what might happen to her. Or you. Now let's go. We have to be ready when your sister shows up."

30

Olivia was saddened but not surprised to discover that the old neighborhood had really gone downhill. It had never been all that nice back when she lived there, but at least the houses were all occupied by ordinary, working class families.

Now, more than half of them were vacant. Some seemed to be optimistically for sale, and others were simply boarded up and abandoned. Her old house was one of the latter.

At some point after the fire, it had been haphazardly rebuilt and painted a weird mint green. Someone had been parking a car on the front lawn, leaving behind a rectangular dead patch of oily dirt and a set of deep tire tracks. But some things remained exactly as she remembered them.

The rickety porch where Randall used to sit and drink. That wonky third step that had never been fixed, and you had to skip over it on your way up to the front door or you were likely to fall through the rotten wood. The now-broken window of her old bedroom on the second floor, the one that she had shared with Rachel. She used to look out that window at the cars passing on the street below, and fantasize about hitching a ride out of that place forever.

It was like a ruin of an ancient civilization—one that practiced human sacrifice. A dark, brooding place haunted by evil memories. Only one of those bad memories had come back to life, and was waiting for her inside.

Olivia crept up the porch stairs, avoiding that third step without even thinking about it. The front door had been padlocked at some point, but the lock was gone, the rusty hasp left hanging and empty. She cautiously reached out to push it open, half expecting to see her nine-year-old self standing on the other side of the door with a gun.

She didn't of course. All she saw was a dim, empty, and squalid room. The layout was just as she remembered it. To the left, the archway leading into the now-empty kitchen. In the back, the door to the downstairs bathroom and the stairs up to the second floor. Someone had started a half-assed tag on the right hand wall, but had either been caught or just lost interest before he finished. In the far corner was a soggy pile of discarded clothes and newspapers, all wet from spilled beer and urine and something else.

Blood.

She took a reluctant step closer to what she had first mistaken for a pile of dirty clothes. That was when she spotted a gaudy fake-gold glint in the pile. A woman's earring.

She was looking at a corpse. And not just any corpse, but the corpse of the homeless man from her waking nightmare. His head was tipped too far back, dust and clumps of hair sticking to the clotted slash in his grubby throat. The cloudy surfaces of his wide-open eyes were also dusty, and something about that seemingly minor fact made it so awful and so real. It made him seem so much more dead than the ugly gash in his throat.

If you were alive, she thought, *you would blink and wipe the dust from your eyes.*

Olivia felt a rush of nauseous revulsion as she took an involuntary step back, her hand flying up to cover her mouth. She always assumed, naturally, that she would eventually encounter dead bodies—both in the military and in her career as an FBI agent. She had always felt sure that she would be able to handle it with calm, reserved professionalism.

Now that she was actually confronted with a real corpse for the first time, she was repulsed, and appalled at her squeamish, girly response.

Get it together, Olivia, she silently told herself. *This is just part of the job. It's just part of the job.*

She forced herself to think—not about the dead man, but about his killer. To shut down her natural disgust and look at the body as a clue, instead of a person.

The man's throat had been cut, so clearly the killer had a knife. Of course, that didn't mean he wasn't carrying other weapons, but she knew that at the very least, she'd be dealing with some kind of bladed weapon. The cut was clean and decisive, the work of a person who had done this before. It made her realize how totally out of her league she was.

Just because she'd been able to get the drop on him once before, hitting him with the car door outside the police station, she'd let herself get cocky. Now reality was starting to sink in. She was an unarmed sixteen-year-old girl going up against a violent and disturbed adult with law enforcement training and a clear lack of remorse.

She had no gun.

She had no plan.

All she had was her wits and her ferocious love for

her little sister. She was smart and level-headed, and willing to do anything to save Rachel. It had to be enough. She couldn't let herself be intimidated into giving up.

All she could do was keep focusing on Rachel. Whatever happened, even if she had to trade her own life for her sister, she had to make sure that Rachel was safe.

In the process of fighting through this raging inner battle with herself, Olivia had put her inexplicable waking nightmare out of her mind. Instead of dwelling on the corpse, she made herself search slowly and meticulously through the first floor.

No sign of the killer—or Rachel.

Then she heard a cry that sounded almost like a baby, followed by a quick scuffle coming from upstairs. Her head whipped around toward the sound.

"I'm here!" she called, climbing up the first couple of stairs, fighting to keep her voice strong and steady. "I'm here to give myself up—now let Rachel go."

There was a muffled, mewling sound that made her think that Rachel might be gagged. Then she heard the bastard's voice.

"Why don't you come up and join us?" he asked, as if she was an old friend who had just popped in for a visit.

"Send Rachel down first," she said. "I want to see my sister."

"She's fine," he replied. "Why don't you come on up and see for yourself?"

She didn't answer, and took a deep breath, marshalling her courage. He could be waiting up there with a gun, ready to blow her brains out as soon as she was in range. But Olivia knew that she didn't have a choice. Somehow, she managed to keep her feet moving, and climbed the rest of those creaky old stairs.

At the top was a small landing with three doors.

To her left was the first one, which led to the upstairs bathroom—a cramped and windowless space that had been young Olivia's sanctuary. The only door in the house with a lock, where she could sit in the bathtub with a book and be safe from Randall, even if only for a few fleeting minutes at a time.

Now the doorknob was gone, along with the lock, leaving a round hole in the splintered door. She toed the door open and peered into the dark space. She was pretty sure it was unoccupied, but the unbearable stench that wafted out was enough to discourage further investigation.

She quickly recoiled and let the door swing shut.

That left the two bedrooms. The doors were side by side on the other end of the L-shaped landing. On the left was the narrow room she'd shared with Rachel. It was so small that when their cheap, white metal trundle bed was open at night, it took up more than half of the floor space. They couldn't get into their closet while Rachel's bed was out, so they had to slide it back underneath Olivia's bed every morning so they could get ready for school.

She pressed her ear against the door. Silence. But she couldn't hear any sounds coming from the other room either. Why wasn't Rachel making any noise? Was she okay? Olivia reached out an unsteady hand to push the door to her old bedroom open.

No one was inside. Just an old, black-laminate dresser with no drawers, tipped over on its back. The room looked half the size of what it was in her memory, like a prison cell. Under the broken window was a large water stain on the grubby carpet, where rain had blown in.

That left only one last option. The larger master bedroom on the right. Randall's lair.

Many were the times the sisters had been forced to

tiptoe around the entrance to that sinister cave, for fear of waking the hungover dragon. If they made even the softest sounds before he was ready to wake up, there would be hell to pay. On weekends, the girls would have to sit silently in their room until well after noon. Olivia vividly remembered a Sunday morning, just a few weeks before the shooting, when Rachel had wet her pants because she was too scared to walk past Randall's door to get to the bathroom.

It made a terrible kind of sense that Olivia would be forced to confront this monster from her past inside the abandoned lair of another.

Suddenly, she was overwhelmed by the strangest feeling of timelines intertwining, of who she used to be, who she was in this moment, and who she would be once she pushed that door open. Pathways intersecting and melding together. She paused for a moment with her palm against the door, fighting to slow her breathing and heart rate.

To clear her head. To forget about the past and the future and concentrate on *now*.

She pushed the door open.

31

Inside Randall's old room, backlit and silhouetted against the dusty window, stood the one-armed cop.

He had Rachel kneeling in front of him with duct tape over her mouth. Her eyes were red and puffy and her nostrils flared with rapid, frightened breaths. Her hair was a stringy, tangled mess, several wispy tendrils stuck under the right side of the tape. She was dressed strangely in ill-fitting pink polyester slacks and a blue T-shirt featuring a Persian kitten in a flower pot. On her feet were clunky brown orthopedic shoes.

She was cradling a little black girl in her arms. A toddler around two years old in a pink T-shirt and a diaper.

But Olivia's attention immediately locked onto the most important detail.

There was a sinister black knife blade at Rachel's throat, forcing her chin to tip up and back.

It took a second for Olivia to realize that the one-armed cop wasn't actually holding the knife. He'd replaced the hook on his prosthetic arm with this wicked-looking blade.

"Rachel," she cried, taking a step toward her sister. She

glared at the cop. "Let her and the baby go, you bastard!"

"That's close enough," he said, pressing the blade harder against Rachel's dirty, vulnerable throat.

Rachel let out a tiny muffled whimper, and her eyes went huge. In her arms, the baby started crying.

"Look," Olivia said, palms held up and out. "I did what you told me to do. I'm here. Alone. Now you have to honor your end of the bargain."

The cop stuck his good hand in his pocket and dug around for a second, then pulled out a red bandana. He balled it up and tossed it to Olivia, who caught it against her chest.

"Tie that around your eyes," he said. "And no tricks. I can tell."

Olivia looked down at Rachel—who was pleading silently with her eyes—and then back up at the smirking cop.

"Then you'll let my sister go?" she asked.

"Then I'll let your sister go," he replied.

Olivia frowned down at the bandana. It wasn't very clean. She shook it out and then folded it over a few times until it was a flat, wide strip. Holding the ends of the strip in each hand she raised it to the level of her chin.

"Okay, let her go," she said.

"Not until your eyes are covered," he said. "Take your time. We've got all day."

Olivia cast one last glance at Rachel, then tied the soiled bandana as he had demanded.

"Now put your hands behind your back," the cop said.

Olivia did what he asked, fists clenching against the small of her back and teeth clenched hard enough to crack.

The toddler continued to wail, making it difficult for

her to hear anything else that was happening.

"Shut that damn baby up, Rachel," he snapped.

Olivia could hear her sister making muffled soothing sounds, trying to comfort the little girl. Whose baby was that, anyway, and why did Rachel have her in the first place?

It didn't matter. Olivia wasn't going to let anything bad happen to the baby *or* her sister.

"Let them go," she said, her voice tight.

The baby stopped crying.

Nothing happened for several seconds. She strained her ears, listening, and thought she heard soft footsteps to her left, but couldn't be sure. Then the cop spoke up again and he was suddenly so close that Olivia could feel his rank breath on her cheek. She jumped, startled, but managed to hold her position.

"I just did," he said. "Or did I?"

"Rachel?" Olivia called, frowning. "Rach, are you still here?"

No reply. Had he let Rachel and the baby go, or silently slit her throat and left her to bleed to death, just inches away from Olivia's feet? Her hands flew up to the bandana, but froze when she felt the point of his blade against the hollow beneath her right ear.

"No cheating," he whispered.

Olivia dropped her hands and put them slowly behind her back. She had managed to get herself into the worst possible position. While she'd already resigned herself to doing whatever it took to save Rachel— including risking her own life—here she was in a totally helpless situation with no idea if Rachel was safe or not.

How could she have let things go so wrong?

Tony couldn't help prolonging the moment as much as possible. He'd waited seven long years—a lifetime it seemed—to have this special moment with Olivia.

As soon as she'd blindfolded herself, he'd hustled Rachel out the door, shooing her like an annoying pet. She stayed silent, as she'd agreed, and had taken the baby. From there, she was free to stay in the house or run away screaming. Tony didn't care one way or the other. He had everything that he wanted in that room.

He reluctantly stepped away from the blindfolded demon girl and bent down to retrieve a claw hammer he'd stashed off to the side. He smiled and raised the hammer above his head.

Olivia had her blind face tipped up and slightly to the right, her lower lip caught between her teeth. The temptation to touch her soft, slender neck was almost overwhelming. He didn't want this special moment to end, but he knew he had no choice.

Shooting her would be far too impersonal, and too quick to be satisfying. So he'd decided to knock her unconscious, so she wouldn't be able to burn him with her hellish powers. Then he would cut her throat while she was out of it. Watch the life drain out of her.

He was about to strike, when he was overwhelmed by an epiphany so staggeringly profound that he nearly dropped the hammer.

He realized in that moment that from the very start, his thinking had been all wrong. Suddenly, he knew that, in seeking simply to end her life, he'd been circumnavigating his own destiny.

Tony let the hammer drop to the floor and put his good arm around the demoness, pinning her arms to her side and pulling her to him. She resisted, but he outweighed her by a good measure. Then he used the blade on his prosthetic arm to cut the bandana from her face.

He needed to be able to see her eyes.

"Burn me," he whispered. "Burn us both."

Olivia struggled against the sick cop's sweaty embrace, twisting her face away from him and squinting against the flood of light that streamed in through the filthy window.

"Burn me," he whispered. "Burn us both."

She had absolutely no idea what he was talking about, but his words brought back terrible, vivid memories of the night the house had caught fire. The night she shot Randall.

They were close to the window, and through it she could see the front yard. Rachel was standing there, clutching the crying baby and looking just as lost and terrified as she had that night, years before.

She'd torn off the tape, and there was blood on her mouth and neck.

On the other side of the street was a man wearing a dark suit and a fedora hat. He looked like some kind of detective from an old black-and-white movie. But why was he just standing there? Why wasn't he helping Rachel, or calling the cops, or doing *anything* other than just watching?

He didn't even seem to notice Olivia's sister—just watched the house like it was a blank screen, and he was waiting for a movie to start.

Then her own fear and anger all mixed together inside her, and began to form an emotional tidal wave. It grew in size and intensity, until she felt as if she was drowning in toxic waste.

Then, in a flash, everything was different.

To her shock and horror, she realized that she and the cop were falling. Her mind barely had time to process the fact that the two of them seemed to be suspended in midair, about twenty feet above a massive scrapyard of some kind. Then they were plummeting helplessly together toward the trash-covered ground.

The cop let out a shout of surprise as he let go of Olivia and shoved her away, twisting, cat-like, in the air beside her. Then her body slammed down on a pile of jagged engine parts, filling her mind with blinding white-hot pain that left her breathless.

She blacked out and came to in a series of vertiginous stutter flashes. For a surreal moment, she thought she saw a large dirigible, drifting overhead, but then she realized that she couldn't see the sky at all, because she was somehow trapped in the dusty crawlspace beneath the house, with barely an inch of room between the splintery boards and her nose.

Then more blackness, followed by sirens and shouting and hands clutching at her, grabbing her by the ankles and dragging her out into the light.

She thought she saw a policewoman carrying the mysterious toddler toward a squad car, but she couldn't see the killer anywhere. The pain in her torso and left arm was unbearable, but she didn't want to scream because she thought she saw Rachel's worried face at her side, and didn't want to scare her little sister.

But as she was lifted onto a stretcher, she couldn't hold it in anymore. The echo of that hoarse, agonized scream followed her down as she spiraled into the blackness once more.

32

Tony woke up alone. There were two nurses and a doctor in the room with him, but he was alone. For the first time in seven long, tortured years, there was no one in his head but him.

Olivia was finally gone. Dead. She had to be. Her heat inside him had been extinguished, torn out by the roots. He had won. Slain the dragon and saved the world.

It should have been a relief, knowing that the demon girl was dead. He should have been elated, but he felt bereft and empty. Crushed beneath a depression so profound that he could barely breathe. He hadn't realized that she was his reason for living—until she was dead.

They should have died together. That's how it was meant to be, their destiny. Yet here he was, alone and useless, like an old, broken Christmas decoration someone forgot to take down long after the holiday was over.

He reached out to the nurse, desperate to tell her about how much he missed Olivia and how unfair it was that she had died without him, but nothing came out of his mouth. Words seemed to elude him like skittering bugs under a lifted rock, leaving him mute and hopeless.

"What's the current prognosis?" Doctor Eric Lansen asked, standing over Olivia's hospital bed and pushing a stray lock of blond hair back from her slack, unconscious face.

He felt like a little boy, waiting for the x-ray specs he'd ordered from the back pages of a comic book. He could feel it in his gut that she would be the one.

The trauma surgeon who'd pieced her back together for him was Doctor Maureen Westfall, a brusque blonde with a profile like a pickax and chilly gray eyes. She was physically in the room, but her mind had already moved on to the next emergency.

"She has a broken arm and a few broken ribs," Doctor Westfall replied, pointing to a thick corset of bandage around Olivia's midsection. "Along with some internal bleeding caused by penetrating trauma here and here. But her overall prognosis is good, and I expect her to make a full recovery."

"What about head trauma?" Lansen asked. "Brain damage of any kind?"

Doctor Westfall shook her head.

"Not that we're aware of at this time," she said. "Of course, she has to remain heavily sedated while her body heals, so you'll need to conduct more extensive tests once she regains consciousness. However, there's no swelling, cranial bleeding, or obvious tissue damage."

"Excellent," Doctor Lansen said.

"Speaking of head trauma," Westfall said. "What's the word on Orsini?"

"He's been relocated to a state-run lockdown facility," Lansen replied. "Since he's not a Cortexiphan-positive adolescent female, he has nothing to offer as an experimental subject. He might have provided some interesting data as a victim of Olivia's most severe pre-adolescent neuroquake, if he hadn't suffered such a severe concussion from the fall. According to our tests, the part of his brain that I suspect may have been activated during the original encounter was damaged.

"As a result, he is utterly convinced that Olivia is dead now, that what he perceived to be a profound spiritual connection has been severed." He shook his head. "It's funny, if you think about it. The poor bastard was never really crazy, was he? He was just trying to find an explanation for something he didn't understand."

"You don't feel sorry for him, do you?" Westfall asked. "After all, you almost lost your new toy because of him."

"Of course not," Lansen said. "I'm just amazed by how far the human mind will go to explain away the things that don't fit into the accepted world view. And maybe that's for the best. Most people couldn't handle the truth."

"I never liked dealing with the brain," Westfall said. "It's much too fussy, and hard to work with. Give me a nice, simple, meat-and-potatoes organ, like the liver or the intestines. You can yank them out, throw them around, remove half and then toss what's left back in, and they'll work just fine. The brain's a goddamn diva. Just one neuron out of place, and it has a total screaming meltdown."

"But that complexity is what makes it so seductive," Lansen said, running his thumb over the curve of Olivia's forehead.

"That's all you," Doctor Westfall said, handing over Olivia's chart.

She left without saying another word.

Doctor Lansen stayed with Olivia until the sun went down, holding her unresponsive hand and staring at her pale forehead as if it were possible to see through skin and bone and into the labyrinthine mystery beneath.

Rachel sat alone in a windowless room with a table and chairs, but nothing else. There was a camera up in one corner of the ceiling, and she had shouted and waved her arms at it until she was hoarse.

Nothing happened.

Now she'd turned her chair around so that her back was to the camera. There was nothing to do at all, and she felt ready to burst into flame from frustration and worry.

Finally, after what felt like forever, two government agents came into the room. One guy was Asian and the other was white, but other than that they looked a lot alike. They both obviously went to the same barber, and shopped at the same boring old-guy store. They even had on the same shoes.

"I'm Special Agent Steven Lau," the Asian guy said, flashing her a badge like she couldn't already tell what they were from their shoes. "My partner Dana Reinbold."

She frowned.

"Isn't Dana a girl's name?"

The white agent smiled and shook his head.

"Nope," he said. "It can be a man's name, too."

"Whatever," she said. "Where's Olivia? I want to see my sister!"

"Your sister is at the hospital, recovering from her injuries," Lau said. "She's going to be just fine."

"But for right now," Reinbold said, "we really need to talk to you about what happened in Jacksonville."

"I already told those cops," Rachel said. "I ran outside with the baby, and then I heard that banging sound coming from under the house. That's all I know."

"So you have absolutely no idea how your sister and your abductor wound up in the crawlspace underneath the house?" Lau asked.

"If I knew, I swear I would tell you," Rachel said. "Why wouldn't I?"

"Try to remember, very carefully," Reinbold said. "Even little details that don't seem important could help." He took a step closer to her and put his hand on the table. "Just picture yourself standing there on the front lawn. You've just walked out of the house with the baby in your arms. What happens next?"

"I heard that banging, like I said," Rachel told him. "And then the cops came and got her out."

"You didn't see your sister exit the house and enter the crawlspace under the porch?"

"I think I *might* have noticed that," she said. "I'm not stupid."

"There's only one way to get into that crawlspace," Lau said. "And that's the hatch under the porch. Are you absolutely certain that you were watching the front door the whole time?"

"She couldn't have, maybe, slipped out?" Reinbold added. "Maybe while you were looking at the baby?"

"I already told you a zillion times," Rachel said. "Can't I please go now? I want to go see my sister."

The two agents looked at each other for a long moment, then they both nodded. Lau turned to look at her.

"I'll make some calls," he said.

The two of them left Rachel alone for another interminable century. She was seriously considering curling up under the table and taking a nap when the

door opened and Mrs. Gilbert—Olivia's dorm mother—
came into the room.

"Rachel, honey," she said. "Are you okay?"

She was about to tell Mrs. Gilbert that she was fine,
to try and be all cool and tough like Olivia, but she burst
into tears instead. All the terror and pain and torment of
the past few days ganged up on her at once, and she lost
it, throwing her arms around Mrs. G and sobbing.

"Oh, hey now," Mrs. Gilbert said, patting her
shuddering back. "Let's get you out of here."

33

Olivia didn't wake up all at once. It was more like a slow leak of reality into her endless drug-induced dreams. A slanting spill of afternoon light through a distant window. A warm hand with a smooth gold ring. Deep, serious voices saying words like *exploratory laparotomy* and *ultrasound*.

A stinging needle.

The scratchy texture of overly starched and repeatedly bleached sheets.

There was one word stuck in her throat like a bone, for days on end, and trying to get it out was the hardest thing she'd ever done.

"...Rachel..."

She didn't realize that she'd finally said it out loud until the owner of one of the voices appeared out of the dreamsick fog.

"She's conscious," someone said, sounding far away.

"Olivia?" This from a closer, female voice. "Olivia, can you hear me?"

The female voice turned out to belong to a tall, broad-shouldered nurse with dark, watchful eyes and a neat black bun with a pen stuck through the middle of it. There was another backlit, blurry figure in a white coat over by the window, but she couldn't make out the face.

"Do you think you can try to suck some of these ice chips?" the nurse asked, holding up a blue-and-white paper cup.

"Rachel," Olivia managed to whisper again. "I need to call my sister."

"Your sister is just fine," the nurse said. "She's safely back at school, and has been informed of your accident and current condition. You don't need to talk to anyone right now, you just need to concentrate on getting better."

"Kieran…" she said.

Then the fog closed in again, bringing with it more unsettling images and fragmented dreams.

The next thing Olivia knew, it was nighttime, and she was shivering beneath her thin blanket, which provided little protection against a blast of chilly winter air. She muscled her reluctant eyelids open and saw a scrawny, brunette girl about her age with a buzzcut and a cigarette, standing by the open window. She had the top tie of her hospital gown unfastened so that it revealed a deep V of her nearly flat, bony chest, but didn't seem at all bothered by the cold.

"They don't open all the way," the girl said, taking a drag of her cigarette and blowing the smoke out the open window. "Have you noticed? They only open enough to tease you with a taste of real air, but not enough to jump."

"They…" Olivia began, feeling like her voice was an unfamiliar instrument she had to relearn. "They let you smoke here?"

"They can't stop me," the girl replied, taking the

cigarette from between her lips and crushing it out on the inside of her left wrist without flinching. "Name's Annie."

"Olivia." She wrinkled her nose at the rich greasy stink of burnt skin.

"So what's your story, new fish?" Annie asked, flicking the cigarette butt out the window. "What's your superpower?"

"I don't have a superpower," Olivia said. "I just had an accident."

"Accident, eh?" Annie smirked. "Radioactive spider bite?" She let out a dismissive chuckle. "Don't tell me you actually think this is a normal hospital."

An unfamiliar chubby Asian nurse with a mannish haircut appeared in the doorway.

"Annie! What are you doing out of your room at this hour?" She frowned. "Are you smoking again?"

"No, ma'am," Annie said, glancing at Olivia. "I was just helping my new friend Olivia here get a little fresh air."

A burly redheaded man in green scrubs appeared behind the nurse.

"Everything okay in here?" he asked, his voice unexpectedly soft and high-pitched.

"Larry," the nurse replied. "Will you please escort Ms. Pagliuca back to her room?"

"Come on, baby," Annie said, hauling the wide-open neck of her gown to one side and flashing the stoic Larry. "Let's go back to my place for a nightcap."

"Knock it off," he said, taking one of her fragile, scarred arms. "You want to go back to wearing the anti-strip jumpsuit again?"

"No, sir," Annie said. "Teal is *so* not my color."

Larry led Annie out of Olivia's room, while the nurse closed the window. Olivia's shivering slowly subsided, but her healing ribs still throbbed from the shiver's achy echo.

"What was that all about?" Olivia asked the nurse.

"Just a fellow patient," she replied. "She's a little eccentric, but harmless."

"What did she mean by saying that this isn't a normal hospital?"

"Annie likes to make up stories," the nurse said. "She's just looking for attention. Don't pay her any mind." She checked Olivia's bandages and then pulled the blanket up to her chin. "Try to get some rest."

Olivia nodded and closed her eyes.

As soon as the nurse was out of the room, however, she opened her eyes again and looked around. The door was shut, and there were no footsteps or voices in the hallway beyond. She waited a minute, then another, and then slowly, cautiously eased herself into a sitting position.

It hurt like hell, and nearly took her breath away, but she was able to tough it out. When she felt as ready as she was ever going to be, she swung her shaky legs over the edge of the bed until her bare feet touched the cold linoleum.

It took several attempts to get her battered and disused body upright and find her balance. Her legs felt like spaghetti and her chest felt like it'd been stepped on by an elephant. But her curiosity drove her on, and she made herself take one wobbly step toward the window, and then another.

When she finally reached it, she had to rest for several minutes with the palm of her good hand against the cold glass and sparkles dancing around the edges of her vision.

When her head cleared, she looked out the window. Nothing visible but dark pine branches. No lights or other buildings or highways. No parking lot so she could check license plates and see what state she was in. It was obviously way too cold to be Florida, but other than that, there was no hint of where she might be at all. Just those taciturn pine trees.

She couldn't see the ground, but she wasn't above the treetops, so she estimated herself to be on the third floor of the building. She slid the window slowly open. Sure enough, it only slid about three inches before hitting some kind of block that kept it from opening any wider. Upon further examination, she discovered that the glass was reinforced with a thin wire mesh.

What kind of hospital has locking, unbreakable security windows?

She didn't like the answer to that question. She didn't like it one bit.

When the day nurse with the bun appeared the next morning to check Olivia's vitals and dole out medication, she refused to allow herself to be examined.

"I want to call my sister," she said. "I'm not taking any more pills until you let me talk to Rachel."

"I'm sorry," the nurse said. "That's just not possible right now."

"Make it possible," Olivia snapped. "Because if you don't, I'm out of here. I don't care if I have to walk back to Deerborn with no shoes and my naked ass hanging in the breeze. You can't keep me a prisoner!"

"You're not a prisoner, honey," the nurse said, reaching out to push a button on the side of the bed. "You're just very badly hurt, that's all. You need to take it easy. Relax."

"Fine," Olivia said, struggling to her feet. "I'm leaving."

"Please, Ms. Dunham," the nurse said, putting a strong hand on her shoulder. "You'll tear your stitches."

Larry appeared in the doorway, blocking it with his

big freckled arms crossed.

"Just relax," the nurse said, taking a capped syringe out of her uniform pocket.

Olivia knocked the syringe out of the nurse's hand with the hard cast on her left forearm and then shoved the older woman away. The pain shooting through her ribcage was blinding, almost unbearable, and she could feel cold sweat pouring down the channel of her spine.

Then Larry had ahold of her, hauling her up and trapping her arms at her sides. She could smell his failing deodorant and his black-coffee breath, weirdly intimate and creepy in that panicky and irrational moment before she felt the sting of a needle in her right thigh.

As the woozy red nothingness swallowed her up, she thought she saw a fleeting glimpse of Annie in the hallway outside her door, mouthing the words, *I told you so.*

34

Olivia sat in Doctor Lansen's office, one leg bent. She was picking at the fraying toe of her non-skid slipper sock.

She'd been in this place for more than two weeks now, and was slowly starting to get the lay of the land. It had been obvious from early on that aggressive resistance wasn't the way to get out of there. She learned very quickly that behavior like that earned her nothing but restraints, both physical and chemical.

She needed to focus and direct her energies. Be smarter, patient, and meticulous. She started toughing out the pain and palming her meds, flushing them down the toilet. Because the longer she stayed there, the clearer it became that she needed to get out, and soon. She needed a clear head to make that happen.

Although she couldn't get any real details out of anyone—about exactly what had happened to her that night—Doctor Lansen claimed she had suffered some kind of mental breakdown during a fight with that crazy cop who had abducted Rachel. She had no memory of anything from that day at all, so it was hard to argue about what may or may not have occurred. But she was pretty damn sure that there was nothing mentally wrong with her now.

There was, on the other hand, something very wrong with this place. And a big part of that wrongness was Doctor Lansen himself.

It wasn't something she could easily put her finger on. He was in his early forties and not bad looking. Kind of like a blue-eyed, American version of Jeremy Irons. Neat and impeccably groomed. Always wore a tie. But there was something in the way he looked at her that made her deeply uncomfortable. It wasn't a sex thing, or at least it wasn't *just* that.

Olivia never considered herself a hottie or anything, but she was far from unaware of the effect her developing body had on the male gender. Yet this wasn't about her boobs or her legs or anything like that. It was like he was perving on something about her that she couldn't see.

"Tell me about your boyfriend," he said.

Olivia shrugged, refusing to give this creep even the tiniest sliver of her feelings about Kieran.

"Are you sexually active?"

Olivia glared at him through her tangled hair.

"Are you?" she replied.

"It's nothing personal, Olivia," he said. "I'm only asking because there appears to be a connection between the onset of sexual activity and your... disorder."

She wanted to smash in his perverted face, but she bit back on the urge and took a long, slow breath instead.

"Well," she said, "I hate to spoil your pet theory, but no, I'm not. Besides, correlation does not imply causation. Didn't they teach you that in medical school?"

"That's absolutely right," he said with a condescending smirk. "Which is why we're so grateful to have you here, to help us learn more about this unique condition."

Condition.
Disorder.

Olivia hated those words. All this tip-toeing around what was supposedly wrong with her, but offering no real information. Like she was a cat at the vet who couldn't possibly understand what needed to be done to her. Like she needed guys like Lansen to do things to her, for her own good. She might be sixteen, but she wasn't a child.

She'd been taking care of herself and Rachel for years, and was perfectly capable of watching out for her own good. As far as she could tell, there was nothing wrong with her besides a broken arm.

"All right then," he said, closing his notebook. "That's all for today. I'll see you tomorrow."

"Whatever," Olivia replied.

Larry was there, right outside Doctor Lansen's office, waiting to escort her through what she liked to refer to as "the airlock."

It was the elevator area in the crook of the L between the ward and the row of labs and offices. Both wings were behind key-card locked security doors, and to travel from one to the other you had to pass through both doors. They were programmed so that one couldn't be opened until the other was closed and locked.

Neither could be opened while the doors to one or both of the two elevators were open. Olivia had been over and over every possible scenario in which she might be able to steal a key card, or find a way to get unsupervised access to the elevator area.

So far, no dice.

Larry gripped her upper arm in his big fist and marched her through the airlock and into the ward. Once the ward door clicked closed behind them, he left her to her own devices while he ferried one of the other patients—a quiet little Hispanic girl named Lindsey—through the airlock in the direction of Lansen's office.

Walking down the corridor to her room, Olivia wondered for the hundredth time what was behind the other locked doors on the ward. There was Annie, Lindsey, Corrine, and Olivia, but there were twice that many rooms. The nurse claimed the extra rooms were empty, but if there was no one inside, why were they locked?

The door to the janitor's closet popped open and a skinny white hand reached out to grab the sleeve of Olivia's hospital gown, pulling her in.

Annie.

She pulled Olivia close, hissing inches from her ear.

"Let's get one thing straight, babydoll. I'm the teacher's pet around here. Not you. I'm the one he really wants."

Olivia shoved her away.

"What's the matter with you?" she whispered, frowning. "I'm not anybody's pet, and neither are you."

"You think you're special just because you're all shiny and new," Annie said, grabbing her arm way too hard. "But see how fast he gets sick of you, once he realizes that you can't control it like I can."

"What are you talking about?" Olivia said, wrenching her arm loose. "Get off me."

Free of the other girl's grip, she took a deep breath. Poor Annie was clearly nuts—most likely paranoid and delusional—and Olivia couldn't help but feel a little sorry for her. If Lansen was doing things to Annie that made her imagine there was some kind of romantic relationship between them, that was his fault, not hers. After all, he was the adult.

"Look," Olivia said, softening her voice. "You shouldn't let him touch you."

"You have no idea," Annie said, opening the closet

door and slipping out. "You don't know anything at all."

Olivia followed her out into the hallway. Corrine was there, sliding along the wall toward her room with her head hung low. She was very dark skinned, chubby and slump shouldered, with a sad, defeated demeanor. She had a pretty face, with widely spaced almond eyes and high cheekbones, but you almost never saw it, because she always kept her chin tucked in and her face turned down and away.

She hadn't spoken a single word to anyone in the whole time Olivia had been there.

As Annie passed Corrine, the chubby girl suddenly slammed backward against the wall as if shoved by a giant invisible hand. She let out a whimper and crumpled to the floor, her hands covering her face.

35

The new girl had to go.

It was becoming clear to Annie that something had to be done about Olivia. Blond, tall, and haughty, walking around the ward like she was some kind of supermodel. Wiggling her cute little ass in Doctor Lansen's face and acting like she didn't notice the effect she was having.

Annie had been here for a little more than a year. Before that she'd been in and out of various foster homes, juvenile detention centers, and psych wards, but had been transferred here shortly after the not-really-accidental death of her abusive junkie mother on her thirteenth birthday.

Her mother, Angela Pagliuca, was originally from New Jersey. Third daughter out of seven. She'd gone to Daytona Beach for Spring Break one year and never went home. A year later, she was strung out and knocked up, turning tricks out of her boyfriend's van.

Police found baby Annie forgotten in a Butchie Burger bathroom stall, wearing an unchanged diaper and nothing else. Her grandparents Sal and Rita in Jacksonville were awarded custody, and for the first five years of her life, Annie had enjoyed a happy, unremarkable childhood. She had a pool and a Chihuahua named Bitsy and her own room full of toys and books. She got to do fun things like go to Disney World and play miniature golf and be part of a cool science program where she played educational games with this friendly doctor.

She was loved.

Then Grandma Rita died. Less than a month later, Grandpa Sal suffered a stroke and had to go live in a home. Bitsy had to go to the dog pound, and Annie went to a foster home.

That first foster home was okay, even though the parents were very religious and strict and made all the kids do chores all day long, like they were slaves. But then one day, Angela showed up, claiming to be sober and wanting to start a new life with her precious little girl.

That lasted just long enough to get custody. By the end of the first week, the cute purple canopy bed Angela bought to impress the social worker had been sold for dope, and Annie had to sleep on some old couch cushions pushed together to form a makeshift bed. Two months after that, they were evicted and had to sleep in the car, or in the apartments of Angela's various male "friends"— many of whom seemed to think Annie was part of a package deal.

Angela would berate Annie every day, calling her a worthless trick-baby whose birth had ruined her mother's life. She pulled Annie out of schools constantly, moving her around from state to state. She would abandon her daughter in fleabag motels for days on end and Annie would get so hungry that she would be forced to go into fast-food restaurants and eat the discarded scraps and extra ketchup packets that other people left behind on their trays.

If there were no scraps, she would sometimes ask the

employees if they had anything they were just going to throw away. Sometimes she got lucky and someone might buy her a fresh burger because she was so thin and they felt sorry for her. But when Angela overheard Annie telling a stranger that she was hungry, she dragged her back to the motel by her hair and beat the crap out of her, threatening to kill her for "making me look like a bad mother."

That was when Annie first realized what she could do.

Back then, she couldn't control it. It was more like a sneeze, a burst of random kinetic energy that fanned out in jagged waves, knocking things off shelves and cracking glasses. It had happened a few times in the past, but she'd never realized that she was the one who was making it happen. But that day she'd been so scared, and sure that Angela really was going to kill her.

When she felt the sneeze coming on, she'd done something she'd never tried before. She aimed it, pushed it out at her shrieking harpy of a mother, and Angela had staggered backward like she'd been slugged, tripping over a pile of dirty clothes and sprawling on her ass.

Shortly after the "bad mother" incident, Angela was arrested for solicitation and possession, and Annie wound up back in a foster home. This one featured "special chores" for the female children. Annie was already well used to those kinds of chores, and was just thankful to have food. So thankful, in fact, that she immediately gained more than fifty pounds.

She started stealing and hoarding candy and carried a pilfered butcher knife to protect her stash. When she used that knife on a fellow foster kid for taking one of her chocolate bars, she was sentenced to her first stint in juvie.

The girls in the junior joint were absolutely merciless about Annie's weight. They teased her and bullied her and beat her up until she tried to hang herself with a bed sheet. She got sent to a children's psychiatric hospital for that little stunt. She was finally away from her tormentors, but their hateful voices had followed her.

Annie was eleven when she decided to stop eating.

Hunger was familiar. It was something she was used to, just like she was used to letting men do what they wanted with her body. It was easy, and it felt safe. More importantly, it made her feel in control.

At first, she went too far with it, and wound up with a feeding tube stuck in her nose. But she soon learned how to eat just enough to stay alive and keep the doctors off her bony back, while still maintaining that cold, hungry sharpness. That iron-willed control. Mind over matter.

And as she gained more and more control over her body, she also started to gain control over her mind. She devised little games for herself, trying to push small objects or move paper. Then she tried lifting things. Then people.

Experimenting on fellow patients in the psych ward was easy, because no one believed them when they complained about what Annie was doing to them. Pushing was relatively easy, almost reflexive, but she wanted finer control. So she started practicing pinching, twisting, and plucking out single hairs.

But her psychic instrument was too blunt, despite repeated experimentation, and she found herself ripping out chunks of scalp, instead of individual hairs. But it *did* seem to be getting stronger, more powerful. The day she got her first period, she'd punched a six-foot-wide hole in the bathroom ceiling.

Angela was hit by a car during an argument with Annie. The young girl was out on a day pass for her thirteenth birthday. The driver and several witnesses claimed that the older woman had either jumped or fallen backward into the path of the oncoming vehicle.

Annie had both hands over her face at the time. Even if she hadn't, at eighty-nine pounds she wasn't strong enough to shove a grown woman off her feet and send her flying six feet back into traffic.

Even though she'd hated her mother, and wished her dead a thousand times, Annie suffered a near-fatal mental breakdown after the "accident." She was tortured by conflicted feelings of guilt and self-loathing, and eventually stabbed herself with a homemade shiv six times in the chest and belly. She only survived because she didn't do a very good job with the knife, and it wasn't as sharp as it should have been.

After that little adventure, she'd been transferred over from the psych ward to this place. When she asked why, she got no explanation. She spent the first week systematically testing the boundaries, like a shark that explores an object by biting it.

She was on lockdown almost every day for one infraction after another, driving the nurses and aides up the wall with her self-destructive and hypersexual antics. Then she met Doctor Lansen.

Unlike all the other adult men in her life, he seemed to have little or no interest in her body. He was only interested in her mind, and seemed to really listen to what she had to say. He wanted to know all about her, and not in that nosy, judgmental kind of way—like all the other shrinks, who just wanted to put her in a box and stupefy her with pills.

He looked at her like she was special. Not a freak, but something beautiful.

At first she hid the full strength of her ability from

him, with the deliberate intention of making him feel like he was teaching her, helping her improve. She made it seem as if she couldn't have done it without him. Like he was the wise father figure, and she was just raw material for him to mold any way he wanted.

She made him trust her, so that she could nose around in his office without arousing his suspicion. And once she started to see the true shape of what he was planning to do to her, she fell hopelessly in love with him.

She knew at that moment that she would do anything for him.

Then Blondie showed up and ruined everything.

Now Doctor Lansen spent all his time testing Olivia, like he was prepping her to take Annie's rightful place as his one true love. Like everything that he and Annie had shared was meaningless, forgotten.

It infuriated her to no end, because Olivia didn't have a clue. Even if she did have special abilities, she didn't seem to know about them, and certainly couldn't control them like Annie could. So why had Doctor Lansen shifted his focus? Why had he abandoned her?

Was it something Annie did, or said?

No way of knowing.

But what she *did* know was that she had to figure out a way to get the blond interloper out of the picture, and prove to Doctor Lansen that she could give him everything he needed. To remind him that no one could ever love him as much as she did.

36

Eric Lansen stood behind his desk, telephone receiver in one hand and the results of Olivia's latest tests in the other.

"Preliminary results on the Dunham girl are off the charts," he said. "It's clear that this current involuntary manifestation of her Cortexiphan-induced abilities has been intensified—as well as complicated—by her fluctuating adolescent hormones.

"At an early age she showed a tendency to cause electrical disturbances and even fires when emotionally agitated, including the documented events on file from Jacksonville. Since the onset of menstruation, however, she has developed—like all our female subjects—a bit of a hair trigger. In each of them the Cortexiphan-affected area of the brain is activated with less provocation, and in response to a wider variety of emotional stimuli. Just as a normal adolescent reacts to ordinary situations with heightened emotional intensity.

"I feel that this particular manifestation of their abilities may subside when they reach full adulthood." He paused, then continued. "Maybe 'subside' is the wrong word. Perhaps 'mature.' Transform into something unprecedented. We have no way of knowing what the final shape of Olivia's abilities will be. But there's no question that she is by far one of our most promising test subjects.

"I'll need a minimum of three months to…"

"We've given you ample time to provide relevant results." The voice on the other end of the line cut him off. "You have two more weeks to wrap up your psychological tests, and collect whatever DNA samples and data you need for your continued analysis. At that point, your highest-functioning patients will be released and monitored from a distance, while those who are not capable of sustaining an independent lifestyle will be transferred to the new experimental campus.

"Allowing you to monopolize any of our Cortexiphan-positive subjects for your own private study is no longer financially viable. We now have far superior facilities available to meet the subjects' needs, while providing shared access for a variety of researchers from different fields." The voice softened slightly. "I'm sorry, Eric. This is not negotiable."

The line went dead.

Eric slammed the phone back into its cradle. It wasn't that he didn't know this day was coming, he just hadn't expected it so soon.

For more than two years now, he'd been engaged in an elaborate ongoing subterfuge with his financial overlords at Massive Dynamic, presenting one set of results to them while keeping the real nature of his work a closely guarded secret.

Because he had discovered something staggering. Something that would change the world.

He had invented and perfected a serum that worked in tandem with the unique chemicals released by the female Cortexiphan-positive brain, while it was deep in the roiling flux brought on by puberty. Cortexiphan needed to be administered to children, while their minds were still open, and his new serum had a similar restriction. It had to be given to adolescent females while their reproductive hormones were in flux, chaotic and wild and full of seething potential.

But while Cortexiphan unlocked the powers of the mind, his serum enabled an unprecedented control over the very structure of human DNA. It harnessed the power of a newly blossomed woman, to create life itself. And through that power of creation, Eric hoped to father a new race of superhuman progeny who exerted total control over both mind and matter.

And now—when he was so close to his most significant breakthrough—this narrow-minded interference from a bunch of corporate bean counters. He'd planned to run at least a month's worth of additional tests before he attempted the delicate and crucial insemination of Olivia. Now, he'd have to distill his preliminary research down to the most critical steps, and move the big day up to the middle of next week, at the latest.

Once he'd confirmed that fertilization had occurred, he'd submit a report regretfully detailing Olivia's suicide through self-immolation, leaving behind no remains for an autopsy. He could let the other patients in the upper ward go without protest. While the Pagliuca girl had shown some excellent potential early on—including a level of voluntary control unmatched by any of his other subjects—he'd recently discovered that she possessed an arcuate uterus. Not a deal-breaker *per se*, since it wasn't unheard of for such females to successfully carry a fetus to term, but it would be a crapshoot.

A crapshoot Eric saw no reason to take, now that he had Olivia.

37

Olivia lay strapped down on a gurney with wires stuck all over her head and face. There was a monitor mounted on a flexible arm that had been positioned so that it was directly above her face, making it impossible for her to look anywhere but at the screen.

"Okay, one more time, Olivia," Doctor Lansen said. "When you see each image, say the first word that pops into your mind. Ready?"

She didn't bother to answer.

She was getting so sick of this lab rat routine.

"Right," he said. "Here we go."

The first image in this latest series was a man helping a little girl learn how to ride a bicycle. He was smiling and beatific in a plaid shirt and jeans. She was blond, looking exhilarated and terrified and not unlike Olivia at that age. Her bicycle was pink. There was a word balloon above the dad's head that read: BE CAREFUL.

"Bicycle," Olivia said.

A second image came up, this one showing a couple having an argument in a restaurant. The man looked like the villain in a Spanish soap opera, showing his nice white teeth like an angry animal. His word balloon read: YOU ARE STUPID. The woman was a little bit chubby, and was crying.

"Restaurant," Olivia said.

The third image was a house on fire. A woman and her daughter were standing in the street in their nightgowns, with their arms around each other, and their shared word balloon said: OUR DOG IS INSIDE!

"House," Olivia said.

"Come on, now, Olivia," Lansen said. "You're editing your responses again. You need to be honest, and say the real first thing that comes into your mind."

Olivia felt a hot rush of anger and heard a little cascade of corresponding beeps from the machine. She wasn't stupid, and could easily see that these images had been designed to provoke an emotional response. She refused to be manipulated by this kind of ham-handed psychological strip search.

The next image was a photo of Rachel and Randall. It had been taken on the front porch of their old house in Jacksonville, before the fire. Rachel was maybe four and was being held by Randall. He had a grip on her little arm and was making it wave to the camera. Her eyes were wide and scared, like she was about to start crying.

"Oh, come on," Olivia said, twisting her head away from the screen. "That's a cheap shot."

"Last one," Lansen said. "Please, try to stay open-minded and respond honestly."

That last photo was of Kieran, and looked like it had been taken by a surveillance camera in the Westley police station. His body language was pleading, desperate, his face anguished and still blotchy with the fading bruise. She couldn't even imagine how worried he must be about her.

She was suddenly desperate to see him, to be with him. She'd never felt such a physical and powerful connection to another person and before she could stifle it, a hot wave of aching emotion washed over her.

There was another frantic symphony of beeps, ascending in pitch until the screen above her cracked with sudden static, and went black.

"Fantastic," Doctor Lansen was saying over and over as he fussed around his machines. "Fantastic. Absolutely fantastic."

"Too bad your monitor broke," Olivia said, anger smoldering in her belly. Anger at herself for giving that creep the reaction he wanted. "I guess this means we're done."

He ignored her for another minute, still enthralled with whatever results he'd managed to trick out of her. Eventually he came to her side and removed the crown of wires from her head.

"That was excellent, Olivia," he said. "Please step into my office for a few minutes, if you'd be so kind."

He gestured toward the doorway that led between the lab and his office. Olivia got up off the gurney and made a sour face.

"Haven't you had enough for one day?"

"Almost," he said with a condescending smile. "Just a few more minutes, and then you'll be free to go back to the ward."

"Like I have a choice," Olivia muttered, walking ahead of him into his office.

She'd spent the last week obsessively trying to figure out some kind of ruse that would allow her a few minutes alone in there. Whenever she entered that office, all she could do was stare longingly at the telephone. So that day, like every other day, her eye went right to it as soon as she walked in. With Kieran still on her mind, she was dying to find a way to call him. Dying to hear his voice.

She sat down in her usual chair, arranging her body into the most hostile, unreceptive position she could manage.

"Tell me more about your relationship with Kieran McKie," Lansen said as he sat down behind his desk.

"We're just friends," Olivia said, still staring at the telephone.

"Do you have a lot of friends?" Lansen asked.

"Sure," Olivia lied. "Tons."

"I see," Lansen said. "And do you normally form such intense emotional attachments to all your friends?"

Olivia wasn't really paying attention to the doctor, because she'd suddenly noticed something right next to the telephone. She'd been so busy wishing she could use the phone that she'd never even noticed the stack of stamped outgoing mail sitting in a plastic tray marked OUT.

Suddenly, Olivia had an idea.

"Why do you keep asking me about my emotions?" she asked, just to keep him talking while she set up her plan of attack.

"Well, Olivia," he said, "I have reason to believe— and this latest barrage of tests seems to have confirmed my hypothesis—that the manifestations of your disorder are linked to intense emotions."

He was still talking, going on and on about hormones and her period and other gross and embarrassing things she didn't really want to hear, but she blocked him out completely and concentrated on making a meticulous inventory of the items currently populating the surface of his desk.

A leather blotter. Telephone. Black plastic inbox on the left side of the desk, currently empty. An outbox on the right, containing the outgoing mail. A spread of papers, charts, and folders in the center of the blotter, along with a pen and a half-full cup of milky coffee that looked like it had been sitting there congealing for some time.

Perfect.

"So you see," he was saying. "While I initially thought the onset of sexual activity might be your trigger, it appears that sexual thoughts or feelings, even if they haven't yet been acted upon, are enough to…"

That was enough.

"You're a pig," Olivia said. "A disgusting, perverted pig!"

She got to her feet and flipped the blotter up and into Lansen's chest. Papers flew like startled pigeons and the coffee cup bounced off his shoulder, splattering its contents all over his lab coat.

Just as she'd planned, the in- and outboxes remained undisturbed on either side of the blotter.

Lansen let out a funny little cry of surprise, batting at the papers flying around his head, and then looking down at the spreading stain on his lab coat. In that precious moment of distraction, Olivia reached out and snagged the top letter in the stack, swiftly stuffing it into the top of the cast on her broken left arm.

Then Lansen hit the panic button on his desk, and Larry was in the office in a flash, grabbing Olivia from behind and hauling her out into the hall. But she didn't care. She had what she needed.

She let herself go limp and compliant against Larry as he dragged her back to the ward and deposited her without protest in her room.

She heard the sound of her door being locked, and Larry's heavy footfalls moving away down the hall. She waited a full minute after he'd gone, and then pulled out the letter she'd stolen. It was addressed to BioCen Filtration and Separation Ltd, in Foxboro, Massachusetts.

But that wasn't as interesting to Olivia as the return address.

S-CCGR
Doctor Eric Lansen, Suite 301
100 Red Oak Road
Potsdam NY, 13676

Potsdam. That's where she was. The "suite" number on that address was the familiar number on the door of his office, so this was where she was now, not his home address.

But why didn't the address say something like "Whatever Hospital?" This was a medical facility of some sort, right?

And what did S-CCGR stand for?

Olivia went into her bathroom and closed the door, turning on the hot water full blast. As the sink began to fill with steaming water, she held the envelope over the steam until the glue loosened enough to allow her to open it.

Inside was a terse letter complaining about a faulty replacement part for something called a Veronesi disk stack centrifuge, and demanding a refund. It was signed "Dr. Eric Lansen," and featured the same mysterious address as the outside of the envelope.

They weren't allowed to have writing instruments in their rooms, but Annie had given Olivia a stolen marker as an inexplicable peace offering after that strange interlude in the janitor's closet. She turned the letter over and wrote a swift message on the back.

Dear Kieran,

I'm being held against my will at this address. It's some kind of psychiatric hospital, and they won't let me leave or make any calls. There's nothing wrong with me at all, just a broken arm, but this creep Dr. Lansen is doing all these weird experiments on me and talking about sex all the time. I need you to find a way to get me out of here right away. But don't tell Rachel, okay? I don't want her to be scared after everything she's been through already.

Please hurry!
— Olivia

She folded the letter and put it back in the envelope, and then resealed it and stuck it back into the tight space between her arm and her cast. The next step would be to try and score a bottle of correction fluid from the nurses' station so she could change the BioCen address to Kieran's address at Deerborn. Then, once she managed that, she'd need to find a way to slip the doctored letter back into the outgoing stack, and hope that nobody bothered to look at each envelope in the bundle before dumping it into the mailbox.

Or if they did, that they didn't know who Kieran McKie was, or care why Doctor Lansen would be writing him a letter.

It wasn't the best plan in the world, by any means, but it was better than no plan at all.

38

Kieran sat on the edge of Rachel's bed. Boys weren't normally allowed in the junior girls' dorm, but the residence supervisor had made an exception for Kieran, since he was the only person she would talk to since she got back from being debriefed by the authorities.

She'd been refusing to eat, or even get out of bed, for the past few days, and Kieran was really starting to worry about the poor kid. Not that he was doing all that much better himself.

"But where is she?" Rachel was asking for probably the dozenth time in the past hour. "Where? Why doesn't she call us?"

"I'm sure she'd call us if she could," Kieran said.

"You think she's dead?" Rachel asked, squeezing his hand way too hard. "Is that what you're saying? If she was alive she would call, right?"

"I don't know, kid," Kieran said. "I wish I did, but I don't."

Rachel started crying again, and Kieran felt his own tears welling up to match. He couldn't stop blaming himself for not staying by Olivia's side, no matter what—

for being a coward, just like always, and letting her down when she really needed him. She'd told him not to follow her when she ran away, and so he didn't. But he should have, because now she was gone and he might never see her again.

His girl, his beautiful Enigma.

She needed him, and he had let her down.

In an effort to make up for it, he'd spent nearly every waking hour pestering various officials to find out what had happened to Olivia. He'd worn out his welcome at the local police station, called every law enforcement agency in the state of Florida, and even made an attempt to contact the FBI. All that happened was that he got transferred around to various people who had no information of any kind, and no inclination to help him whatsoever.

He was on his own and out of ideas.

So now, all he could do was try to be there for Rachel. He knew that Olivia loved her more than anything else in the world and that if—god forbid—she really was dead, Kieran felt that she would have wanted him to look out for her kid sister. It was a daunting task—terrifying really, because he'd never been very good at taking care of anyone, not even himself. But he owed it to Olivia to do his best.

Was she dead? Wouldn't he feel the loss of her somehow, somewhere deep inside his defective heart? He loved her so much that it seemed impossible for her to be dead, when he could still feel the brush of her hair against his skin and her warm palm pressing against the center of his chest.

But that line of thinking was way too painful. So he just let Rachel hold onto his hand, tried to get her to eat some of her favorite candy, and told her stupid jokes to make her smile.

39

Operation liquid paper was in full swing.

It had taken several days to fully case the nurses' station and formulate a solid plan. The station had a door, which was generally open. To the right of it, there was an open, glassless window through which the nurse on duty could keep an eye on what was happening in the lounge. When Olivia peered over the edge of the window, she saw a desk directly on the other side.

On the desk sat a cup of pens, a pad of adhesive notes, a roll of tape, and the coveted bottle of correction fluid. It was too far for her to reach without help, though.

So Olivia had used her teeth to tear one of the ties out of her hospital gown, and fashioned it into a little lasso. She'd been practicing using it to pick up a variety of small, lightweight objects, and felt as if she had her one-handed technique perfected. The only difficult part was the little flick of the wrist that tightened the loop around the object. If it wasn't fast enough, it would knock the bottle over before the loop could tighten.

Once the bottle was on its side, it would be impossible to lasso, and she would have to wait until the nurse came back to the desk and set it right, then wait for her to turn her back again. If it happened more than once, the nurse would become suspicious and put the bottle away in a drawer, where Olivia would have no hope of ever getting it.

She just had to time the strike perfectly, and get it right with the first attempt. Failure was not an option.

When Olivia entered the lounge, the nurse on duty was Mrs. Andrada, a petite older woman from the Philippines. She was tiny and sweet faced, but ferociously strict, with dark, predatory eyes like a hungry mink. Olivia considered waiting until the next shift change, but that would be nearly four hours away. Which would mean that she couldn't get her SOS into the mail until the following day.

Every minute that she spent in this creepy medical prison was one too many. She had no choice. She had to act now.

When she sidled up to the nurses station, Mrs. Andrada was sitting at the desk, reviewing a file folder full of paperwork. The second Olivia got within six feet of the window, Mrs. Andrada looked up and clocked her, eyes narrow and wary.

Olivia looked away, trying to appear nonchalant, and leaned against the wall as if she was lost in thought. Mrs. Andrada watched her for a full minute, but Olivia forced herself to stay Zen under her scrutiny. Eventually, the nurse went back to her paperwork.

Then, a lucky break. The phone rang.

The phone in the nurses' station was on the wall on the other side of the door. In order to answer it, Mrs. Andrada had to get up and stand with her back to the desk.

The moment she picked up the receiver, Olivia leaned over the lip of the window and let the lasso drop down out of her sleeve.

Fully unrolled, the loop dangled just a quarter of an inch from the bottle top. Olivia was afraid that maybe she'd misjudged the distance, but if she stretched up on her tiptoes and reached her arm all the way over the lip, she could close that final quarter inch between the loop and the bottle.

Just a little more...

"What are you doing?"

Olivia jumped and spun to face Annie. The girl was standing there with a smug smile that said she knew perfectly well what Olivia was doing. She folded her arms across her chest and arched a dark eyebrow.

"Oh..." Olivia said, fumbling with her lasso, bunching it up in her fist. "Well... I..."

Mrs. Andrada had finished her call and come back to sit at the desk. She looked up through the window at the two of them.

"Can I help you, girls?" she asked, her chilly tone anything but helpful.

"We're good," Annie said with a wink.

Olivia was silently furious. Annie had blown her best shot. There was no way to know how long it would be before the nurse's attention was distracted again.

Oblivious to her anger, Annie hooked her arm through Olivia's and dragged her over to the other side of the lounge.

"Spill," she whispered. "No wait, don't tell me. Let me guess. You want to steal the correction fluid so you can drink it and off yourself, right?" She shook her head, pulling an overdramatic sad-clown face. "Sorry, sweetie. It won't work. It just makes you sick. Trust me, I've tried it all."

"I don't want to off myself," Olivia said. "I want to get out of here!"

"And stealing the liquid paper will help you do that?" Annie shot her a skeptical smirk. "You really *are* crazy."

Olivia looked over at the nurses' station, and then back at Annie. She didn't trust the girl, but Annie had made it abundantly clear that she didn't want Olivia spending so much time with her beloved Doctor Lansen. So maybe she'd help—not out of charity, but out of the desire to get her rival out of the picture.

It was a risk, but having a partner in this particular crime would make it so much easier.

"Okay, look," Olivia said, leaning in to Annie as if she was sharing a special confidence. "I'm trying to send a letter to my boyfriend." She hit the word boyfriend with extra emphasis. Subtext: *See, I already have a boyfriend, and have no interest whatsoever in stealing Doctor Lansen away from you.*

"I miss him like crazy," she continued, "and I want him to come bust me out of here. I need the correction fluid to cover up the address on a stamped letter I swiped from Doctor Lansen, so I can write in a different address."

Annie looked skeptical. She seemed to be sizing Olivia up, to figure out if she was trying to pull a fast one. But it was the truth, and it seemed like Annie could tell.

"Will you help me?" Olivia asked.

At first, Annie didn't answer. She just held Olivia's gaze, her dark eyes slitted and challenging, that smirk still lazing around the corners of her lips. Then, she turned slowly away and strolled over to the open doorway that led into the nurses' station.

"Hey, Ratchet!" she said, leaning against the doorframe. "Come here, I want to tell you something."

Olivia's breath caught, and her heart was in her throat. Was Annie going to rat her out? If the nurses searched Olivia, and took away the envelope she'd stolen, she might never have an opportunity to get another one, and all her hard work would be for nothing. Had she made a terrible mistake trusting Annie?

Mrs. Andrada got up from behind the desk and stepped over to the door to talk to Annie.

"What do you want, Miss Pagliuca?" she asked coldly.

Annie looked back over at Olivia for a second and winked. Then she turned toward the nurse and slammed her own head as hard as she could against the doorframe.

The nurse swore and hit the button to summon help.

Larry arrived almost instantly with another orderly, a big, fat Samoan guy with lots of tribal tattoos. The two of them grabbed Annie by the arms and hauled her away from the doorframe, but not before she got in two more solid knocks to her own head. Blood was running down between her eyes as she stood up on her tiptoes and licked Larry's face.

He flinched away from her with his face screwed up like a little boy who'd just been kissed by his aunt. If he'd had a free hand, he probably would have wiped his face on his sleeve to rid himself of cooties.

"Hold her, dammit," the nurse said, filling a syringe.

This was Olivia's chance.

She walked as casually as she could manage back to the station window. No one paid her any mind.

Annie was screeching and kicking while the nurse was trying to find a place to stick her with the needle. Olivia slung her little lasso over the lip of the window one more time, stretching as far as she could. The loop brushed softly against the bottle a few times before finally sliding down around the cap. She held her breath, lower lip clenched between her teeth, and flicked her wrist.

It worked. The noose tightened perfectly, and she was able to quickly pull the little bottle upward. There was a scary moment when it hit the lip and wobbled, threatening to slip free, but the noose held and she was able to pull the bottle the rest of the way up and over.

Once she had it, she used the string to flip it up into her good hand and palm it.

Behind her, Annie had knocked over a chair with her kicking legs, startling her and nearly making her drop the bottle. She edged cautiously around the melee, clutching her hard-won correctional fluid so tightly the little cap dug painfully into her skin. She paused, hesitating by the sofa and trying to calculate if she should wait until the orderlies dragged Annie away before leaving or try to slip past them into the hall.

An unfamiliar blond nurse grabbed Olivia's good arm.

Her whole body went rigid with panic, ready to fight for her prize. Her skittering mind was racing, desperate and clutching at the disintegrating fragments of her precious plan.

"Go back to your room," the blond nurse said, shoving Olivia toward the lounge door. "And stay there until this situation is under control."

"Yes, ma'am," Olivia said, weak with relief.

She did what the nurse instructed.

Once she got her prize back to her room, she ducked into the bathroom and pulled the letter out from its hiding place inside her cast. She set the envelope on the lip of the sink, and then used her teeth to unscrew the bottle cap. Once it was loose enough for her to open it with her good hand, she set it down on the other corner of the sink, pulled the tiny brush out, and wiped the excess fluid against the neck of the bottle.

The commotion from the lounge increased again, and she froze with the brush poised above the letter. She held her breath as she heard the Doppler effect of Annie, shrieking and swearing, as she was dragged past Olivia's cell and down the hall to the quiet room. She still didn't move for a beat or two after the screaming stopped, waiting to see if the orderlies would come charging into her room and rip the hard-earned brush out of her shaking hand.

When that didn't happen she went to work, carefully covering up the old address. She plastered a thick layer of the chalky white fluid over the front of the envelope and waved it in the air, blowing on it and wrinkling her nose at the smell.

Once the fluid had fully dried, she took her pen and wrote Kieran's address over the rough white patch. As soon as she was sure it wouldn't smudge, she slipped the envelope back into her cast, address facing away from her moist skin.

This had to work.

Olivia sat in Doctor Lansen's office, staring at the modest stack of outgoing mail like it was the Holy Grail. She'd already slipped the envelope out of its hiding place and tucked it under one thigh, ready to grab it as soon as an opportunity presented itself.

The session was almost over, and she was running out of time. She had to do something and quickly.

As she stood to leave, she staggered, swung her cast, and knocked the outbox off the edge of his desk and onto the floor.

"Sorry," she said. While he picked up the box, she bent down to help pick up the fallen mail. There were several envelopes, and she slipped her own into the middle of the small stack.

"Here," she said, handing them over.

"Thanks," he said absentmindedly, slipping the envelopes under the rubber band and setting the box back on the desk.

40

Kieran trudged through the melting slush along the path that led to the rec hall, lost in thought, gloveless hands stuffed deep in his pockets. The day was gloomy, and there was a threat of rain or snow. This time of year, it was a toss up which it would be.

Just inside the front door was the campus post office, such as it was. It was really just a wall of individual mailboxes for all the students, along with a letter drop slot and a coin-operated stamp machine. His box was number 331.

He opened the box with a tiny brass key and pulled out a hastily scrawled postcard from his mother, who was vacationing in Costa Rica. There was a slip of paper that let him know he had a larger package waiting for him up at the front office—probably also from his mother, and undoubtedly full of questionable herbal supplements and protein shakes specially formulated for "hard gainers." Instead of actually caring about him, she was constantly sending him junk he didn't need.

Also wedged into the narrow box was the latest issue of *Video Watchdog* and a padded envelope from his Hong

Kong tape trader. It had to contain his long-awaited VHS copy of *Heroic Trio* with Michelle Yeoh, Maggie Cheung, and Anita Mui. Last and definitely least, there was a white, letter-sized envelope from some doctor.

Probably junk mail or some kind of alternative medicine scam. Thanks to his mother, he was on a lot of strange, health-and-wellness-related mailing lists.

He carried the mail over to one of the study tables and tore open the padded envelope from the tape trader. Sure enough, it was *Heroic Trio*. The tape was in a plain black sleeve with a Chinese label on the spine, and the English title had been handwritten with a black sharpie over the red characters. He had to restrain himself from kissing the cassette. He'd have to make sure to put his name down on the VCR sign-up sheet ASAP, so he didn't get tape-blocked by some girl who wanted to watch *Sleepless in Seattle* for the fifty-billionth time.

He put the empty padded envelope and the junk mail off to one side, to toss in the trash on the way out. Then he put the precious tape into his backpack. He was about to put the magazine in there, too, but hesitated. He just couldn't resist flipping through it for a few minutes.

He read through the Oliver Stone interview and an article about one of his favorite action movies, *The Crow*, but decided to save the rest for later. He always read each new issue of *Video Watchdog* way too fast, and was trying to stretch them out, to make them last.

He tucked the magazine away in an outside pocket of his backpack, and then grabbed the stuff he was going to throw away. When he picked up the junk mail from that doctor, he noticed something odd about it. The texture of the front of the envelope was rough and chalky in the center, where his address had been written.

Looking at the envelope more closely, he realized

that the original address had been covered with a thick layer of correction fluid. He scratched at it with his thumbnail and revealed a few letters of a different, typed address beneath.

That seemed odd. If whoever sent the letter wanted to correct the address, why not just retype it? Why would they have handwritten his address?

He used his mailbox key to scrape off the rest of the correction fluid, creating a dandruffy flurry of white flakes all over his lap. The address that appeared beneath was some kind of scientific instrument wholesaler.

Seriously curious now, he ripped the envelope open, and sure enough, inside was a letter from a doctor to a scientific instrument wholesaler, complaining about a faulty part. He couldn't imagine why on earth anyone would want this letter to go to him, instead of the intended recipient.

Then he turned the letter over and saw the handwritten message on the back.

Kieran waited in the hallway outside of Rachel's math class, feeling like he was going to lose it. He forced himself to breathe slowly and stay calm.

The second he'd seen the message from Olivia, he'd almost run right to the parking lot and driven away, but he couldn't leave without telling Rachel first. She was so fragile these days, and had only agreed to start going to class again this morning.

He couldn't just disappear on her.

So he waited. It felt like forever, but eventually the bell rang and she and a chattering flock of junior high kids came tumbling out the classroom door. He noticed she wasn't participating in any of the chatter, though.

"Kieran," Rachel said, her worried eyes going right to him. "What is it? Did you find her?"

"I got a message…"

Before he could say anything more, she flung herself against him, squeezing him around his waist so tightly that he could barely breathe.

"Easy, kid," he said. "Let me finish, will you?"

"Is she okay?" Rachel asked, breathless and flushed. "When is she coming back?"

This was the tricky part. Olivia's note had begged him not to tell Rachel that she was in danger, but he didn't want her to be scared if he just took off without any explanation.

"Listen to me," he said, gripping her arms. "Listen, okay? I got a message from the hospital where Olivia has been recovering. They said she's all healed up and ready to be discharged, so I'm going to go pick her up and bring her back to Deerborn."

"That's fantastic!" Rachel said. "But why didn't she call me?"

"I don't know," Kieran said. "But…"

"Whatever," Rachel said, cutting him off and grabbing his hand. "Let's go!"

"Whoa, wait a minute," Kieran said. "You're not going anywhere. You have classes."

"Screw my stupid classes!" she said. "I'm going with you."

"Come on, Rachel," Kieran said, fumbling for some kind of answer that she would accept. "You've missed so many days already this semester, and you're getting seriously behind on your coursework. You know Olivia would be pissed if you skipped any more, just to pick her up. Especially when she'll be back here before you know it."

Rachel stopped, and looked as if she wanted to cry. But she just sniffed and nodded, wiping her nose on the back of her hand.

"Okay," she said. "Okay, but you bring her straight back. Seriously, don't even stop to pee."

Kieran smiled and put a hand to his heart.

"Deal," he said.

41

As Kieran drove down the long, winding road to the town of Westley, a rough plan started to form.

He thought about the package his mother had just sent him, via SpeedyShip. She always used SpeedyShip.

Kieran remembered a time when she'd sent him a huge, utterly ridiculous celebrity exercise machine that he couldn't have used even if he wanted to, because of his heart. She'd gotten it as a free gift from some kind of television endorsement deal, and decided to ship it to him "for his little friends at the school to use."

Of course, if she ever actually spoke to him, she would have known that he didn't have any friends, big or little. Not to mention the fact that Deerborn already had a full, state-of-the-art gym facility for the athletically inclined, and didn't need a MegaFit Thigh-Blaster 2000.

He'd had to convince one of the custodians to give him a ride in his pick-up truck, so he could go get the damn thing from the SpeedyShip warehouse over in Waltham. They took it straight to the nearest thrift shop and donated it without even bothering to open the box.

But thanks to that particular misadventure, he knew

where the SpeedyShip warehouse was, and remembered the fleet of distinctive red trucks parked out back. He also remembered the motley crew of slackers and befuddled bimbos who worked there.

It was a pretty industrial area, with minimal foot traffic and no sidewalks. There was an electrician, a metal shop, and a motorcycle dealer on the same street. He parked down the block from the unremarkable cinderblock building that housed the SpeedyShip office and warehouse. Got out of the new car his mother had bought for him, and glanced up and down the street. There was a guy messing with a vintage Indian motorcycle out in front of the dealership, but he was paying way more attention to his bike than to Kieran.

Gnawing anxiety about Olivia made it difficult to concentrate, but he needed to stay sharp if he was going to pull this off. He arranged his face and body into what he hoped might be a relaxed but businesslike demeanor, trying to give off the impression that he was just an ordinary working stiff doing exactly what he was supposed to be doing.

These are not the droids you're looking for.

There was a driveway down the right side of the SpeedyShip building that led to the parking lot in the back. On the left was a chainlink fence that separated the driveway from the lot for the metal shop. Standing in the metal shop lot, beside a beat-up old Chevy Nova, was a lone man in a dark suit and fedora-style hat. He didn't look like the sort of person who would work at a metal shop. He seemed to be watching Kieran from under the shadow cast by the brim of his hat.

That made Kieran nervous, so he tucked his chin down into the collar of his jacket and kept on walking like he had every right to be there. Like maybe he was late for work, and didn't have time to worry about some weird guy staring at him. He thought he did a pretty good job, but still felt much better once he turned the corner into the SpeedyShip parking lot.

Out back, there was a wide-open loading dock stacked high with packages of all different shapes and sizes. A girl in an unflattering red polyester uniform was sitting on the edge of the dock smoking a cigarette. She had a curly, strawberry-blond bob haircut and big hoop earrings, and was flirting with one of the drivers, a burly guy with a shaved head and a goatee. He was also smoking.

They both seemed too into each other to pay much attention to Kieran.

He slipped between two of the delivery trucks and peered into them through the side windows. One was clean and orderly inside, and the other was full of fast-food wrappers and crumpled paperwork. The messy truck was perfect for two reasons. First, because the lazy driver had left his red uniform jacket on the passenger seat, balled up with one sleeve pulled inside out. But more importantly, he'd also left the key in the ignition.

So Kieran stuck his head around the back of the truck to look over at the smoking lovebirds on the loading dock. They had finished their cigarettes and the guy had his thick arm around her waist, leading her over to the back door. As he pushed the door open and chivalrously held it for her to enter, he glanced back around the lot, clearly worried about being seen with his female companion. Kieran ducked back out of sight, and he was pretty sure he'd done so before he could be spotted.

Nevertheless, he waited for a handful of seconds before risking another peek around the back of the truck. The lovebirds were gone—having disappeared into the warehouse for whatever tawdry liaison they had in mind.

Kieran clenched a fist, cheering silently on the inside.

He got behind the wheel of the truck and grabbed the jacket. It was cheap and uninsulated, much thinner than his own parka, but he put it on anyway. It smelled disturbingly like Cheetos. He placed his own coat and backpack on the passenger seat, then keyed the ignition and got the rattling heater going. It brought the interior temperature up from death-by-hypothermia to a brisk, sleigh-ride kind of feel. Far from toasty warm, but better than nothing.

It was going to be a long drive to Potsdam.

42

Red Oak Road was in the middle of nowhere, east of the university and hidden from the highway by a grim platoon of bare, witchy trees. Kieran missed it the first time, and ended up having to double back along US Route 11.

A relentless, sleety rain had begun to fall, and it wasn't making it any easier, but the thought of Olivia trapped in that creepy hospital drove him to keep going. When he finally found the turn-off, the big, bulky messenger truck shimmied and slid across the icy tarmac, nearly dumping him into a drainage ditch. He kept control of the reluctant vehicle, and managed to keep it on the road as he powered through the turn and barreled down the side road.

There were no visible addresses along Red Oak, but there were also no buildings or houses—or structures of any kind—for more than a mile. He finally spotted a large, foreboding L-shaped building that could have been anything, standing on the left side of the road. That had to be it.

When he got closer, he saw a small, unassuming sign that read STEUBENVECKER-COLESON CENTER FOR

GENETIC RESEARCH in a forgettable san-serif font. Beside the name there was a corporate logo, a kind of three-dimensional M.

Genetic research? Not a hospital. Not even a psychiatric treatment facility. Was he in the wrong place? If not, what would Olivia be doing in a facility for genetic research?

What the hell was going on here?

When Kieran turned onto the driveway, he discovered that there was a security booth beside the open gate. The guard inside didn't slide open the steamed-up window until the truck had pulled close beside it.

"This 100 Red Oak?" Kieran asked, trying to sound bored and a little hassled, like he just wanted to get this over with and finish his shift.

"Yup," the guard replied, barely looking up from a small portable television that showed a basketball game on the screen. "Help you?"

He was heavy-set and morose, with thick black eyebrows and a low, werewolf hairline. He couldn't have been more than a year older than Kieran at the most. The nametag above the left-hand pocket of his stiff navy uniform shirt indicated that he was H. Aulard.

"Delivery for a Doctor Eric Lansen," Kieran said.

"Right," the guard replied, gesturing back over his shoulder with a gloved thumb. "Parking garage is on your left." Eyes still on the screen, he handed Kieran a laminated parking pass. "Park in one of the six spaces marked 'delivery,'" he said. "And leave this pass on your dash."

"Will do," Kieran said, but the guy had closed the window before the second word was out of his mouth.

Kieran rolled his own window up as protection against the spitting sleet, and drove to the entrance of the underground parking garage. This was too easy, and that ease made him feel more anxious, rather than less. This was only the first level of the game, and he had no idea how many more levels he'd have to pass through in order to find and save Olivia.

He parked the truck as instructed, left the pass on the dash, and grabbed a package he had doctored up with a fake address label. He picked up a SpeedyShip clipboard, and left the truck unlocked in case he needed to make a quick getaway. The lot was massive and eerily silent, lit with jaundiced yellow bulbs. He felt like he was about to walk into a Hong Kong-style shoot-out. All he could do was channel his inner Chow Yun Fat, and try to stay frosty.

The cars in the lot were all bland, standard models, all gray and blue and tan. Nothing red. Nothing sporty or edgy. The only visible signs of character or individuality were the occasional Darwin fish-with-legs symbol or nerdy stickers that said things like SMEG FOR BRAINS or MY OTHER CAR IS THE DEATH STAR. Nothing that would seem unusual or out of place in a legitimate scientific research facility.

There was a door leading to a stairway on his left, but it was locked and required a key card to open it. To the right there was a bank of elevators sitting beneath a small sign that read: TO LOBBY. Other than walking back up the ramp and around the outside of the building to the main entrance, this seemed like his only viable option.

The waiting area by the elevators was clean, well lit, and utterly devoid of character. There were two cameras that he could see. Probably more that he couldn't. This might have been any corporate office building anywhere in America. He pushed the button and waited, pulling his bored wage-slave act tighter around him like a protective overcoat.

The elevator arrived and he got in. There was just one button, marked L. He pushed it. The doors slid silently closed.

A minute later, they slid back open, revealing a large, open lobby with gray marble tile and lots of floor-to-ceiling windows, currently fogged over and dripping with condensation from the contrast between the cold outside and the hot, stale, recycled air inside. Overhead there was a large, ugly modern chandelier that was obviously meant to look like stylized DNA, but looked more like a drunk and bedazzled ladder.

In the center of the big echoey space was a reception desk made of the same gray marble as the floor, so it looked more like the floor had developed a rectangular tumor. Behind the tumor-desk was a sturdy woman with a wide, low forehead, small, dark eyes, and a white stripe in her black hair that made her look like an exasperated badger. She looked like she might be related to the guy at the gate.

As Kieran approached her, she made her displeasure abundantly clear with a chorus of long, weighty sighs.

"May I help you?" she asked, as if the words themselves were acutely painful.

"SpeedyShip," Kieran said, pointing to the patch on his stolen jacket. "Got a package for Doctor—" He paused and looked at the label, for effect. "—Eric Lansen."

"Fine," she said, holding out a stubby hand with long, French-manicured claws that made the badger image even harder for Kieran to shake. "Let's have it."

When Kieran didn't hand her the package, she looked at him like he was an idiot.

"What's the problem, kid?" she asked.

Kieran had to think fast.

"I need his signature," Kieran said. "The sender paid extra for return receipt."

"I'm authorized to sign for all packages that enter this facility," the badger lady said. "It's not a problem."

Think. Think. Think.

"Look," Kieran said. "My boss has really been riding my ass on these return receipts. If the client wants it hand-delivered, then it has to be hand-delivered, or else the recipient can claim they never received it. Come on, man. This is my last run for the day."

She looked at him as if he was a bug she wanted to squish.

"Lansen's office is on the third floor. That's a level-D security area," she said. "D-clearance personnel only. So, you've got two choices. You can let me sign for it, or you can return it to the sender and tell them to mail it to his house. There's no other option."

Kieran's brain was racing, chasing its tail, desperately scrabbling for some way around this obstacle, when he heard an elevator door open.

A trio of researchers in lab coats stepped out from a second bank of elevators Kieran hadn't noticed before. Two men and a woman. One of the men was older than his companions and was pushing a small cart piled high with overflowing file folders. The younger two were engaged in flirtatious banter, laughing and ignoring the older one.

As they moved closer, Kieran spotted a plastic key card balanced on the top of the stack of files. A large, red letter D was visible on the face of the card.

"I'd better go call my boss," he told the badger lady. "Find out what he wants me to do. I'll be right back."

He backed away from the desk, and then turned at the

last moment, deliberately bumping into the guy with the cart. Several of the file folders fell off the stack, dumping their contents onto the floor, along with the key card.

"Aw, man," Kieran said. "I'm so sorry. Here, let me help you with that."

He set the SpeedyShip clipboard down on top of the key card and helped the bewildered man collect the fallen files.

The couple paid no attention to the spill, and went off to make out in a broom closet or wherever they were headed. The badger lady's phone rang, and she picked it up and started chatting, eyes drifting away.

When all the fallen files were stacked back up on the cart, Kieran picked up the clipboard and the key card beneath it, palming the card and slipping it into his hip pocket.

"Thanks," the guy said without looking at him.

"No problem," Kieran replied over his shoulder, already making a beeline back to the elevator.

Of course, it wasn't there. Kieran pushed the button about a hundred times in the thirty seconds it took for it to arrive.

Stay frosty, he told himself.

He put his hand in his pocket, closing his fingers around the pilfered key card as he stepped through the sliding doors.

The ride down seemed twice as long as the ride up. When he arrived on the garage level, he pretended to check something on his clipboard, surreptitiously confirming the location of the cameras.

One was pointed toward the elevator doors and one was pointed into the garage. Standing by the elevators and looking down the row of cars to the slot where he'd parked the truck, he couldn't see the door to the stairway.

The bulk of the truck was blocking his view.

With luck, it would block the camera's view, too. Of course, there might be other cameras hidden around the parking area, but that was a chance he had to take. Besides, it wouldn't be long before the guy with the cart noticed the missing key card.

The only thing to do now was to go for it. So he walked around the back of the SpeedyShip truck as if he was about to get into the driver's side, and then paused. Standing with his hand on the door handle, he couldn't see the elevator. The locked stairway was about fifteen feet away. If he crouched down in between the rows of cars, he ought to be able to make it to the door without being seen.

Kieran had to force himself to breathe and stay calm. His heart was letting him know that it wasn't thrilled with this covert mission routine.

When he reached the door, he paused for a moment, ears humming with strain as he listened for any sign that security was coming for him.

All he heard was his own skittery, irregular heartbeat.

His hands were sweaty, so he wiped the key card on his pant leg before swiping it through the lock. There was a beep and a click as the light flashed from red to green.

Kieran twisted the knob and pushed the door open.

43

Olivia was standing by her window, staring out at the cryptic branches and wondering for the thousandth time if Kieran had gotten her message. Suddenly, Larry entered the room, along with Mrs. Andrada and another orderly whose name she didn't know.

"How are we today?" Mrs. Andrada asked, not even bothering to pretend that she was actually interested. Then to the orderlies, she said, "Go ahead."

The two men flanked Olivia, each grabbing an arm. Before she could blink, Mrs. Andrada had jabbed her with a needle.

"*No!*" Olivia cried, twisting hopelessly in the grip of the big men. An icy gush of fear filled her belly, and then seemed to thaw and dissipate like smoke as whatever chemical she'd just been given started to take effect. The bulb in her bedside lamp flared up, flickered, and then went back to normal.

"It's taking effect already," Mrs. Andrada said. "Full spectrum suppression of cerebral electrokinetic activity should occur within five to ten minutes."

She checked her watch. "But be careful on the way to

the lab. Tell Doctor Lansen about electrical anomalies of any kind, no matter how minor they may seem.

"Bring the gurney."

Olivia sagged between the two men, feeling boneless and fuzzy. She wanted to fight, to struggle, to do something—*anything*—to stop them from taking her away, but her mind felt dull and scattered.

A new, unfamiliar nurse in surgical scrubs and a paper hairnet arrived with a gurney, pushing it in through the open doorway, and the orderlies lifted Olivia like she weighed nothing at all, dumping her on it like a dropped rag doll. The new nurse started strapping Olivia down with heavy canvas straps, and she couldn't do a thing about it.

Surgery? she wondered. *Are they going to perform some type of surgery on me?*

She found herself thinking of lobotomies and *One Flew Over the Cuckoo's Nest*, and those thoughts should have been terrifying, but they seemed weirdly distant, like the sort of reaction she might have to an unexpected plot twist on a television show she didn't really like.

This was a million kinds of wrong, but all she could do was stare at the bland white ceiling tiles as the nurse wheeled her out of her room. The two orderlies flanked her like a presidential guard as she rolled down the hall. She heard Annie screaming and swearing at the far end of the hallway, and her guards went running to deal with the furious girl.

"*I'm* supposed to be next!" Annie was hollering. "Not that bitch, *me*! I'M SUPPOSED TO BE NEXT!"

There were crashes and more swearing, but then Olivia was being pushed through the airlock, and she couldn't hear Annie anymore. Next thing she knew, she was wheeled into Doctor Lansen's lab.

44

When Kieran reached the third floor, there was another electronic lock, this one marked with a letter D. He slid the pilfered card through the lock, convinced that an alarm would go off, or some kind of automatic lockdown would trap him in the stairwell.

But the lock beeped and clicked from red to green, exactly like the one down below. He cautiously pushed the door open just enough to disengage the lock and pressed his ear to the resulting crack.

No sounds.

No clue.

He had no idea what would be on the other side of that bland, white door. It might be a room full of armed guards. It could be an empty hallway.

Only one way to find out.

He eased the door open wider, wide enough to peer through. On the other side was a hallway, but it wasn't empty. A big, burly, red-headed guy was walking away from Kieran, practically filling the hall with his massive shoulders. Reflexively, Kieran flinched back, pulling the door closed and reengaging the lock.

He swore softly to himself, struggling to slow his breathing and chill out. The guy hadn't seen him. It wasn't a big deal. He made himself count to ten, then swiped the card through the lock and cracked the door again.

This time, the hallway was empty, and he actually had a chance to eyeball the layout. Clean, featureless white walls. Glossy white-tile floor. White drop-ceiling with a double row of recessed fluorescent lighting. Unmarked white doors lining either side of the corridor, four per side. At the far end there was an open, doorless archway on the right hand side, and double doors on the left.

He thought he might try to find and steal a lab coat, and pretend to be a researcher or a doctor. But that thought didn't last. Although he had no problem passing as a believable messenger, he was afraid the lab coat would just make him look more like Doogie Howser. He still had the package, though, and if confronted he could always claim to be looking for Doctor Lansen.

But he couldn't let that happen before he found Olivia.

The corridor wasn't going to get any more empty, so Kieran slipped through the door. He was glad he'd worn his Doc Martens, because their rubber soles were silent on the slick white tile.

The first door that he tried was locked, as was the second. The third, however, was not. He was about to peer inside when he heard footsteps at the other end of the hall.

A nurse with a black bun stepped out of the open archway and began checking some sort of chart on the wall. Then she was turning toward Kieran, head down and reviewing something on a clipboard. If she looked up, she'd see him.

He had no option.

Pushing through the unlocked door, he found

himself in a spare, square room with a single bed. The bed was occupied by a soft, bloated person with a shaved head, a slack mouth, and heavy-lidded, unseeing eyes. Kieran guessed the person was female, based on the lack of facial hair on the pale, flabby cheeks, but couldn't be sure. He took a step closer, raising a hand and waving. No response.

That's when he noticed a dry-erase board above the bed with the name Lisa Brachlen, an elaborate "turn schedule" indicating what time the patient had been turned from back to side or side to back, and by whom. Above that, the words COMATOSE SINCE 4/15/94.

Kieran had never before seen a person in a coma—not in real life—and had always assumed that their eyes would be shut. There was something deeply unsettling about those dead, empty eyes.

That's when he noticed something weird going on along the edge of the thin white blanket covering the person in the bed. At first it was so subtle that he thought he might be imagining it. But when he looked closer, he saw that a six-inch section of the hem of the blanket was bunching up and smoothing out, then bunching up again. Almost as if it was being clutched in a small, invisible hand, and then released. Clutched and then released.

The bunching of the blanket seemed to be perfectly timed to match the heavy, irregular breath of the person beneath. But if it was just the rising and falling of the person's chest that was moving the blanket, why was it only bunching up on one side, and not the other?

"Who the hell are you?" a female voice asked, startling Kieran so badly that he nearly dropped his package.

He spun to face the voice and saw a girl with a dark buzzcut standing in the doorway that led into the bathroom. She was pretty in a hard kind of way, with wary dark eyes and a sarcastic mouth. She was dressed in a hospital gown, the top hanging wide open to display her pale, xylophone chest.

"Man, you scared me," he said, trying for friendly and non-threatening. He thought about trying to keep up the messenger pretense, but this wasn't a staff member, so he decided to try a different approach. "I'm looking for Olivia Dunham. Do you know where she is?"

"I might," the girl responded. "Why do you want to know?"

"I'm her boyfriend," Kieran said, knowing it was a risk, but hoping his admission would gain the girl's sympathy. "I'm really worried about her. Is she okay?"

"Define okay," the girl said. "Okay like me? Okay like Lisa Broccoli over there?"

"Broccoli?" Kieran frowned.

"As in she's a vegetable, genius." She rolled her eyes. "You'd better be smart, because you're certainly not badass. In fact, you may be the lamest action hero of all time. Still, you get an A for effort, I guess. Got a cigarette?"

"I don't smoke," Kieran said, frustration digging its nails into his gut. "Do you know where Olivia is, or don't you?"

"Sure I do," the girl said. "She's in the lab with Doctor Lansen. She's his little favorite now. He's prepping her right now for his 'special treatment.'"

The toxic, white-hot jealousy in her voice was so strong it could've stripped paint. It made Kieran sick to think of some weird doctor having his way with Olivia, but as his head spun to catch up with all of this new information, it also gave him an idea.

"Then we need to stop him," he said. "It sounds to me that you don't much like Olivia. You must want her out of the picture—don't you? Well, I want her out of here, too.

We both want the same thing, so help me find her and I'll take her away. You'll never have to see her again.

"Okay?"

The girl squinted at him, skeptical.

"Okay?" he repeated, his desperation building.

"How did you get in?" she asked.

"I stole a key card."

"D level?"

"Yes." What was she getting at?

She looked him up and down like she was sizing up a racehorse.

"Okay, listen," she said. "At the end of the hall is the lounge, and a set of double doors. I'm going to go set off the Lindsey bomb in the lounge, and when all the orderlies come rushing in to handle it, we'll slip out through those doors."

"What's a Lindsey bomb?"

"Trust me, okay," she said. "Just be ready to make a break for those doors. They'll let you out into the elevator area, and on the opposite side will be the door to the lab wing. Locked of course, but you have the key. Doctor Lansen's lab is the second door on the left."

Kieran didn't exactly trust this strange, intense girl, but he also didn't have a better plan.

45

Doctor Lansen watched nervously as the nurse wheeled Olivia into the lab.

He felt like a man on a first date. He'd already prepped and scrubbed in for the procedure, but kept finding himself raising an involuntary gloved hand to smooth back his cap-covered hair, and being forced to stop himself at the last minute.

The nurse transferred Olivia to the operating table and removed her underwear before strapping her legs into a pair of metal stirrups. Doctor Lansen watched anxiously as she started an intravenous drip in the crook of Olivia's good arm. While it would allow the insemination process to proceed without protest or undue distress on the part of the subject, general anesthesia was out of the question. The Cortexiphan-enhanced part of the brain often remained active even while the subject was unconscious.

Conversely, the psychic suppression agent required to calm any neuroquakes either counteracted the standard anesthetics, or caused potentially dangerous cardiac arrhythmia when combined with other, more uncommon formulations.

The trickiest part of the process would come when the psychic suppression agent wore off. He'd learned the hard way—with previous subjects—that a kind of involuntary rebound effect occurred sometime between six and twelve hours after the initial dose was administered. Clustered neuroquakes of varying severity would hit like an internal storm and, depending on the particular Cortexiphan-induced abilities of the subject in question, a wide spectrum of potentially catastrophic phenomena could occur.

Given Olivia's predilection for electrical and pyrokinetic disturbances, he had prepared a special recovery room for her in the lower ward, fully insulated in non-conductive, non-flammable material and equipped with a lightning rod to attract and safely ground any power surges. She and the unique zygote she would soon be carrying were too far precious for him to take any chances.

"That will be all for now, Helen," he said to the nurse. "Thank you."

The nurse gave a curt nod and left the room. He was alone with Olivia.

46

The hall outside was empty. The skinny girl with the buzzcut went first, padding down the hallway in her textured slipper-socks. Kieran followed close behind.

When they reached the open archway, the room beyond was revealed. A dull, blandly decorated dentist's-waiting-room kind of area with two uncomfortable-looking, easy-to-clean vinyl couches and two bolted-down tables with ugly, dated chairs.

A scattered game of checkers lay ignored on one table. A few sad, dog-eared fashion magazines on the other. A sturdy television was bolted to the wall, currently showing an episode of *Friends*. On the far side there was another open doorway that looked like it led into a nurses station.

There was a single occupant in the room, a tiny Hispanic girl with a sad, heart-shaped face and thick, chapped lips. She seemed shy and child-like in her demeanor, although the curvy body beneath her hospital gown was much more grown up. Her thick, curly hair was held back with a pink-and-red scrunchie that matched the plush bunny in her arms.

"That's Lindsey," the skinny girl whispered to Kieran as she slunk over to the archway that led into the lounge. "Whenever her dad, well, you know... Her mom would scrub her with bleach and a wire brush." As he let that horrifying concept sink in, she added, "You'd better stay back."

Kieran did as he was told, adrenalin racing through his veins. He had no idea what to expect. All he could do was keep his eye on the big double doors, and be ready to bolt through them as soon as he had a chance.

"Lindsey's dirty!" the skinny girl called into the lounge. "DIRTY!"

It was hard to see exactly what happened next, but there was a furious, almost inhuman wail and a burst of fluffy white stuffing like the aftermath of a pillow fight.

"I'm not!" Lindsey wailed. "I'M NOT DIRTY!"

An ugly chair came flying out into the hallway, followed by the sound of shattering glass. As the girl had predicted, a pack of orderlies came rushing through the double doors, running for the lounge, while nurses poured out of the nurses' station like angry hornets.

Mad chaos, flailing limbs, and flying furniture filled the lounge and the skinny girl just smirked and cocked her chin toward their destination.

"Let's go," she said.

Annie led Olivia's white knight out through the airlock and over to the entrance to the lab wing.

"Gimme that key," she said.

"I got it," the knight said with a suspicious squint.

Maybe he wasn't so dumb after all.

She looked back over her shoulder toward the ward as the knight slipped the pilfered card through the lock.

The door clicked open, and he motioned for her to come with him.

"Hurry," he said.

She slipped through, and then paused with one hand on the door to Doctor Lansen's office.

"Give me sixty seconds," she said. "And then go through that door and get your girl."

He nodded, so earnest and clueless. He seemed like a sweet guy, but honestly, if this was Olivia's hero, she'd better hope for a miracle.

Annie slipped into Doctor Lansen's office and pulled the door closed behind her. His warm, bookish smell made her feel a little dizzy, and she found herself tempted to roll around in his possessions like a cat. But she had more important things to do. Like get rid of that Olivia, once and for all.

As soon as Doctor Lansen saw how far she was willing to go for him, he'd have to realize that she was the one and only subject he would ever need. That they were meant to be together… forever.

She counted another handful of heartbeats and then smiled. An excited giggle welled up as she stretched her arms up over her head. Going up on her toes, she reached her fingers toward the highest shelf, and tipped several books down until they fell with a loud, rustling thump.

"What is this?" Olivia demanded, craning her neck around the lab. Her voice was a little slushy, a side effect of the psychic inhibitor. "What are you doing to me, you pervert?"

"Nothing perverse, I assure you," he replied as he prepped the dosage of the genetic plasticity serum. "I'm a scientist."

"Then why are my underpants off?" she asked. She struggled weakly against her bindings.

"Please try to remain calm," he said. "The procedure should be over in approximately twenty minutes."

"Procedure?" She twisted her head, and her eyes were wide. "What procedure?"

It was times like this when he really wished his research could be conducted using animal models. He was already keyed up, and the last thing he needed was a lot of irrelevant chit-chat to distract him from the process. There was so much riding on the outcome. If it failed, then all of his work up to this point would be wasted.

He took a deep breath and steadied his hands, then gripped the IV bag and injected the serum through the port. The dark, viscous, and intensely concentrated serum swirled into the lactated Ringer's solution, and started sending tendrils down the tube.

Toward Olivia's arm.

From somewhere he heard a stifled giggle, and then a crash coming from inside his office.

What the hell...? No one was allowed in there—not when he wasn't present. There were things no one else should ever see.

But he couldn't interrupt the procedure—not at this critical juncture. So he stepped over to the door and cocked his head, then used his elbow to hit the panic button, keeping his sterile hands up and away from his body.

No response.

He hit the button again, and then stalked over to the door to the hallway, seething. He expected to hear the sound of running orderlies, or security guards coming to deal with whatever was happening in his office. But there was nothing.

He didn't want to touch the knob, so he just banged

on the door with his knee. He miscalculated, and a shot of pain ran up his leg, causing him to curse under his breath.

"Security?" he called. "Hello? Does anybody besides me actually work in this place? I'm scrubbed in here!"

More thumps and giggles from his office.

"Oh, for Christ's sake," he said, stripping off his gloves and throwing them way too hard at the flip-top trash can. One went in, but the other bounced out and landed on the floor near his feet.

Jerking open the door, he stormed into his office, furious at this ill-timed interruption. He wasn't all that surprised to find Annie there, sitting cross-legged on his desk in a pile of books.

47

Her head clearing a bit, Olivia systematically tested and retested the straps that held her down. She tried repeatedly to close her legs, but found that it was impossible.

There was less than a fraction of an inch of wiggle room in every direction. She'd never felt so infuriatingly helpless, but the thick, narcotic strangeness from the drug she'd been given made her anger feel slippery and difficult to grasp. The thick, inky substance that Doctor Lansen had injected into her IV bag was working its way down the clear coil of tubing toward the needle in her arm.

She had no idea what it was but she knew she didn't want it in her body.

When she heard the door open behind her she felt a spike of nausea, and hollow dread.

"Liv?"

It was Kieran. He was wearing an ill-fitting, bright red jacket. The sight of him made it feel like someone was squeezing her heart inside her chest.

He ran to stand next to her.

"Get…" Her throat felt raspy and dry, her voice unwieldy. "Get this needle out of my arm. *Quick*…"

He looked up at the tube, frowning. The dark liquid was less than an inch from the butterfly needle tenting the skin of her inner arm.

"What is this?" he asked.

"*Now!*" Olivia hissed. "Hurry…"

"Okay, okay," he said, wincing a little as he ripped the tube from the coupler that connected it to the needle.

It hurt like hell, causing the needle to twist beneath her skin. Once the tube was disconnected, blood started shooting out of her arm in a thin stream, while a mix of saline and that black chemical compound from the IV bag sprayed all over the floor.

"Whoa!" he said. "Here, let me just…"

He peeled off the white medical tape holding the needle down and pulled it out of her vein. Blood continued to trickle from the puncture in her skin, but at a much slower rate.

Then he swiftly unbuckled the straps that held her down, pulling her up and into his arms.

"Jesus, Liv," he said, crushing her in a breathless embrace and then taking her face between his hands. "Are you okay? What the hell is going on here?"

"I don't know," she said. "They gave me some kind of drug. I think Doctor Lansen was trying to test some sort of weird serum on me." She shuddered, and pressed her face into his neck, smelling his safe, familiar, clean-laundry smell as if it were all she had to hold on to.

"Kieran, get me out of here."

"See, I told you," Annie's voice spoke from the doorway. "She brought that boy here because she doesn't want to be with you. She doesn't love you like I do."

Doctor Lansen pushed her aside roughly and came charging through the door.

"Who the hell are you?" he asked Kieran.

Annie caught up and clung to Doctor Lansen's arm, staring up at him.

"Please," she said. "Listen to me."

He ripped his arm out of her grip and shoved her back.

"Get away from me, you stupid girl," he said. Then he turned back to Kieran. "Do you have any idea what you've done?"

"But," Annie said, regaining her balance, "I *love* you." Oblivious to Olivia and Kieran, she threw her arms around Doctor Lansen, trying to kiss him. He backed up into a table full of lab glassware that tumbled to the ground and shattered around their feet while the two of them struggled.

"Let's go!" Kieran said, gripping Olivia's arm and pulling her toward the open doorway that led to Doctor Lansen's office.

"God *dammit!*" Lansen said, hauling off and letting Annie have it in the face.

She crumpled into a sobbing heap as Kieran shoved Olivia through the door ahead of him. From behind them in the lab, her sobs became a wail, and they heard a disturbing series of crashes. Suddenly Lansen was crying out in pain, the sound growing until it overwhelmed Annie's wail, but Olivia didn't look back to see what was happening.

Once they were inside Lansen's office, Kieran slammed the door, and then put his shoulder to the bookcase beside them, motioning for Olivia to help him. Together they were able to shove it in front of the entrance to the lab.

But once they'd moved the one bookcase, it revealed the edge of a sliding panel, set into the wall.

"Is that a door?" Kieran asked.

"I have no idea," Olivia said. "I never noticed it before."

He pried the panel open, and behind it was a dark elevator shaft. Meanwhile, Olivia could hear pounding on the door to the lab, and thundering footsteps in the hallway. She grabbed a steel paperweight from the desk, ran over to the entrance to the hallway, and used the paperweight to smash the keypad. She hoped that would seize up the electronic lock.

Now the only way out of Doctor Lansen's office was that dubious elevator shaft.

Olivia went over to stand beside Kieran, and together they peered into the shaft. She could barely make out the roof of an elevator car, all the way at the bottom. Harsh light leaked through a ventilation grate. To the left of the door, there was a rickety metal maintenance ladder and some kind of panel.

"Think you can climb down that ladder with your broken arm?" Kieran asked.

"I don't exactly have a choice, do I," Olivia replied.

"Let me go first," he suggested. "I think I can disable the elevator from that panel there." He cast an anxious glance at the shuddering bookshelf that was blocking the lab door. "We don't want the car coming up under us, and then squashing us against the top of the shaft."

"Right," she said, hoping to sound more confident than she felt.

She watched with her heart in her throat as Kieran leaned into the yawning shaft and grabbed the top rung of the ladder. He swung his long legs onto a rung below and hung on with one hand while yanking at the wires that sprouted from the maintenance panel. Sparks shot out, making him cover his face with his forearm.

Down below, the light in the elevator car went out.

"Come on," he said, holding a hand out for Olivia to grasp.

With only one good arm, she was unable to hold onto the edge of the door while reaching for that top rung. She just had to go for it, and hope she didn't miss and tumble to her death.

Kieran gripped her shoulder, steadying her. She was able to grab the top rung, but then her center of balance shifted and she had no choice but to follow-up with her legs.

She crashed into him, her feet slipping so that she dangled for a brief, terrifying moment by her one hand. Kieran hooked his arm under her armpits and squeezed her broken ribs so tightly she had to bite back a scream.

"I got you!" he said, his breath coming fast. "Hang on, Liv."

She peddled her bare feet in the air before her toes found a lower rung on the ladder. For nearly a minute, all she could do was hang on and try to get her panicked heartbeat under control.

"Are you sure you can make it?" Kieran asked, still clinging to her.

"Sure I'm sure," Olivia rasped, gripping that rusty rung with white knuckles and trying not to look down. She didn't want him to know how scared and wobbly she felt.

"Here," he said, climbing down until he was holding onto the rung at her waist level. That placed his arms around her on either side. "Go down one, and then I'll go down one, like this. That way, if you slip, I'll catch you."

Olivia smiled and shook her head. If she slipped again, they were probably both going to plunge to their deaths, but it was sweet of him to offer.

They'd worked their way down two floors, and it

actually seemed like they were going to make it, when armed security guards appeared in the open doorway. They shouted, then started shooting at them.

"Jesus!" Kieran said, flinching and burying his face in the small of her back.

She cringed, tucking her face down and involuntarily trying to move her broken arm to cover her head as a bullet ricocheted off the concrete just inches from her cheek. She only succeeded in banging the cast against a metal rung, sending a shooting pain up to her shoulder.

They were easy targets.

Olivia's entire body was clenched and ready for a bullet when she heard Doctor Lansen's voice echo down the shaft.

"Are you *insane*?" he asked. "Stop! I need her alive, you idiots!"

The shots stopped. The shouting ended, and almost immediately the voices were gone altogether.

Kieran and Olivia had to get to the bottom of this shaft and fast.

48

"Go," she hissed.

After what seemed like forever on the spindly ladder, they finally reached the roof of the elevator car. The only light came from high above, so Olivia and Kieran had to get down on their hands and knees and feel around the filthy, grease-caked roof before they found the maintenance hatch.

More precious time passed before they could find the pull ring and get their grubby fingers under the edges of the hatch to lift it open. Kieran sat on the lip of the opening with his legs dangling into the car, and then lowered himself down.

"Come on!" he said, his disembodied voice rising from the pitch-black interior of the car. "I'll catch you."

Olivia had no idea where he was, but she sat down on the edge of the opening just like he had, lowering her legs into the darkness. She felt his hands gripping her calves as she slid forward. It wasn't until his hands slid up to grip her bare hips beneath her hospital gown that she remembered she didn't have on any underwear.

She'd never been so happy it was dark.

She slid down into his arms until her feet touched the elevator floor. There was a thin sliver of light coming from the crack in the elevator doors, and Olivia could just barely make out the silhouette of Kieran's shaggy head, just inches from hers. He held on for a moment, and she could feel her heart racing.

"Let's get the hell out of here," she said, gently pulling away. "We need to figure out where we are."

"This should let us out in the underground parking garage where I left the truck," Kieran said, struggling to pry the elevator doors part of the way open. "Based on how far down we've climbed."

It didn't.

Instead, they found another bland white hallway almost exactly like the one they'd left up on the third floor.

"Is this the bottom of the shaft?" Olivia asked. "Or are there other floors beneath this one?"

There hadn't been any other doors in the shaft, on the way down, so it was impossible to count how many floors they'd passed.

"I don't know," Kieran replied, squinting back up through the open hatch, and then over at the control panel. "There are only two buttons, and they're both unmarked. This has to be the basement level... I think."

"Well, we can't climb back up," Olivia said. "And we can't stay in here."

"Right," Kieran said, forcing the reluctant steel doors the rest of the way open. "Come on."

As soon as they were through, and Kieran let go of the doors, they snapped shut like an angry mouth. Standing in the hallway, they scanned their surroundings. The elevator was at one end, and at the far end stood a heavy steel security door with an electronic keypad. Smaller, less imposing doors lined the hall.

The two of them ran for the security door and Olivia pressed her ear against the cool surface, listening, while Kieran messed around with the key card.

"Can you open it?" she asked.

"It doesn't take a card," he said. "It requires some kind of code." He pulled a Swiss army knife from the pocket of his cargo pants. "But, I think I can bypass it manually."

He used the stubby little knife to pry off the beige plastic cover of the keypad and started messing around with the wires beneath. Olivia stood by, tense and anxious.

That's when she noticed that the door to her right was open, just a crack. She pushed it open a little wider, to peer inside. As soon as she did, a sour, chemical stench wafted out, like ammonia and spoiled milk and dissected frogs in biology class.

She flipped on a light and found what appeared to be a small morgue. Stainless-steel drawers lined the far wall. Several steel gurneys were parked along the left side of the room, one empty and the rest occupied by black vinyl body bags.

She told herself that there was nothing weird about a morgue in a hospital basement. But shapes inside the body bags seemed all irregular, and disturbingly proportioned. Some seemed to sag, causing the bag to appear nearly empty, while others looked ready to burst at the seams.

Stepping into the room, Olivia couldn't bring herself to go near the body bags, but she was curious enough to try the doors on some of the large metal cabinets, thinking she might find a scalpel or something she could use as a weapon. She instantly regretted this decision when she revealed row after row of specimen jars.

Some contained organs, or other unidentifiable lumps of tissue, but most contained what appeared to be an extensive collection of fetuses. Not the normal kind, though.

There were fetuses with massive, fragile heads like gray aliens, and fetuses with low flat heads like crocodiles. One in particular that caught her eye had no features at all—just a red, fleshy blossom like a carnation where the head should have been.

This is a research hospital, she said to herself. *They study genetic defects. It's completely reasonable for them to have a collection like this.*

Yet why were they down here in the morgue, and not in a lab? They couldn't all be recently deceased? Could they?

Olivia backed out of the room and pressed close to Kieran.

"How much longer?" she asked.

"I'm trying," he replied. "Almost there…"

There were no sounds coming from the other side of the locked door, but Olivia could hear sounds coming from behind the doors that lined the hallway. Soft—barely more than whispers at first, but becoming louder and more agitated. Scraping and scuffling. Staccato thumps. Low, garbled voices that didn't sound like English. A sound that may or may not have been crying.

That's when Olivia noticed that none of the doors had knobs.

"Kieran," she said. "We need to get the hell out of here… *now*."

Then they heard someone scrabbling around behind the elevator doors at the opposite end of the hallway.

"Someone's coming!" she hissed.

Kieran wiped sweat from his eyes with his jacket sleeve and continued to work, swearing under his breath and pleading with the wires like he could sweet-talk them into doing what he wanted.

The elevator doors scraped open a scant inch, then slammed back shut.

"Hurry!" Olivia said.

"Come on come on come on," Kieran muttered, pulling one wire loose from its moorings, and then another.

Then, suddenly, several things happened at once.

Kieran crossed the wrong two wires, causing sparks to shoot out from the keypad, making him drop the knife and leap back.

The lights flickered and went out—then a harsh, stark, white emergency lamp over the door clicked on, throwing jagged shadows across the walls and ceiling.

The door to the stairway remained stubbornly closed, but all along the hallway, the other doors slid slowly open.

49

For a seemingly endless moment, nothing happened. No drooling maniacs came tearing out of their cells. No armed guards. Nothing.

Then a familiar voice.

"Smooth move, Exlax."

Annie, stepping out of the shadows at the far end of the hall.

Olivia strode down the hall toward her, fists clenched and ready to let her have it. Kieran was right behind.

"What the hell do you want?" Olivia hissed.

"I've had it with this place," Annie said. "I want out. Take me with you."

"Why did you tell the doctor about me?" Kieran asked. "We could have made it to the stairway, if you hadn't given us away."

"I thought…" Her voice caught, and she looked down. "I thought I could make him love me. But he doesn't. He never will."

Olivia stepped forward in front of Kieran.

"Why should we trust you?" she asked.

"You can't, I guess," Annie said. "I wouldn't trust me."

She shrugged, chewing at a torn bit of skin on the edge of a ragged fingernail, and looked away.

Olivia frowned.

"We can't just leave her here with that crazy bastard."

"Why not?" Kieran asked. "I really don't think…"

"Something's coming out of that door," Annie interrupted, eyes wide and pointing back toward the exit.

"Where?" Olivia asked, squinting against the glare of the emergency lamp.

"There," Kieran said. "Second door on the left."

Sure enough, there was something. Something small and white, low down near the bottom of the doorframe.

A hand.

A child's hand.

A little blond girl came toddling out from the doorway. She was maybe three years old, with big, scared eyes, naked except for a plastic hospital wristband. She was dirty and shivering and seemed wretchedly thin. She turned toward Olivia and held out her scrawny little arms, silently pleading to be picked up.

Olivia suddenly flashed back to another little girl, scared and confused, not understanding what was being done to her.

"Jesus," she said, taking a step toward the child.

"What is going on in this place?" Kieran asked.

"I thought I knew," Annie said. "But now…"

"It's okay, honey," Olivia said, squatting down and holding out her arms. "It's okay, come here."

The little girl took a few wobbly steps, then fell back on her bottom and started crying.

That's when something else appeared from the doorway opposite from the morgue. Something that was not a little girl.

50

Olivia had an impression of a very tall, pale, morbidly obese person with no hair. But as the person turned toward them, it became clear that what looked like rolls of fat were actually fluctuating waves of flesh that moved like molten wax over that abnormally massive frame.

There was also something very wrong in the loose, rubbery, double-jointed way those long arms and legs moved.

"Becky?" Annie said, frowning. "What happened to you? We thought you were dead."

"Becky" cocked her big, lumpy, stone-idol head and then lunged toward the child. Dozens of greasy red tumors erupted like mushrooms along the inside of her long, reaching arms, blossoming into bouquets of jagged, translucent teeth.

Before those grasping, abnormal hands reached the wide-eyed toddler, the steel door at the end of the corridor opened, causing Becky to whip around to face it.

A brace of four guards in security uniforms came through. Olivia's eye went straight to the unfamiliar rifle in the lead man's hands, and she quickly realized that it was actually some kind of air gun, like the kind used to dart large animals.

Becky's attention also went right to the gun. She let out a bizarre, inhuman wail that sounded like it had passed over more than one set of vocal cords on the way out. She lurched forward and grabbed the man's head with one hand. The fingers on that hand suddenly doubled and then tripled in number, the impossible new digits long and fleshless, with hooked tips that pierced easily through the screaming victim's skull.

With a flick of her wrist, she flung the body in their direction. Olivia shoved Kieran toward the wall, shielding him as the guard flew past them and landed upside-down and crumpled against the elevator door.

The other men fell back into the stairwell visible on the other side of the door, and opened fire with a variety of sidearms.

Bullets pinged off the tiles and took chunks out of doorframes all around her, but Olivia didn't even stop to think about her own safety. She just ran over and grabbed the terrified child, then ducked into one of the open doors and out of the line of fire.

Seconds later, Annie dove through the same door, with Kieran in tow.

Taking a quick look around the room they were in, Olivia saw that it was an empty hospital room, the bed sheetless and bare.

"Block the door!" Olivia said, protectively cradling the clinging child against her chest.

"Help me tip up this bed!" Annie said to Kieran.

The two of them worked together to wedge the heavy old-fashioned bed frame into the doorway.

Suddenly, the shooting out in the hallway just stopped.

"Now what the hell are we supposed to do?" Annie asked.

"There's no way out," Kieran whispered, his jittery gaze all over the featureless dimensions of the small room. He looked pale and terrified, a thin sheen of sweat on his anxious face. Olivia needed to keep him calm, to avoid too much stress on his heart.

"Stay frosty," she said, borrowing one of his little catchphrases. "Look there."

She gestured at the right-hand wall, which seemed to be hinged in several places, as if it was retractable.

"Another elevator?" Kieran asked.

"I don't think so," she said. "But I do think we might be able to slide it open and go through into the next room."

Annie ran to the edge of the dividing wall and started running her fingers over the surface, looking for some kind of latch or lock.

"Then what?" Kieran said.

"Climb back up the elevator shaft?" Annie suggested.

"Even if that was a good idea—which I'm not sure it is," he responded, "Olivia will have a hard time climbing back up with her broken arm. Especially carrying that little boy." Kieran turned back to Olivia, holding out his arms. "Here, let me carry him."

Olivia frowned, looking down at the toddler in her arms. The girl stuck her thumb in her mouth and turned her head, laying it against Olivia's shoulder.

"Kieran," she said, hand on the child's back. "She's a girl, not a boy."

He frowned.

"You're kidding, right?" he asked. "I mean, last time I checked, girls don't have..." He gestured at the naked child. "You know."

Olivia held the child away from her body, looking

her over. What the hell was Kieran talking about?

"You're on crack, dude," Annie said over her shoulder, still searching for a way to open the wall. "She's a girl. In fact, she looks just like me when I was that age. And I certainly don't have…" She smirked at Kieran. "You know."

Olivia looked at Annie, with her black hair and dark eyes, then back at the child. The child had blond hair and green eyes.

Just like Olivia.

She felt a cold flush of fear in her belly.

"Something is wrong here," she said, slowly putting the child down on the floor and backing away.

"Is he…" Kieran said. "Or she… I don't know. Controlling our minds? Making us see her… differently?"

"For that matter," Annie said, "What does she, or he, *really* look like."

And at that moment, the fragile glamour around the child *shattered*, peeling back like a shed skin and revealing the face beneath.

51

The child had a large, pale cloven head with two distinct lobes and a deep crease between them. Its shrunken, bony torso was no bigger than a soda can and its long, insectoid limbs seemed too weak and spindly to support the weight of its huge, spatulate tree-frog hands and feet.

The face seemed almost vestigial, like the face of cave-dwelling fish that had never seen the sun. Its tiny, slitted eyes were solid matte black, with no visible distinction between white, iris, and pupil. There were three identical slits in the lower face that looked like the watertight nostrils of a marine mammal, though one of them had to be a mouth of some kind. All three were crusted with gummy discharge. Its grayish skin was covered with a pustulent rash and it smelled bad—fishy and rotten, but weirdly sweet too, like the dumpster behind a Chinese restaurant.

Olivia involuntarily wiped her hands on her hospital gown, disgusted by the fact that she'd touched that thing. How could she not have noticed that smell?

As hideous as the creature was, it seemed more

sickly than scary. Hopeless, like a dying thing too weak to chase away the vultures. It sat where Olivia had placed it on the floor, its heavy malformed head drooping down and shivering.

"What is it?" Kieran asked.

"We can't just leave it here," Olivia said.

"What if it's contagious?" Annie asked.

"Jesus," Olivia said, wiping her hands again.

At that moment, that weird harmonic scream sounded in the hallway and something slammed against the bed that was blocking the doorway.

All three of them jumped, startled, as thousands of questing, hair-thin red cilia squeezed in around the edges.

The child lifted its head toward the commotion, a thin breathy whine coming from the slits in its face as it reached toward the bed frame.

"It's Becky's baby," Annie said, face lit with incredulous realization. "Look at it. It wants mommy."

The cilia wrapped around the frame and snapped it in half, flinging the two pieces in separate directions while the intact mattress fell forward, toward the child.

Olivia lunged forward to catch the mattress and prevent it from falling on the helpless child, but to her amazement, she didn't have to.

It stopped, suspended in midair just a foot away from the child, then eased back and away, toppling off to one side.

Becky came through the doorway like a trapdoor spider, snatching the child up with way too many uneven arms and clutching it close, cooing softly as bloody tears filled her bulging eyes.

Olivia was utterly transfixed. Her mind was relentlessly picking at all these impossible details, twisting them into theories and rejecting one after the other. She thought of all the preserved fetuses in the morgue. What was Doctor Lansen doing here anyway? Messing with the human reproductive system?

Was he trying to do to her what he'd clearly done to Becky. Impregnate her? But *why*?

"Um... guys...?" Annie said quietly. "I think we really ought to..."

Olivia snapped out of it.

She looked over saw that the girl had managed to locate the electronic latch that allowed her to push back the dividing wall, just enough for them to squeeze through. She was already slipping through, and was motioning for Olivia and Kieran to follow.

Olivia gave one more glance back at the monstrous Madonna and child. The sobbing mother's unruly liquid flesh was curling in tongue-like tendrils around the dying child's body, and the child's own flesh responded by rippling like a pond around a dropped stone.

Then she slipped through the gap in the dividing wall, leaving the monsters behind.

But not the questions.

When she turned to take in the new room, she realized that it was occupied.

52

On the bed lay a massively pregnant woman. Her face was wizened and skull-like, both childish and ancient at the same time, like a starving kid in one of those charity commercials.

There was a rubber feeding tube hanging from one of her nostrils and an IV needle in her bony right arm. Heavy canvas straps kept her bound to the bed, completely immobilized. The entire left side of her body was riddled with tumors, some small and smooth like clustered pink grapes and others weighty and irregular with a texture not unlike the surface of a human brain.

Although it took a minute for Olivia's mind to process what her eyes were telling her, she realized that the girl's huge bare belly had a variety of small floating objects orbiting around it, like an asteroid belt.

A plastic cup.

A catheter.

A box of tissues.

A bottle of liquid soap.

Her belly was horribly bruised and blotchy, speckled with pinpricks of blood and as they watched, Kieran's keys sailed out of his jacket pocket and started to bash themselves repeatedly against the traumatized skin. The woman opened her dry lips and let out a barely audible mewling sound of hopeless misery.

Kieran reached out a shaking hand and, with a struggle, snatched the keys out of the air. This action caused all the other objects in the asteroid belt to jitter and jump, and then swoop down to peck at the girl's belly like attacking birds. Her cries of pain got louder and more desperate.

"Come on," Olivia said, grabbing the soap bottle and wrestling it free from the vengeful gravitational force. "Help me!"

The three of them caught the flying objects, one by one, and—following Olivia's lead—threw them into a metal cabinet with a latch to hold it closed. Once all the objects were locked up and safely out of reach, the thing in the girl's belly started flailing in mindless fury, punching and kicking against the flesh from inside with what looked like far too many limbs, tenting the tortured skin.

All around them, the cabinets and drawers shook as if rattled by an earthquake. This lasted for a terrifying thirty seconds, then subsided.

"My god," Kieran said. "What kind of place is this?"

Olivia was standing by the bed, trying to figure out what to do next, when the emaciated girl feebly gripped her hospital gown in one bound hand. She was trying to say something, but her voice was the ghost of a whisper. Olivia bent down to put her ear closer.

"…eating me…" the girl was saying.

"What?" Olivia asked, wrinkling her nose at the appalling smell of the girl's strange, almost fishy breath.

"It's… eating me… from inside." Her voice cranked

up to raspy, breathless shout. *"It's eating me!"*

Olivia flinched away, turning to Kieran with wide eyes. Then she saw Annie.

She was leaning back against the far wall, shaking her head with both hands over her mouth and tears rolling down her pale cheeks.

It's hitting her—Olivia realized—*what Lansen has been doing here.*

But there was nothing she could do to comfort the girl right now.

"Kieran," she said. "Unbuckle those straps."

"Why?" he responded. "We can't save her."

"Just do it!" Olivia snapped, turning away and rummaging through the drawers and cabinets until she found what she needed.

Kieran did what she asked. As soon as her arms were free, the girl grabbed Kieran's jacket.

"Help me!" she begged. "Please... Don't leave me like this."

Kieran turned, anguish and pity and revulsion all mixed up in his eyes. Olivia ignored him and concentrated on selecting the largest hypodermic needle she could find. She removed it from its sterile paper packet and began to fill it from the vial she'd chosen.

It wasn't easy with the cast on her arm, but she managed.

She walked back to the girl's bedside, shouldering Kieran aside.

"Listen to me," Olivia said, putting the loaded hypodermic in the girl's good hand and closing her fingers around it. "This is morphine. Five hundred milligrams, a lethal dose. Do you understand?"

The girl nodded, bright tears in her tormented eyes.

"Thank you," she whispered. "Thank you."

"Come on," Olivia said to Kieran. She didn't want to stick around to watch that poor girl put an end to her own suffering. "Let's get the hell out of this house of horrors."

53

Back out in the hallway, the area around the stairwell had been transformed into an abattoir. Blood was everywhere, shattered bones and glistening organs scattered like party favors. The rich, coppery stench made Olivia feel sick, but if they wanted to get out of this underground hell they were going to have to walk right though that mess.

Meanwhile, Kieran didn't look so hot. He was pale and sweating, eyes wild and too wide. Olivia was worried about him. About his heart. If they got into some kind of physical confrontation, she could try to step in and protect him, but if they had to run, he might not make it.

Suddenly, the overhead lights came back on and the side doors all slid shut. Whatever damage Kieran had done had been rectified. However, the door to the stairway remained propped open—held that way by a boot with the previous owner's foot still in it.

A white-coated figure appeared in the stairway, on the other side of the door. It was Doctor Lansen.

He stepped into the gory hallway with his attention riveted on Annie, as if she were holding a loaded gun. He had a split and swollen lip and blood was crusted around his hairline. His lab coat was torn and there were lurid bruises blooming around his neck and jaw.

"Annie," he said, taking one step toward them, then another. "Listen to me. I'm so sorry I got angry with you. You know how I get wrapped up in my work sometimes. I didn't mean to hurt you."

"Don't listen to him, Annie," Olivia hissed, putting a hand across Kieran's chest and backing him toward the elevator. "Remember what he did to you! He doesn't love you—he's just using you, like he's been using all these girls."

"Shut up," Lansen snapped. "You don't know what you're talking about.

"Annie," he continued, pitching his voice low and soft. "You know we have something special. Something that other people don't understand. Please, come back upstairs with me."

She took a hesitant step toward him, her expression conflicted and pained, tears welling in her eyes.

"That's it," he said. "Come on."

Annie cast a guilty glance back at Olivia, then walked slowly down to the end of hallway, where Lansen stood waiting.

Olivia was out of back-up plans. The doctor stood between them and the exit, and she didn't think she could make it back up the elevator shaft. And even after everything Annie had done, Olivia didn't want to leave the girl in that scumbag's clutches.

Lansen was holding out his left hand, his right hand slipping into his lab coat pocket. His body was turned toward Annie so that she couldn't see it, but Olivia could. As she took one more step back, she saw the glint of a syringe in his hand.

"Annie!" she called. "Look out!"

Her heel bumped against something soft, and when she looked back she saw the body of the guard with the tranquilizer gun. His fallen rifle was just three feet away.

If she took the time to think about it, she'd be too late. She just pictured herself back at Deerborn, running drills with the rifle team. Hands moving confidently, automatically. Gauging the distance, locking in on the target.

An icy calm flooded her veins as she grabbed the air rifle and drew a bead on the little slice of skin between Lansen's ear and his collar. She blew all the air out her lungs, and squeezed the trigger.

Lansen yelped and dropped the syringe, hands scrabbling at the dart now protruding from his neck.

Annie turned back toward Olivia with anguish in her eyes, then bent to scoop up the broken syringe. As she held it up to examine it, Lansen went down on his knees, sagging against the wall and collapsing onto his side.

For a few heartbeats, the three of them all just stood there.

Then, from behind one of the closed doors came that weird harmonic wail, only this time it wasn't a sound of rage. It was a heart-wrenching sound of bottomless grief. The terrible, unmistakable sound of a mother who has just lost her baby.

Becky.

Annie turned toward the sound, and then back to the syringe. In that moment of realization, all his lies seemed to peel away as the terrible reminder of what kind of man her beloved doctor really was sank in. A deep flush reddened her pale face.

"Annie," Olivia began, dropping the air rifle.

To her amazement, Annie let out a furious shriek, and Doctor Lansen's limp body levitated up off the floor.

It started whipping back and forth like a toy shaken by a dog, slamming into one wall and then the other. Olivia could see his bones cracking and snapping in the air, flesh being pulverized as if he was being crushed from inside.

Within seconds, his body was reduced to a pulpy, lifeless rag, but it didn't stop flying back and forth, over and over.

"Annie," Olivia said. "Jesus, Annie, stop it!"

The girl turned, her face splattered with Doctor Lansen's blood and eyes wide and bright with jagged madness. She covered her face and dropped to her knees, drooping into a sobbing C shape.

Olivia ran to her side, then exchanged a glance with Kieran, who was making frantic gestures toward the stairway.

"Annie?" she said softly.

"Just go," the girl responded without uncovering her face.

"I won't leave you," Olivia said, putting a hand on Annie's shuddering shoulder.

Annie's head jerked up, and Olivia could see the skin of her face straining from within. Straining and tearing, veins bulging as black hematomas spread across the surface of her eyes. Olivia backed away in horror as Annie started to levitate off the floor, blood flowing down her cheeks like sacred tears.

A throaty, earthquake rumble started deep in the walls around them.

"GO!" Annie cried.

Olivia grabbed Kieran's arm and ran for the stairwell, as the ceiling and walls started to collapse all around them. Massive cracks appeared in the floor, forcing them to zig zag.

By the time they reached the stairs, the entire

hallway behind them had caved in, filling the air with blinding dust.

The wild destruction poor, crazy Annie had started in the basement set off a chain reaction of tremors through the core of the building. If they didn't get out soon, they would be buried under thousands of tons of concrete and steel.

She had to get Kieran out of there.

54

She could barely see him through the swirling dust, but she held tight to his wrist and started making her way up the stairs. By the time she reached the next landing, the dust was so thick that she felt like an arctic explorer, trapped in a white-out blizzard. She could barely breathe, and could hear Kieran coughing and hacking beside her.

"Liv," he said, wrapping an arm around her waist. "Here, I think I found a way out."

She reached out in the direction he led her, and found the door. Together they pushed on the bar that should have opened it.

Nothing.

It was locked.

"Do you still have that key card?" Olivia asked, pulling the neck of her hospital gown up over her nose and mouth.

"I think so," he said. She could barely make out the shape of his arms, fumbling through his pockets. "Here. Where's the lock?"

"It's to the right of the doors, up on the ward," Olivia said.

"Found it," Kieran said.

There was a beep, then a click as he pushed the door open. Together, they tumbled through and found themselves inside the parking structure.

"Yes!" Kieran said with a little fist pump.

"Don't start celebrating now," Olivia said, pointing to a shifting network of cracks forming all around the doorway. "We're not out of here yet."

Kieran looked around the massive underground parking area, scanning the rows of cars.

"I can't figure out where we are," he said. "But this definitely isn't the same stairway I used before. I think we're all the way on the other side of the building." Futility reflected in his expression. "Hell, I don't even know if this is the same floor where I parked the truck."

"Well then, we better start looking for another car," Olivia said running to the nearest row of vehicles and trying one locked handle after the other.

"Even if we find one that's unlocked," Kieran said, his voice tight and panicky, "how are we supposed to start it? Do you know how to hotwire a car? Because I sure as hell don't!"

"Stay frosty," Olivia said. "We just need to…"

Before she could finish her sentence, a massive tremor rocked the building. More cracks spider-webbed across the low concrete ceiling, and chunks rained down all around them, some the size of hailstones, others as big as softballs.

"We have to get out now," Olivia said, hands over her head as she sprinted toward the ramp at the far end of the garage. "Run!"

She made it to the ramp in seconds, and turned back to find that Kieran wasn't behind her. He was more than halfway down the row of cars, doubled over and gasping with his hands on his knees.

She ran to his side, and put an arm around his shoulders.

"Are you okay?" she asked, terrified that he wasn't.

"Peachy," he said with a shaky smile that confirmed Olivia's worst fears.

"Where are your meds?" Olivia asked.

"In my backpack," he said.

"What backpack?" Olivia asked.

"The one on the passenger seat of the truck," Kieran said with a rueful smile.

"Are you crazy? You know you're never supposed to go anywhere without your meds!"

"Yeah, well..." Kieran shrugged. "I guess I had other things on my mind."

"Well, you can't rescue anyone if you drop dead," Olivia said, her worry causing her tone to come off harsher than she intended. She deliberately softened her voice and took him by the arm. "Come on, we need to find that truck."

They had to go agonizingly slow, and Kieran kept having to stop to catch his breath. It was freezing cold in the unheated garage, and Olivia shivered beneath the thin hospital gown. Her bare feet were nearly frozen.

The roof over by the stairwell collapsed, and large slabs of concrete came crashing down all around them. If they didn't find that truck soon, they'd never make it out of there alive.

"Look," Kieran said, once they'd traveled the entire length of the structure. "I don't think it's on this level."

"You're right," Olivia said, dodging a toaster-sized hunk of concrete with a crooked length of rebar sticking out like a spear. "Look, that ramp leads up to another level. Can you make it?"

"No problem," Kieran replied. She had a feeling he was lying.

They walked up the ramp, while behind them, the lower parking level was swiftly blocked by a collapsed roof. But the upper level was pure chaos, packed with panicked people trying to get to their cars. The driveways were jammed, everyone honking and swearing out their open windows. Emergency personnel were struggling to help people evacuate on foot, and move people who were injured.

Olivia spotted the SpeedyShip truck almost immediately.

"There," she said. "Hurry!"

When they got to the truck, Kieran grabbed his backpack and his own coat. He took the time to put his coat over Olivia's shoulders before digging out his meds.

"We can't drive out of here," Kieran said, dry swallowing a pill. "We'd better go on foot."

"I can't," Olivia said. "I have no shoes. I'll freeze to death out there!" She paused for a moment, then said, "You go."

"Like hell," he answered.

Up at the top of the exit ramp, a white SUV had just reached the exit when a sedan rammed into it from behind. The driver, a pudgy young man in a stained lab coat, got out of the SUV and—to Olivia's surprise—hauled the older Asian man out from behind the wheel of the car and starting belting him with wild haymakers.

Emergency personnel ran to split up the fight and the chubby guy went wild, screaming and flailing and headbutting a firefighter so that his helmet flew off.

"Let's go," Kieran said, suddenly lunging into action

and pulling Olivia with him toward the still-running SUV.

Olivia realized what he had in mind and silently cheered. The fight had spread down the ramp, and panicked people were shoving and stampeding wildly all around them. When they got to the SUV, Kieran flung open the passenger-side door, shoved Olivia in, and tossed his backpack into her lap, then got in behind the wheel.

People dove out of their way as Kieran punched it and roared up the ramp, then out into the driveway. He had to swerve several times, barely missing an incoming emergency response vehicle and two parked fire engines.

Just as he made it out onto Red Oak Road, the left wing of the building shuddered and bowed outward, and then came crashing down in a vortex of dust and flying paper.

55

Kieran and Olivia drove for several hours without stopping, trying to put as many miles as they could between them and Potsdam.

Finally, they stopped at a department store on the way to pick up some clothes, shoes, and a coat for Olivia. Fully dressed in normal things for the first time in ages, she started to feel like a person again.

She felt free.

"What do you think was really going on back there?" Kieran asked as he pulled out of the store parking lot.

"Honestly, I don't know," Olivia replied, turning her face to stare out the dark window at nothing. "The part I just can't figure out is, why me? Why did Doctor Lansen want me?"

"Do you have... you know, powers?" Kieran asked. "Like that crazy chick?"

"Of course not," Olivia replied. "And if you would have asked me a month ago if I thought that kind of thing existed at all, I would have laughed in your face. Now, I'm not so sure."

"Maybe that black stuff Doctor Lansen was trying

to inject you with has something to do with it," Kieran suggested. "Like maybe that was some kind of formula to activate psychic abilities in the brains of his subjects."

"But what was the deal with the babies?" Olivia asked, shuddering at the memory of all those bottled stillbirths.

"I'm just glad I got you out of there before you had a chance to find out for yourself," Kieran said, reaching across the seat and taking her hand.

They planned to make it to Albany, but by the time they reached Schenectady, they were both utterly exhausted. They found a forgettable franchise hotel called the Co-Z Inn, and while she waited in the car, Kieran checked-in using the credit card his mom had given him.

Their room was on the far end of the second floor, with an uninspiring view of the highway.

They'd been there for several minutes before it fully dawned on Olivia that she was alone in a hotel room with a boy.

"Well," she said pointlessly, but she didn't have any idea what to say next.

"You can have the bed," Kieran said, suddenly flushed and his head bowed.

"What, are you gonna sleep on—the floor?" Olivia asked.

"I thought..." he shrugged with a crooked smile. "I don't know."

"I have a rule," Olivia said, a smile of her own blossoming across her lips. "Anybody who saves my life gets to sleep with me."

Kieran looked up at her.

"Sleep with you?" he asked, looking back at the bed. "Or, you know... *sleep* with you?"

Instead of answering, Olivia kissed him.

At first he seemed almost flabbergasted by this turn

of events, shoulders hunched and hands up and open. But moments later, he had his arms wound tight around her and was kissing her back like his life depended on it.

She pulled him toward the bed and then shoved him down on his back. He bounced comically on the springy mattress, causing one of the pillows to fall off the side.

"Wow," he said, running his fingers through his hair. "I guess I'm still feeling a little shaky."

"Then I'd better be on top," Olivia replied, pulling her brand new T-shirt off over her head.

Afterward, he lay with his head on her chest for a few quiet minutes.

"Are you thirsty?" he asked, tracing the shape of her jaw with his fingertips. "I think I saw a soda machine out in the hall."

"Actually," she said. "I'd love a glass of water."

"Cheap date," he said, getting up and pulling on his boxer shorts. He padded over to the bathroom, and Olivia watched him peel the paper wrapper off a drinking glass then fill it from the tap. He took a deep drink himself, and then refilled it and brought it back to her.

"Thanks," she said, sitting up in bed to take the glass, and feeling suddenly shy and awkward.

She drank the water and handed the glass back to Kieran. He took it and looked down at it, as if it held some kind of important clue. Neither one of them spoke for several long seconds.

"Come back to bed," Olivia said, reaching out to touch his sharp hipbone where it poked above the boxers' elastic waistband.

"Okay," he said, setting the glass on the bedside table and sliding his legs under the covers beside her. Instead of lying down, though, he remained sitting up and turned toward her, slipping one arm around her waist and pulling her close.

"I guess you know how bad I wanted this to happen," Kieran said. "I mean, not you getting kidnapped and everything."

Olivia laughed and shook her head.

"I know what you mean," she said.

She kissed him lightly and pushed his tangled hair back from his face.

"I..." He was flushed, jaw clenched, and his gaze dropped to the left. "I think I love you. I mean, I *know* I do." He looked up at her, eyes raw and vulnerable. "I love you, Liv."

Olivia felt her breath catch, her heart beating way too fast. She knew she was supposed to say it back to him, but those three little words felt so loaded, so serious. The kind of thing that, once said, couldn't be taken back.

She'd never said those words to anyone but Rachel and her late parents, and they seemed so different now, suddenly layered with complicated nuance and meaning. Like magic words you say to open the doorway to a mysterious new world.

She thought again of Rachel, who claimed to be in love with a different boy every day of the week and tossed those words around like heart-shaped confetti. Why couldn't she be like that?

Why did everything have to be so serious all the time?

Besides, she was fairly certain that she was in love with Kieran, and had been even before he rescued her. Looking into his familiar eyes and seeing such open, guileless trust made her feel safer than she'd felt since her father died. So why did she feel so conflicted? Why did working up the nerve feel like jumping off a building?

Guess that's why they call it "falling in love."

Just jump, she thought.

"I love you, too," she said.

He took her face between his hands and kissed her a little too hard. As she kissed him back, she felt some deep inner floodgate open, unleashing a deluge of overpowering emotion.

She broke the kiss and looked up into his eyes, placing her hand in the center of his bare chest.

That's when it happened.

It started with the baby-fine hairs on her forearm prickling and standing up as a crackle of static shot through the cheap polyester comforter beneath her. The overhead light flickered and Kieran frowned, lips twisting into a grimace as he reached up and put his hand over hers, clutching at his chest.

"Kieran?" she said, cold fear surging through her veins. "Kieran what's wrong? Is it your heart?"

His mouth moved, but nothing came out. His shoulders hunched down, spine curling inward as veins bulged in his temples.

"Hang on!" She pulled her hand free from his iron grip and ran to his backpack, unzipping it and frantically pawing through the contents. "Hang on, Kieran!"

When her desperate fingers closed around the orange pill bottle, she turned back to Kieran and he was no longer on the bed. She ran around the side and found him lying on his side on the scratchy carpet, unmoving.

He wasn't breathing.

56

"No," she said, pill bottle dropping from her numb fingers as she ran to him. "Jesus, no."

She grabbed the phone and dialed the front desk.

"Call 911," she said, her voice sounding much calmer than she felt. "My boyfriend had a heart attack. Room 207. Tell the paramedics I've started CPR."

She hung up the phone without waiting for a response, and rolled the unresponsive Kieran over on his back to begin chest compressions.

She had completely forgotten about her broken arm.

Unable to perform the standard, two-handed compressions, but with no time to lose, Olivia stood over him and put her full body weight behind her right hand, like she was doing one-armed push-ups on his sternum. It worked at first, but the strength and energy required to maintain the correct pace was exhausting, and she could feel herself getting winded less than a minute into the effort.

But she couldn't give up on him.

She had to keep going no matter what.

Yet panic was winning. She tried to keep it at bay, but

she could feel it gaining the upper hand, devouring her from the inside out. Fear and love and anxiety and anguish and a thousand other unnamed emotions swarmed inside of her like angry hornets as Kieran remained inert and lifeless. Her one hand just wasn't strong enough, and her recently healed ribs began to send sharp jolts of painful protest through her body.

She had to come up with another idea, but she was afraid that he would die if she stopped. Somewhere, someone was chanting breathlessly, "No... no... no... no..." She desperately wished they would stop, and then realization dawned.

It was coming from her.

The panic was mounting, cranking up to an eleven, and she could smell a sharp, metallic ozone scent in the crackling air.

Then there was a massive, blinding flash, as if lightning had struck every wall of the room at once. All three lamps exploded, every outlet gave off a burst of sparks, and the television screen shattered into a thousand flying daggers. Olivia threw her body over Kieran, barely feeling the sting of glass fragments in her bare back. She used her arm to protect her eyes.

When she looked up, the room was lit only by flickering blue flames shooting from the electrical outlets and crawling up the wallpaper. It was rapidly filling up with acrid smoke. She had only seconds to act.

She grabbed the first piece of clothing her fingers found, Kieran's crumpled T-shirt, and pulled it on over her head. Then she got herself into a squat position and rolled him onto his stomach, hooking her elbows under his shoulders and pulling him up and toward her so that his chest was pressed against hers.

She grabbed his wrist and pulled his arm over her

shoulder, into a fireman's carry. Her aching ribs screamed in protest, but she ignored them. Settling his weight onto her back, she gripped his arm in her good hand, hooked the elbow of her broken arm around his thigh, and staggered toward the door.

Opening it, she had to turn sideways to get him through.

Out in the hallway, she found that all the lights were out and flames were pouring out of every electrical outlet and light fixture. The smoke was so thick she could barely see, but she could hear shouting and running feet as panicked guests fled the flames and ran for the stairs.

Stairs.

Olivia was going to have to carry Kieran down the stairs and out of the building.

She'd practiced the fireman's carry, briefly lifting other students in her CPR class for a few seconds at a time. But it was one thing to lift a conscious, standing person, and something altogether different to carry an unconscious, unresponsive one down a flight of stairs.

But she didn't have a choice. So she shut out the noise and chaos around her, and focused intensely on each step, one after the other, as if she was doing a particularly hard set at the gym. She could feel the heat of the flames on her skin, making her sweat and rendering her grip treacherous and slippery. Smoke filled her mouth and nose, making her lungs feel as if they were loaded with rusty nails.

By the time she made it to the stairway at the end of the hall, her legs were already shaking, her spine and ribs throbbing with the pain of his crushing weight.

Looking down the first flight of metal stairs, the task seemed utterly insurmountable. While going down was certainly easier than going up, she was close to the end of her endurance, and was absolutely terrified of falling and dropping Kieran.

But every second that ticked by—during which he wasn't receiving CPR, while the flames and smoke were spreading—made it less and less likely that he would survive.

She squared her shoulders and took the first shaky step. With only one good arm, she was unable to steady herself using the railing, but she managed to stay upright. She had to take each step slowly—excruciatingly so—placing one foot down, then bringing her other down beside it.

Each time, she paused to catch her balance and her breath. She kept on pushing herself to go faster, picturing mothers lifting cars off their endangered children, and reaching deep down inside herself to find hidden reserves of strength she never even knew she had.

It wasn't enough.

57

She made it to the first landing before her legs gave out and she collapsed to her knees, a frustrated scream of anguish wrenched out from between her clenched teeth.

All her life, Olivia hated to be told she couldn't do something, just because she was a girl. She fought every day to prove that she could outrun, out-shoot, and outwit any boy in school. Her endurance was top-notch, and she constantly pushed herself to go heavy, to beat her previous best.

Now, when it really mattered, she just wasn't strong enough.

It didn't even occur to her that by getting him this far, she'd already accomplished an impressive feat of strength and willpower. She was facing what could be the darkest, most brutal failure of her young life, and all she could think about was that she couldn't stop.

She couldn't give up.

She struggled to lift her right leg so that her bare foot was flat on the floor, then shifted her weight forward and tried to bring her other leg up into a squatting position. She made it for a precious second, but misjudged her balance as she tried to rise, and wound up falling backward instead.

Kieran slipped off her shoulders and thudded bonelessly to the floor.

For a second, all she could do was lie there with her head on his belly, dizzy and gasping with black and red shapes dancing in the corners of her vision.

"Kieran," she said, spinning toward him and gripping his clammy hand. His face was the color of skim milk, eyes rolled back but not completely closed. "Kieran, stay with me. I'm gonna get you out of here, or die trying. Do you hear me? You stay with me!"

She hooked her elbows under his armpits and started dragging him toward the next flight. Bouncing him down the steps on his ass was far from ideal, but so was leaving him to die on the landing. She was so beyond exhausted that she wasn't even sure that she could make it down the stairs on her own, but she didn't hesitate. She backed down as quickly as she could, pulling him with her.

His head lolled against her thighs, flopping from side to side.

Halfway down the flight, she slipped and bloodied her bare knees against the metal edge of a step but still managed to stay upright and hang on. Kieran's rumpled boxer shorts were starting to scrunch down off his skinny ass, but she couldn't risk her grip to try and pull them back up.

It was all about the next step. And then the next one, and the one after that. She blocked out the agony in her lungs and ribs and knees. She blocked out the fear of failure and death. She blocked out everything but making it down *each and every single step*.

And then there were no more.

She'd hit the first floor landing.

She collapsed back on her ass, clutching Kieran against her chest and graying out for a precious handful of seconds. With no idea of how much time had slipped away, she snapped back into focus, feeling like she was going to throw up and gasping desperately for oxygen in the smoky stairwell.

Forcing the rising bile back down, she lurched to her feet, pulling him the last few feet to the stairway door.

She pushed the door open with her shoulder and backed into the chaos of the hotel lobby.

Firefighters in heavy turnout coats and frantic hotel staff members were managing the evacuation, helping coughing, terrified guests and guiding everyone out the big, double glass doors into the parking lot. Many were in their pajamas, nightgowns, or robes, and some just had sheets or blankets wrapped around their shoulders. Mothers herded crying children and maids helped frail, bewildered seniors. Paramedics triaged the injured, tending to burns and administering oxygen.

"Paramedic!" Olivia called in what she intended to be a clear, strong voice, but came out was a strangled, croaking wheeze. "*Help*!"

An older black female with a man's haircut and a flyweight boxer's build responded immediately to her cry. She ran to Olivia's side and began to methodically and efficiently check Kieran's vitals.

"Heart attack, from a congenital heart defect." Olivia said, the act of talking like broken glass in her smoke-scoured throat. "He's been unresponsive for approximately eight to ten minutes. I started CPR but was unable to continue when the conditions in our location became unsafe."

The gruff paramedic made a terse, non-verbal sound in acknowledgement, without turning her head or stopping her ministrations. A second paramedic, this one white and male with glasses and a shaved head, joined the first. Seconds later, the female paramedic looked up at her partner and shook her head.

"Wait," Olivia said. "Wait, no…"

"I'm sorry," the woman said, her hard, dark eyes softening. "There's nothing more we can do for him. He's been gone for some time. Most likely died instantly."

"No," Olivia said, shoving the paramedic aside and putting her hand on Kieran's cold, unmoving chest. "No, that's not possible. Don't you have a defibrillator?"

"Defib can't bring back the dead," the male paramedic said. "It ain't a magic wand, kid."

"No," she said again. "You just need to…"

She stopped, and leaned into Kieran, starting up her desperate one-handed compressions again.

"Come on," she hissed between clenched teeth. "Come on come on come on."

"Honey, don't," the woman said, putting a gentle, calloused hand on Olivia's shoulder.

The compressions had shifted to angry hammer-fists, slamming into Kieran's bony sternum again and again as a tortured, rusty scream welled up inside her.

Echoing Olivia's unleashed scream, a wall of raging flame surged through the lobby like the leading edge of a nuclear blast. The female paramedic grabbed Olivia and dropped to the charred carpet, using her own body to shield her from the flash fire.

Olivia's last thought as she slipped into dizzy blackness was that she was the one who was supposed to be doing the protecting.

And she had failed.

58

When Lorna Gilbert arrived at the Co-Z Inn, it was total chaos. She'd been on her way to New York City to report in at the Massive Dynamic head office, when she'd gotten a call saying there had been a blip on the trace that had been put on Kieran's credit card.

They'd done it as soon as she'd reported him AWOL from the school. But when the call had come across the police band, reporting an explosion at that location, she'd floored it all the way there.

Lorna had been working for Massive Dynamic for twelve years, keeping a watchful eye on high-functioning Cortexiphan positives under the guise of a teacher, guidance counselor, or dorm mother—whatever the situation required. Before that, she'd worked in private security, and could still stand and bang with the boys without breaking a sweat.

Although she referred to herself as "Mrs. Gilbert," and often told her charges that she had children because it made her seem more motherly, in reality she'd never even married. When she was younger, she'd experimented a bit, thinking that her disinterest in men meant that she was into women. By the time she was forty, though, she realized that she just wasn't interested in intimate relationships at all.

On the other hand, she got a lot of satisfaction from taking care of her young charges, and often developed strong bonds with them, despite the fact that the relationship was built upon false pretenses.

Just now, she was worried sick about Olivia.

Olivia was a strange one, she had to admit that. She was so reserved, so quiet, so mature. Not shy at all—just intensely private. A loner. It had taken a lot of work to put her at ease, to get her to let her guard down, even just a few precious inches. But once she did, Lorna discovered that she was ferociously smart and thoughtful and even funny in her own quirky, deadpan way.

She'd sent one of their best security teams after Olivia when she foolishly went after that rogue cop on her own, giving them strict orders to protect her at all cost. But somehow, a sixteen-year-old girl had managed to give MD's finest the slip, a fact she would never let them live down.

Lorna just wished that she could have found a way to communicate with Olivia, to let her know that those men were there to help her, not hurt her.

Through some kind of miracle, Olivia had found a way to beat that cop and save her sister, although to be perfectly honest, Lorna didn't understand exactly what had gone down inside that house. It didn't matter. She'd learned early on that there were a lot of things she didn't fully understand, and she was okay with that. All that had mattered was that Olivia was safe, and being cared for at a Massive Dynamic research facility.

Until now.

Lorna didn't know if the two explosions that occurred

that day were both caused by Olivia, but this second one had to have been, since she was the only Cortexiphan positive in the building.

The parking lot outside the Co-Z Inn was blocked off by emergency vehicles, so she had to park across the main road and run over on foot to the burning hotel.

Firefighters were battling the blaze while paramedics and the walking wounded helped evacuate those who couldn't walk. Crowds of fearful, shivering guests milled about the parking lot, unsure of what to do or where to go.

She found Olivia sitting on the pavement with a silver thermal blanket around her shoulders and a black female paramedic dabbing at a cut on her forehead. Her face was smudged with soot and her body language was slumped and utterly defeated.

In her eyes, the thousand-yard stare.

"Olivia," Lorna said, squatting down beside her. "Thank god you're okay." She looked around, then back at the girl. "Where's Kieran?"

Olivia shook her head, her face mask-like and emotionless.

"You mean you don't know where he is?" Lorna asked. "Or…"

"He's dead," she said flatly. Then she lifted her head. "He's *dead*, okay?" she snapped. "He's dead, and there's nothing I can do about it."

"Oh, honey," Lorna said, wrapping her arm around Olivia's shoulders. "I'm so sorry. Was it his heart?"

Olivia turned away and nodded. Lorna looked to the paramedic.

"Is she okay," she asked.

"Physically," the woman said, and she nodded. "She'll be okay. But mentally?" She shrugged and started packing up her equipment.

"Come on, Olivia," Lorna said. "Come back to the school. Rachel misses you. She needs you."

Olivia looked up at her, a slight frown creasing between her pale brows.

"Rachel," Olivia said. "Jesus, what am I gonna tell her?"

"Tell her the truth. Tell her that you stopped at a motel on the way home from the hospital, because you were both so tired," Lorna said. "And then Kieran had a heart attack. It's not a lie, it's just not the whole story." She helped Olivia to her feet. "Sometimes, people are better off if they don't know the whole story."

"I suppose you're right," Olivia said, leaning heavily against her.

EPILOGUE ONE

SEQUOIA NATIONAL PARK
2008

Junior Agent Olivia Dunham unholstered her sidearm and got out of the Crown Vic, nodding silently to her partner, Special Agent Dan Considine.

Considine was in his early fifties, lean and tough as beef jerky. What hair he had left was shaved down to silver stubble, and his eyes were an unusual shade of pale, grayish brown behind his wire-rimmed glasses. He had a humorless and taciturn disposition that made for dull company on long assignments, but he was also a patient and skilled teacher with years of knowledge and practical on-the-job experience that Olivia soaked up like a sponge.

She trusted him with her life.

Considine got out from behind the wheel and drew his own gun, aiming over the roof of the car to cover her as she moved cautiously toward the door of the cabin.

It was one of many small, seedy vacation rentals clustered around the outskirts of Sequoia National Park in central California. Built for free-range families back in the optimistic, post-World War II boom years, when a vacation didn't have to be a 3-D, interactive, corporate-sponsored, consumer circus meticulously designed to inspire brand loyalty in jaded and entitled offspring, cabins like these were places to spend lazy summers catching fireflies and telling ghost stories.

Now, the fireflies had been driven to the brink of extinction by the undying electric glow of a jacked in modern existence, and no one could pay attention long enough to find out what happened at the end of the ghost story. As a result, rustic and quaint family cabins like these sat empty, season after season, inhabited only by the occasional tweaker misfit wearing a tin-foil hat, or bewildered foreign tourist who'd fallen for some kind of online bargain.

The owner of the property was named Lee Canliss, an older woman who could have been anywhere from sixty to a-hundred-and-six. She was tall, but deeply stooped and wore her white hair in two long braids like a little girl. Her clothes and boots were utilitarian and gender neutral, except for the quirky addition of a big glittery pendant in the shape of a stylized lion head.

She told Olivia that the occupant had given his name as Mark Mitchell, but that she recognized him from the drawing of the suspect in the Jensen case. She'd also said that the man calling himself Mitchell had a girl with him when he checked in—a blonde who "looked young." She claimed the girl had been sitting in the passenger seat of the car the whole time, and mostly kept her face turned away, but that the hair looked kind of like the girl on TV, so she'd phoned the FBI tip line.

As soon as the call came in, Olivia came running.

This deeply personal vendetta had started out as a low-priority Jane Doe case involving two sets of unidentified female remains. The burnt skeletal fragments had been discovered in two different states more than four hundred miles apart, but they were both found to contain traces of the same brand of lighter fluid. Both had been burned elsewhere and then later dumped. Both were Caucasian females between fourteen and seventeen years of age.

Olivia wound up with the case partly because no one else wanted it. She tinkered with it in her spare time, but got nowhere until she got a blip from a small-town sheriff who had a complaint from an underage prostitute named Makayla Wayne. The girl claimed a john had tried to set her on fire, but she had escaped and provided a description of her attacker. The drawing based on her description was laughable, like an evil pirate in a kid's cartoon, but one element of this mythical pirate stood out to Olivia.

He had a hook for a hand.

His right hand.

When she called up a mugshot that showed the victim, she felt sick to her stomach. Blond hair. Green eyes. That girl could have been her little sister.

Olivia had been overwhelmed by a flood of complex, dark, and bittersweet memories that she'd tried to leave buried in the past. Her life was good now, exactly what she wanted in every way. She had an exciting job that challenged her, and an active and carefree love life. Rachel was married and mother to a beautiful little girl of her own, and while Olivia couldn't imagine settling down herself anytime soon, she enjoyed being an aunt to the precocious Ella.

There wasn't a single thing Olivia wanted that she did not have.

But now this unquiet spirit from her difficult past had raised his ugly head, to remind her of things that were better off forgotten. She was angry at first, but as the pieces started to fall swiftly into place, she began to realize that this unexpected resurrection was actually a good thing. The right thing. Closure after all those years.

She paid a visit to Makayla Wayne, and it wasn't the slam dunk she'd hoped for. The girl was cranked to the gills during the interview, and positively identified a control photo of Dan Considine as her attacker, before changing her mind and picking out the photo of Tony Orsini.

Unwilling to let it go, Olivia started slogging through female missing person reports in which the juvenile subjects were between the ages of fourteen and seventeen and had blond hair and green eyes. Once she had eliminated the ones who didn't look anything like her, or lived more than a thousand miles away from the dump sites, she narrowed it down to a solid dozen possibilities.

She'd had to sweet talk a lab tech into slipping her request into the forensic queue, but it still took more than six months to get results. It was worth it, though, because she got a DNA match between one of the missing juveniles and one of her charbroiled Jane Does.

The match turned out to be a hard-partying high school dropout named Amanda Lindstrom, from Omaha, Nebraska. Olivia paid a visit to Omaha to talk to Amanda's grief-stricken parents and friends. She got lucky when one of the girl's friends told her about a one-armed man who had bought liquor for them, and "seemed weird." She claimed that the local cops had ignored her story, because they had been convinced that Amanda's African-American boyfriend was responsible for her disappearance.

She positively identified the photo of Tony Orsini as the "weird guy."

Still circumstantial and mostly based on the

testimony of unreliable witnesses, Olivia's little pet case was starting to get warmer. What she really needed was some kind of solid evidence, like surveillance footage or a credit card receipt that placed Orsini in the area on the day Amanda went missing.

When she started digging into Orsini's recent whereabouts, she discovered that he had fallen off the grid nearly nine years ago—when he had last been released from an inpatient psychiatric facility. No bank accounts, no credit cards, no utilities, nothing.

He had become a ghost.

So with little or nothing to go on, Olivia continued to work the case in her spare time, sifting through minutia and watching hours of gas station security camera footage until her eyes crossed.

Then Jamie Jensen went missing, and Olivia's cold case flashed white hot.

Sixteen-year-old Jamie Jensen was an all-American girl next door. The only child of Sam and Nancy Jensen from Fort Worth, Texas, Jamie was popular and athletic, She played on the girls' basketball team and volunteered at the local animal shelter. She wasn't a hooker, a junkie or a runaway. She was a nice girl from a nice family.

A telegenic victim, who also happened to look remarkably like a young Olivia.

Nobody cared about what happened to a white-trash tweaker like Makayla Wayne or a bad girl like Amanda Lindstrom, but when Jamie Jensen failed to come home from the library, it sparked a multi-state manhunt and a media feeding frenzy. The drawing based on her brother's description of a suspicious one-armed man he'd seen hanging around the library looked exactly like Tony Orsini.

Because Olivia had already done so much preliminary

legwork on Tony, she and Considine had taken the lead in the Jensen investigation. It was her first major case.

And now, all that legwork was paying off. A second back-up car full of muscle and bullets was prowling down the long dirt driveway, kicking up a cloud of dust in the hot, still afternoon. There was a third team heading up toward the back of the cabin via the strip of woods that separated it from its neighbor, in case Orsini decided to make a run for it.

Olivia felt sharp and confident—everything was going exactly the way she had planned. She walked slowly through the long grass, gun drawn and ready. Considine was right behind her. A startled grasshopper leapt away from their invading feet as they approached the cabin door.

There was a warm, summery scent of crushed grass and sun-bleached wood in the air, but beneath it, Olivia could detect another sharper, more unnatural odor.

Kerosene.

An alarmed look passed between her and her partner. He nodded, grim and silent.

Olivia kicked the door in.

Inside, she found Tony Orsini and Jamie Jensen, both soaked in stinking kerosene. Jamie lay on her side on the splintery floor, roughly hogtied and gagged with a knotted bandana. When she saw Olivia, she tried to scream but the sound was reduced to a muffled squeak.

Tony spun to face her, an unlit Zippo lighter in his hand.

The years had not been kind to him. He looked shrunken and worn out. In Olivia's memory, he'd been this towering monster, all-powerful and looming over Rachel like an evil dragon. Seeing him now, he just looked like a sad old man. His hand was shaking, his yellowy, bloodshot eyes wide with disbelief.

"Olivia?" he said, voice cracking and barely a whisper.

She held out her arm to keep Considine back, squinting against the fumes. One wrong move and Orsini would spark that lighter and engulf them all in flames.

"Yes, Tony," she said, gun pointed down and her free hand up, palm out. "It's me. What are you doing?"

"I…" He looked from the lighter in his hand to the bound girl on the kerosene-drenched floor. "I thought…" He looked back up at Olivia. "I thought you were dead."

"I came back for you," she said, holding out her hand. "Now give me the lighter, Tony. We don't need it. Or her."

He looked down at the lighter, and then very slowly held it out to her.

She snatched the lighter, tossed it away and immediately slammed him up against the wall, gun pressed against his neck as she slapped her cuffs around his left wrist. Then she paused, non-plussed. How was she supposed to handcuff that hook?

Considine saw her dilemma and tossed her a flex cuff. Then he ran to Jamie and went to work freeing her from the kerosene-soaked rope that bound her. As soon as her arms were free, she threw them around Considine's neck, clinging to him and sobbing hysterically.

He shot Olivia a baffled look over the top of the girl's head. He was never any good at dealing with crying females.

Thank god you're not like this, his eyes said.

Olivia smiled and used the flex cuff to cinch the solid links at the center of the cuffs to the metal "wrist" of Orsini's prosthetic. Walking him out of the cabin and putting him into the back of the car, she felt a tremendous sense of relief… and closure.

Like she'd slain her childhood demon, and salted his

grave so he could never hurt anyone else again.

As Considine drove them back to the local command center, she found herself thinking again of Kieran, for the first time in years. Finally bringing Orsini to justice made her realize how much weight and significance she had placed on the events of that strange winter. It made her realize that she was still harboring a sense of guilt over what had happened to her first lover, and her inability to save him.

Now that she had conquered her lingering fear of Orsini, it was time to let go of that other baggage, too.

EPILOGUE TWO

Olivia was sitting at her desk and looking at a drawing that her niece Ella had done. The girl had drawn herself, holding hands with Olivia and Rachel.

It would have been hard to tell Olivia apart from her sister in the drawing if Ella hadn't given Olivia a giant badge the size of a gladiator's shield. She smiled and pinned the drawing up on her cork board. The jaunty, colorful picture looked totally out of place amid the crime scene photos, autopsy reports, and maps showing the locations where murder victims had been found.

Considine put down his phone and looked over from his desk.

"Fitterman wants to see you," he said.

"Right," Olivia replied. "I just need to finish up some paperwork."

"Go now," Considine said, with a slight rise in one corner of his thin lips. "It was nice working with you, kid."

Olivia's head snapped up.

"What?" She frowned. "What's this about?"

He didn't answer, just tipped his head in the direction of their superior's office.

Olivia shrugged, still frowning, and got up from her desk. Her curiosity was piqued.

Lieutenant James Fitterman was beaming like a new father when Olivia walked into his office. He was a handsome older man with perfectly styled salt and pepper hair and bright blue eyes. The kind of man who would be cast as a kindly doctor in a commercial for antacid.

He was generally well dressed, but his taste in ties was deplorable. He almost seemed to take a kind of perverse joy in choosing the most eye-wateringly jarring and tacky patterns. That day, it was a delirious swirl of hot pink and lime green, accented with yellow crescents that looked like macaroni elbows glued to a child's art project.

Ties notwithstanding, he'd always been a good boss.

"Great job on the Orsini case," he said.

"Thank you, sir," she replied.

"I think you're ready to have your training wheels taken off," he added. "I'm promoting you to special agent, and assigning you a new partner."

"But I like working with Dan," she said.

"I need Considine to break in another rookie," he said. "You're beyond that now. Besides, I think this will be a good match up for you. Oh, hey, here's your new partner now."

He stood up behind his desk and gestured toward the open door.

"Olivia Dunham," he said. "This is John Scott."

Olivia turned to face her new partner.

He was blond and handsome, with a strong, square jaw and compelling blue eyes. She smiled and took his extended hand. It was large and warm, the broad palm slightly sweaty. She could tell that she made him a little nervous, and that he was working very hard to keep his gaze from dipping down to the open collar of her ivory silk blouse.

She held his hand and his gaze a few seconds longer than necessary, her smile shifting into an unspoken challenge.

This was certainly going to be interesting.

ACKNOWLEDGEMENTS

The author would like to thank Al Guthrie, Steve Saffel, Anna Songco, JoAnne Narcisse, Angela Park, Noreen O'Toole, Rob Chiappetta, Glen Whitman, Joel Wyman, and Nathan Long.

ABOUT THE AUTHOR

Christa Faust is the author of a variety of media tie-ins and novelizations for properties such as *Supernatural, Final Destination* and *Snakes on a Plane*. She also writes hardboiled crime novels, including the Edgar Award-nominated *Money Shot, Choke Hold*, and the Butch Fatale series. She lives in Los Angeles. Her website is christafaust.net.